DAWN OF THE CLANS

WARRIORS

THE FIRST BATTLE

WARRIORS

MANGA

The Lost Warrior

Warrior's Refuge

Warrior's Return

The Rise of Scourge

Tigerstar and Sasha #1: Into the Woods

Tigerstar and Sasha #2: Escape from the Forest

Tigerstar and Sasha #3: Return to the Clans

Ravenpaw's Path #1: Shattered Peace

Ravenpaw's Path #2: A Clan in Need

Ravenpaw's Path #3: The Heart of a Warrior

SkyClan and the Stranger #1: The Rescue

SkyClan and the Stranger #2: Beyond the Code

SkyClan and the Stranger #3: After the Flood

NOVELLAS

Hollyleaf's Story

Mistystar's Omen

Cloudstar's Journey

Tigerclaw's Fury

Also by Erin Hunter

SEEKERS

Book One: The Quest Begins
Book Two: Great Bear Lake
Book Three: Smoke Mountain
Book Four: The Last Wilderness
Book Five: Fire in the Sky
Book Six: Spirits in the Stars

RETURN TO THE WILD

Book One: Island of Shadows
Book Two: The Melting Sea
Book Three: River of Lost Bears
Book Three: Forest of Wolves

MANGA

Toklo's Story
Kallik's Adventure

SURVIVORS

Book One: The Empty City
Book Two: A Hidden Enemy
Book Three: Darkness Falls
Book Four: The Broken Path

DAWN OF THE CLANS

WARRIORS

THE FIRST BATTLE

ERIN
HUNTER

HARPER

An Imprint of HarperCollins*Publishers*

With special thanks to Kate Cary
For Josh, my son (Thanks for all the cups of tea)

The First Battle
Copyright © 2014 by Working Partners Limited
Series created by Working Partners Limited
All rights reserved. Printed in the United States of America. No part of
this book may be used or reproduced in any manner whatsoever without
written permission except in the case of brief quotations embodied in
critical articles and reviews. For information address HarperCollins
Children's Books, a division of HarperCollins Publishers,
10 East 53rd Street, New York, NY 10022.
www.harpercollinschildrens.com

Library of Congress Cataloging-in-Publication Data [tk]
ISBN 978-0-06-206353-3 (trade bdg.)
ISBN 978-0-06-206355-7 (lib. bdg.)

Typography by Hilary Zarycky
14 15 16 17 18   CG/RRDH   10 9 8 7 6 5 4 3 2 1
❖
First Edition

ALLEGIANCES

CLEAR SKY'S CAMP

LEADER

CLEAR SKY—light gray tom with blue eyes

FALLING FEATHER—young white she-cat

MOON SHADOW—black tom

LEAF—gray-and-white tom

PETAL—small yellow tabby she-cat with green eyes

QUICK WATER—gray-and-white she-cat

FIRCONE—tortoiseshell tom

NETTLE—gray tom

KITS

BIRCH—brown-and-white tom

ALDER—gray-and-white she-kit

TALL SHADOW'S CAMP

LEADER

TALL SHADOW—black, thick-furred she-cat with green eyes

GRAY WING—sleek, dark gray tom with golden eyes

JAGGED PEAK—small gray tabby tom with blue eyes

DAPPLED PELT—delicate tortoiseshell she-cat with golden eyes

RAINSWEPT FLOWER—brown tabby she-cat with blue eyes

SHATTERED ICE—gray-and-white tom with green eyes

CLOUD SPOTS—long-furred black tom with white ears, white chest, and two white paws

FROST—pure white tom with blue eyes

JACKDAW'S CRY—young black tom with blue eyes

HAWK SWOOP—orange tabby she-cat

WIND RUNNER—wiry brown she-cat with yellow eyes

GORSE FUR—thin, gray tabby tom

TURTLE TAIL—tortoiseshell she-cat with green eyes

KITS

LIGHTNING TAIL—black tom

ACORN FUR—chestnut brown she-cat

THUNDER—orange tom with amber eyes and big white paws

OWL EYES—gray tom

PEBBLE HEART—brown tabby tom with amber eyes

SPARROW FUR—tortoiseshell she-kit

ROGUE CATS

THORN—she-cat with a short, thick gray coat and bright blue eyes

DEW—mangy tom with splotchy fur

RIVER RIPPLE—silver, long-furred tom

MISTY—gray-and-white she-cat

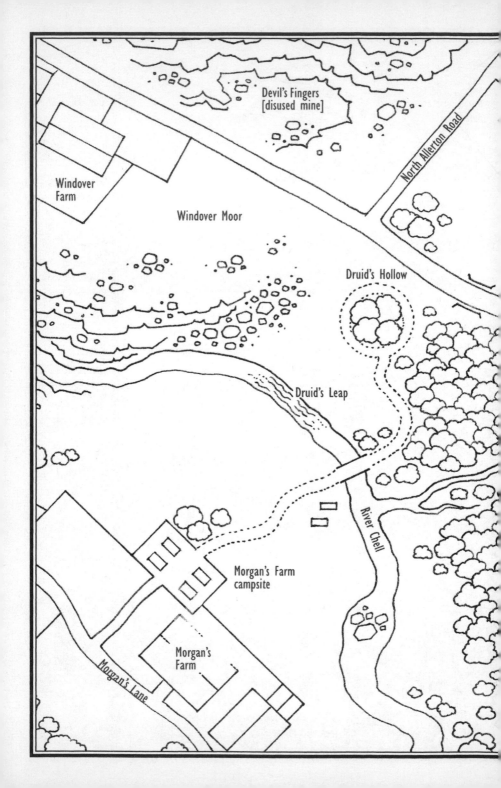

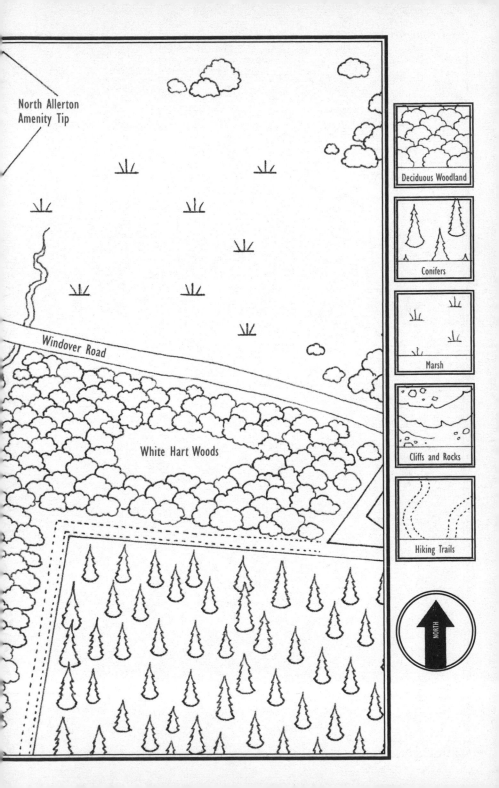

North Allerton
Amenity Tip

Windover Road

White Hart Woods

Deciduous Woodland

Conifers

Marsh

Cliffs and Rocks

Hiking Trails

NORTH

PROLOGUE

❧

Water cascaded beyond the cave mouth. A gray tom watched it tumble past. It muffled the wind and softened the jagged peaks beyond, before disappearing far below into a rainbow of spray.

Cats moved behind him, hardly more than shadows in the dappled light of their cavern. Longing misted the gray tom's eyes. Twisting back his ears, he listened to their murmuring.

"Stones in my nest!" An elder croaked irritably. "Always stones in my nest."

"I'll pick them out." Tiny paws skipped across the cave.

"Come back, Jay Frost," a queen called anxiously. "Your pads are too soft for sharp stones."

"They'll need to toughen up sooner or later," the elder muttered.

The gray tom turned, his sleek pelt pricking.

"Try it, Misty Water." An old ginger tom was nosing a scrawny mouse toward a dull-pelted she-cat.

Misty Water peered at the prey from her nest in the dimpled cavern floor. "Give it to a younger cat." She nodded toward Jay Frost as he picked grit from the elder's nest.

"You must eat," Lion's Roar persisted.

"It's the last piece of prey," the she-cat protested.

"But the hunting party will be back soon. They may have found more," a brown tom called from where he was sharing tongues with a white she-cat at the edge of the cavern.

The gray cat pricked his ears happily. "Twisted Branch! Snow Hare!" He padded toward the two cats, rearing in surprise as four kits charged across his path.

"No rough play!" Their mother hurried after them.

Dewy Leaf. The gray tom blinked at the queen. *You kitted safely! I'm so glad.* A purr rumbled in his throat for a moment, then fell quiet. "If Moon Shadow had stayed to see his kits, he might still be alive now," he murmured.

"Gray Wing?"

A cracked mew made him turn. An ancient she-cat was padding from the shadows at the back of the cave.

"Stoneteller!" Gray Wing hurried toward her. "You can see me?"

"Of course." She stretched her muzzle to greet him. "We share the same dream."

He touched his nose to hers, surprised at how cold it was. He'd lived on the moor for so many moons now that he'd forgotten how the bone-chilling cold of the mountains never entirely loosened its grip.

He glanced around the cave at his old tribe mates. "Can *they* see us?"

"We can see out of the dream," Stoneteller told him. "They can't see in."

Gray Wing blinked. "Am I *here*, or dreaming in my nest on the moor?"

"Both." Amusement lit up Stoneteller's eyes so that, for a moment, they looked as bright as a kit's. "For now, all that matters is here."

Gray Wing stiffened as he saw the speckled pelt of a gray she-cat. "Quiet Rain." His chest tightened as he recognized his mother curled in her sleeping hollow. Her soft eyes clouded as she followed the rippling light playing on the cave walls. "Is she okay?" he asked Stoneteller.

"She's fine," Stoneteller assured him.

"I wish I could tell her we survived the journey, that Clear Sky is well—Jagged Peak, too, despite his injury. She was so worried about us, setting out—even though she told us it was the right thing to do."

"I'll let her know," Stoneteller promised.

Gray Wing hardly heard her. *Jagged Peak and Clear Sky are well.* It was only half true, and that knowledge brought sorrow that stabbed like an icicle at his heart. Should he confess that Jagged Peak was lame now, his hind leg crippled by a fall from a tree? *I swore I'd protect him.*

And what about Clear Sky? Gray Wing's littermate might be safe, but he was so changed that Quiet Rain would hardly recognize her firstborn son. They had found the prey-rich land they had hoped for, but the cats that had traveled through the mountains as one had split into two groups when they reached the warm fields and forests of their new home. Clear Sky had taken possession of the woods with a few of his old tribe mates. It pained Gray Wing to admit it, even to himself, but his brother had become brutal in guarding his share of the plentiful prey.

Shame warmed Gray Wing's pelt. *I failed them—and my mother.*

He felt Stoneteller trying to catch his eye, but could not meet her gaze.

"It's not your fault, Gray Wing." She swung her muzzle toward her skinny tribe mates. "Having *little* makes cats share." She touched her nose to his shoulder softly. "Having much makes us greedy."

Gray Wing lifted his head sharply. Did she know what he was thinking? Clear Sky had once been his closest friend. Now they faced each other like rivals.

"I've lived long." Stoneteller tipped her head. "I must warn you: greed is only the beginning." Her eyes darkened. "There will be war."

Gray Wing swallowed. "With Clear Sky?"

"Don't be scared," Stoneteller soothed.

Gray Wing lifted his head. "I'm not scared!" But his heart quickened. *How can I fight my own brother?*

"Remember the cats who love and trust you," Stoneteller murmured. "You and Clear Sky may be divided, but you still have Jagged Peak."

Warmth filled Gray Wing's chest as he remembered his younger brother's courage and loyalty.

"And Turtle Tail?" Stoneteller's eyes rounded with curiosity. "How is she?"

"She's happy." A loving purr choked Gray Wing's mew.

"You recognized the strength of her love at last." Stoneteller's eyes shone. "I'm glad."

Gray Wing shifted his paws. He could picture Turtle Tail now, sleeping beside him as he walked in his dreams. Pebble Heart, Owl Eyes, and Sparrow Fur would be curled at her belly, still kits but growing each day. Though they were the offspring of a kittypet, he loved them as his own and they loved him, as much as Turtle Tail loved him.

A pang jabbed his heart. He missed them all, even though he knew that his pelt was touching theirs, far away on the moor. *How?* As his mind began to cloud with confusion, he tugged his thoughts back to the cave. *For now, this is all that matters.*

He turned wistfully toward Stoneteller, but she was staring toward the waterfall, faint moonlight dappling her face.

She closed her eyes. "Why have you come here?"

Did I choose *this dream?* Unease flickered beneath Gray Wing's pelt. Something had drawn him deep into memories. But what? Sudden guilt hollowed his belly. Since they had reached the moors, the tribe cats had seen so much death. Gray Wing stiffened as he instinctively thought of Fox, the rogue who had died at his own paws, killed accidentally as they'd fought over boundaries. "We brought death with us."

"You brought change," Stoneteller soothed.

"But must all change be born in blood?" *I only ever intended for my friends to be safe.*

"We are all born in blood," Stoneteller murmured. "But it marks the beginning, not the end."

The beginning? Was there more blood to come?

Mist rolled through the cave entrance, swallowing the Tribe, enfolding Stoneteller until he could no longer see her.

"Stoneteller!" The thick haze swamped his cry. "Don't go!" Grief tightened his throat. He didn't want to lose his old friends again.

"I have faith in you, Gray Wing." Stoneteller's mew echoed through the shrouding haze. "Always."

Fog filled Gray Wing's eyes and clogged his throat. He struggled for breath as it reached into his chest, dizziness muddling his thoughts until the darkness claimed him.

CHAPTER 1

❧

Clear Sky narrowed his eyes. He could see Thunder's bright ginger pelt threading through the ferns. His son was climbing the slope to the moor, leaving the forest with Frost.

I suppose that's what he must do. Clear Sky tried to ignore the regret gnawing in his belly. Above him, a soft breeze whispered through the leaves. Warm sunshine dappled his pelt. Behind him, the gnarled trunks of ancient trees creaked. Musty scents pooled at his paws where leaf litter lay thick on the ground. This was his territory. If Thunder didn't want to live here, then he could leave. Frost *had* to leave, but Thunder had chosen to. Frost was wounded—an injury that was not healing and might grow bad. An infected cat couldn't stay in the camp. His weakness would burden the forest tribe. *Doesn't Thunder understand that?* he thought, clawing the earth with frustration. Why did so few cats understand him? All he wanted to do was protect his cats in the forest—that was all he'd ever wanted to do, since setting up home here. But his own son had called him a monster for caring. *Well, he must leave, then. I won't have my authority undermined.* If Clear Sky kept telling himself this, maybe the pain in his belly would fade. . . .

Tribe! The word rang like a blackbird's cry in Clear Sky's mind. It was the first time he'd thought of the forest cats as a tribe. *No!* He pushed the thought away sharply. *We're not a tribe!* After moons of rich prey, the forest cats were sleeker and better fed than the poor starvelings who'd chosen to stay in the mountains. With the right leadership, they could flourish in lush forest. They could become stronger than any mountain cat. They need never know cold or hunger again.

Flicking his tail, Clear Sky turned and headed through the trees.

White fur flashed at the edge of his vision. Falling Feather was stalking through the tall grass edging the forest.

Clear Sky's pelt lifted irritably along his spine as he remembered Falling Feather's parting words to Thunder. *I almost wish I were coming with you.* Thunder had tried to persuade the white she-cat to desert with him. And she'd actually *considered* it!

Clear Sky unsheathed his claws. "Falling Feather!"

Her head jerked up. "Clear Sky?" She looked surprised.

"I want to talk to you."

She blinked at him over the grass. "What about?"

Clear Sky narrowed his eyes. Didn't she realize he'd overheard her? "I was watching you say good-bye to Thunder and Frost."

"Were you?"

She tried to sound innocent but he could see the fur around her neck rippling guiltily. "Come here." He scowled at her. "Well?"

"I just wished them well, that's all." She pushed through the long grass toward him.

"Thunder asked you to leave with him." He stared at her accusingly.

She bounded from the grass and landed on the leaf-strewn ground a tail-length away. "I told him no."

"You *told* him you almost wished you were going with him." He circled her, his tail twitching irritably. She was acting like she'd done nothing wrong.

"I decided to stay." Her gaze sharpened. "What's it to you? I can go anywhere I like."

Clear Sky showed his teeth. Dumb cat! Didn't she realize how much she needed his protection and guidance? "You are part of my tribe now. If I can't rely on your loyalty, then you might as well leave for good."

"*Tribe?*" Falling Feather's eyes widened in surprise. "We're not a tribe. Half our kin are in the mountains. Half the cats we traveled with live on the moor. We have no Stoneteller to guide us."

Heat scorched beneath Clear Sky's pelt. The word had slipped out accidentally. Did she have to humiliate him? "Okay, we're not a tribe," he snapped. "We're *better* than a tribe. Who needs a Stoneteller? You have *me*." He lashed his tail. "I guide you now. I found our camp. I decide our borders. You should be grateful. Because of me, you will never be hungry or cold again."

"Because of *you?*" Falling Feather snorted. "You act like you brought us here! Have you forgotten that we made the journey from the mountains together? Who saved Quick Water from drowning? I did! Who saved Jagged Peak from the eagle? Gray Wing. We protected each other. No cat is more important than any other—no cat except Stoneteller. She speaks with the ancients. She's wiser than you'll ever be!"

Rage surged through Clear Sky's belly. "Look at this place!" He swept his tail toward the trees. Birds sang in their branches. Prey scuttled among their roots. "If she's so wise, why did she stay in the mountains to *starve*?"

Falling Feather thrust her muzzle close. "She was looking after her cats!"

"That's all *I'm* doing!" Indignation surged through him. How could Falling Feather be so ungrateful? "Because of me you are safe and well fed."

Falling Feather frowned. "It's the forest that feeds us."

"And who makes sure the forest belongs to us and no one else?" Clear Sky jerked his muzzle toward the boundary marking the edge of the trees.

"All you care about is boundaries," Falling Feather accused. "You stretch them farther every chance you get. There's more to life than territory!"

"Really?" Clear Sky spat. "Do you want to share our prey with every passing stray?"

"There's enough prey in the forest to share!"

"But now we have kits! Have you forgotten Birch and Alder?" Clear Sky couldn't believe how shortsighted she was being. "There'll be more kits one day, and more! Do you want them to *starve*, like Fluttering Bird?" Grief echoed in the back of his mind as he recalled his young sister who'd died in the mountains. Guilt soured his memory. *Would she have lived if I'd hunted harder?* "I never want to watch a kit starve again."

"Do you think I do?" Falling Feather hissed. "Stop pretending you're moving boundaries for our sake. You're just greedy!"

Rage roared in his ears. Fast as a snake, Clear Sky raked her muzzle with his claws.

Falling Feather jerked away, her paws slithering on the leaves, and stared as though she hardly recognized him.

He showed his teeth. "Everything I do, I do for all of us," he snarled.

Falling Feather backed away, blood welling on her nose. "Okay," she growled huskily.

"I'm sorry I hurt you," said Clear Sky, "but when the cold season comes and there are new kits in camp, you'll understand what *I* already know: any cat who questions my loyalty puts all of us in danger."

With a whip of his tail, he turned and began to head farther into the forest.

Charred wood scents still wafted on the breeze as they trekked silently through the forest, despite the fact that several full moons had passed since the great fire. When they reached camp, Clear Sky climbed the steep bank edging one side and watched Falling Feather slink across the clearing to the tangled roots of an oak. There she crouched alone, her tongue flicking out to soothe the scratch on her muzzle. Quick Water hurried to join her and the two she-cats huddled, heads close, murmuring.

Clear Sky shifted his paws. Were they gossiping about him? Was Falling Feather complaining about the scratch he'd given her? He wondered whether to interrupt. He didn't want cats to talk about him behind his back. But, if he drew attention to Falling Feather's whining, he might make it worse. His pelt pricked uneasily but he held his tongue.

His gaze flicked to Fircone and Nettle. The two young toms had joined the forest cats only recently. Their loyalty was still as brittle as dry leaves. They'd persuaded Thunder to question Clear Sky's decision to enlarge the forest boundaries. A growl rattled in his throat. He was going to have to strengthen their commitment. *And* teach them some courage! Brave cats would have questioned him themselves.

He straightened, leaping down the bank and padding into the center of the earth clearing.

Leaf, a black-and-white tom, looked up from where he'd been washing his belly at the foot of a smooth rock jutting at one end of the clearing. He searched Clear Sky's gaze. "Is Thunder really leaving?"

"He already left." Clear Sky flicked his tail. He didn't want to think about the past. The future was all that mattered. "Gather to hear me speak." He flashed his gaze around the forest cats.

Quick Water padded toward him. Falling Feather followed. Nettle and Fircone circled him and stopped a tail-length away.

Leaf shook out his fur and joined Nettle, exchanging glances with the young rogue.

A yellow face peered out from beneath a low-spreading yew. "Is there a meeting?"

Clear Sky beckoned her with his tail. "Yes, Petal. Please join us."

As the golden-pelted she-cat slid out from beneath the dark green branches, the faces of two kits peered after her, their round eyes shining.

"Don't worry, Birch." Petal turned and soothed the tom kit. She nodded to his sister, huddled beside him. "Alder, stay there. Make sure Birch stays with you."

She whisked them back into the shadow with a soft flick of her tail-tip and crossed the clearing.

"What's up?" She stopped beside Falling Feather.

Clear Sky hardly heard her. He was watching Birch and Alder as they stared from the yew. They weren't Petal's kits. She'd taken them in after their mother had died.

After I killed their mother.

The words rang unbidden in his head. Guilt moved like worms beneath his pelt. A growl rumbled in his throat. *No! She attacked us! I was just defending my cats.*

She was just defending her kits.

He ignored the reproach echoing in his ears and fought to steady his paws. They were trembling. *I must stay strong if I'm to see my cats through the cold season.* The forest was still blossoming as the warm season gave way to hot. But warmth never lasted. The forest would be frozen all too soon. Prey would go to ground and hunger would stalk the cats with the ruthlessness of a fox, just as it had in the mountains.

"Clear Sky?" Petal's mew jerked him from his thoughts.

He flicked his tail and leaped past Leaf onto the rock.

His cats turned their faces toward him.

"Thunder and Frost have left and they aren't coming back."

Fircone and Nettle exchanged glances.

"There's no room in our forest for cats who aren't loyal." He snapped his gaze toward Falling Feather.

She straightened. "I'm loya—"

He cut her off.

"Falling Feather thought about leaving with them."

"Only for a moment!" Falling Feather protested.

He was pleased to see guilt flashing in her wide green eyes. She looked anxiously around at the other cats. Clear Sky hoped they all saw the same guilt in her gaze. Then, they'd understand what he was about to do. "Even a single moment is too long," he growled. "If we are to make it through the cold season we need to establish strong boundaries and unwavering loyalty *now*." He stalked to the edge of the rock and glowered at Falling Feather. "When times are hard, I need to be able to trust you."

Quick Water lifted her muzzle. "You have known Falling Feather since you were a kit," she called up. "Of course you can trust her."

Leaf's gaze slid toward Falling Feather. "What about the rest of us, not born in the mountains? Can *we* trust her?"

Clear Sky scanned the cats' faces eagerly. Did any other cat share Leaf's doubt?

"Of course!" Quick Water stared angrily at Leaf.

Petal narrowed her eyes. "Clear Sky is right," she murmured. "We need to be able to rely on each other even when times are tough. If we'd wanted to live as rogues, we'd have stayed rogues. But we chose to join Clear Sky because we believed he offered us a better life."

"Exactly!" Clear Sky lifted his tail triumphantly. "I'm glad *you* understand, Petal. I only want what's best. Loyalty will give us strength. It will let us trust one another. It will keep us safe." His gaze flashed back to Falling Feather. "That is why she must be punished."

Falling Feather's snowy fur spiked along her spine. "Punished?" Her mew was barely a breath.

Clear Sky looked around the other cats. "If she shows any signs of disloyalty, it must be reported to me. Immediately!" He waited until Petal nodded and Leaf blinked in agreement.

Fircone and Nettle shifted their paws uneasily.

"*Immediately!*" Clear Sky showed his teeth.

They gave hasty nods.

"Quick Water?" Clear Sky glared at the gray-and-white she-cat.

"I won't need to report her." She glared back. "Falling Feather would *never* be disloyal."

He narrowed his eyes. "Any cat may give Falling Feather orders. Any cat may take her prey if they wish. She is lower than a snake until she has earned our trust again."

Falling Feather's eyes sparked with hurt but she didn't argue. Quick Water moved closer to her friend.

Clear Sky flicked his tail. "But we have more important things to discuss." He looked down at Fircone and Nettle. "*Some* cats have been questioning my decision to expand our boundaries." He saw Nettle unsheathe his claws defensively. His warning had been heard. Content, he softened his tone. "I want to put your minds at rest," he soothed. "It's for your own good. Can't you see that?" He nodded toward the trees crowding the camp. Blackened trunks showed among them. "The fire destroyed much of our territory and it will take time for the forest to recover and prey to return. We need more land to hunt until it does. And with Thunder and Frost gone and small mouths to feed . . ." He glanced toward the yew. Birch had crept from the shadows and was staring up at him while Alder tugged his tail between her teeth, trying to haul him back beneath the branches. Clear Sky went on. "We need to claim as much territory as we can."

Leaf frowned. "Claiming territory is one thing," he called. "How do we *keep* it?"

Clear Sky flexed his claws. "We patrol our borders and we fight any cat who crosses them."

"Even Gray Wing?" Quick Water tipped her head. "He's your brother."

Fury surged from Clear Sky's belly. "He attacked me! He accused me of murdering the kittypet Bumble!" Outrage spiked his pelt. "Me! Murder a kittypet?" He flicked his tail toward Birch and Alder. "I *rescue* cats, I don't kill them." He pressed on before anyone could remind him how the kits had lost their mother. "These are dark times, and the cold season is not yet here. We must work *together* to build a strong, safe home!"

"Together! Together!" Petal chanted eagerly.

"Together!" Leaf joined her.

Fircone joined in with the black-and-white tom. "Together!"

Clear Sky's chest flooded with pride as the cats yowled their support. Even Quick Water and Falling Feather joined in, though their eyes watched their new mates warily. *So what?* He knew that building loyalty and trust among his cats was going to take time. But it would be worth it. By next warm season, the forest would belong to them and they would be well fed and safe. *We must be strong.* Clear Sky lifted his chin. "Let us train until no cat can outfight us!"

"Train?" Leaf stared as the other cats fell quiet around him.

"We will practice fighting until we're better than any rogue or moor cat!" Excitement rushed through Clear Sky like wildfire, his thoughts spiraling. *If we share our skills and our strengths, we'll be able to protect our territory.* "Nettle!" Clear Sky leaped from the rock and circled the gray tom. "I want you to fight Fircone." He padded toward Fircone and nudged his mottled gray shoulder. "Go on," he urged. "Fight!"

"I don't want to hurt my friend!" Nettle objected.

"Then keep your claws sheathed," Clear Sky told him. "I just want you to show us your fighting technique." He nodded to Leaf and Petal. "We can watch." He beckoned Quick

Water and Falling Feather closer with a flick of his tail. "And we can learn your skills, then show you ours."

Leaf was nodding. "Great idea, Clear Sky. I bet they have moves we don't know."

Petal leaned forward. "And I have moves they can learn."

"You can fight next," Clear Sky promised, exhilarated to see his cats so eager to share their skills. He blinked at Fircone. "Are you ready?"

Fircone nodded, his amber eyes shining. "I'm ready."

"Me too." Nettle whisked his tail and dropped into a crouch.

Fircone narrowed his eyes and faced his friend.

Clear Sky padded across the clearing, nudging Leaf, Petal, Falling Feather, and Quick Water back until there was a clear, wide circle for the two young toms.

"Can we watch?" Birch was straining against Alder's teeth as she tugged on his tail.

"Yes." Clear Sky purred indulgently. "You're never too young to learn."

Quick Water flashed him a disapproving look. He ignored it. Hopefully, she'd change her mind when they grew into fearless, skillful fighters.

He stepped aside as Birch and Alder hurtled forward and skidded to a halt beside Petal.

Fircone's tail was sweeping the earth behind him as he stared at Nettle.

Nettle narrowed his eyes, muscles twitching beneath his pelt.

Fircone leaped.

Nettle reared and met him in midair. The thump of their bodies as they clashed rang throughout the camp.

They dropped. Nettle landed on top of Fircone and, raising his forepaws, slammed them down onto his friend's shoulders.

Breath burst from Fircone. He rolled, bunching his hind legs and kicking out as Nettle reared to hit him again.

His back paws caught Nettle on the chin and thrust him backward.

Petal darted out of the way.

Alder and Birch stared frozen as the huge tom careened toward them.

"Move!" Petal ordered.

Shrieking, they scattered like mice, escaping a moment before Nettle collapsed heavily onto the ground beside them.

"Finish him, Fircone!" Clear Sky goaded.

Fircone had already leaped to his paws, rage burning in his eyes. He clearly hadn't expected Nettle to attack him so forcefully. Hissing, he leaped at his friend.

Nettle scrabbled to find his paws too late.

Fircone hit him hard, smashing him to the ground.

Growling, Nettle curled like a caterpillar and grabbed Fircone's hind paws as the mottled tom reared. Clamping his jaws around his friend's leg, he tugged until Fircone staggered and fell. "No one finishes me!" With a hiss, Nettle dived for Fircone's throat, teeth bared.

"Enough!" Clear Sky darted forward and grabbed Nettle's scruff. He tugged him back. "We don't hurt each other."

"He tried to hurt *me*." Nettle glowered at Fircone.

Fircone glared back. "I was defending myself!"

"You both fought well," Clear Sky praised. He was pleased to see such ferocity. If they were this fierce with friends, how fierce would they be with enemies? "That was a good move, Nettle." He nodded approvingly at the gray tom. "Fircone wasn't expecting you to grab his hind legs." He turned to Fircone. "And you moved well in the air. You must teach us all how you managed to twist like that."

"I used my tail," Fircone told him.

Leaf tipped his head curiously. "How?"

"I'll show you." Fircone dropped into a crouch. "When you leap, the twist starts in the tail-tip. If you flick it right, it'll alter your balance just enough." He leaped, twirling as he streaked through the air, then landed gracefully on his paws.

Nettle leaned forward, rage giving way to curiosity. "I didn't know you could do that."

"Try it," Fircone encouraged eagerly.

Clear Sky sat down. The friends' anger was forgotten already. They were only interested in learning how to fight better. Satisfaction warmed his pelt. They were skilled cats. *And, with training, they'll be deadly.*

CHAPTER 2

❧

"*We should meet him face to* face, ready to fight."

Gray Wing watched Wind Runner pace the clearing. Her brown pelt was rippling nervously.

She lashed her tail as she went on. "The sooner we make a stand, the sooner he'll understand."

The wiry rogue had grown plump since joining them. *The steady diet of prey must be doing her good.* Gray Wing glanced at the rest of the moor cats, gathered in the sandy hollow where they had made their camp. Jagged Peak was crouching beside Turtle Tail, his eyes round with worry. Gorse Fur watched through narrowed eyes. Shattered Ice and Jackdaw's Cry sat with ears pricked, as though they were listening beyond the gorse for trouble. Hawk Swoop fidgeted between them, her orange pelt catching the early evening light. In the distance, the setting sun touched the moortop, turning the heather golden.

Gray Wing closed his eyes in frustration. "If we start with a fight, who knows where it will end." His paws felt heavy as stone.

Tall Shadow growled softly, her hackles lifting. "Wind

Runner could be right. If we make a stand now, he'll think twice about attacking us."

"He *won't* attack us!" Gray Wing refused to believe Clear Sky would hurt his own kin. *He's my brother! I grew up with him.*

"What is there to fight for anyway?" Rainswept Flower spoke up. "We don't want Clear Sky's dumb forest. Surely he doesn't want the moor? He *chose* to live in the woods." She stood beneath the drooping brambles that arched over one end of the hollow, the yellow-flowered tips of its trailing fronds resting on her brown pelt. Behind her, Gray Wing could hear Turtle Tail's kits playing in the shadows, sheltered from the wind beneath the arching branches.

The petals rustled and Sparrow Fur tumbled out. "I'll be the mouse this time," she called to her littermates. She'd hardly finished speaking when Pebble Heart and Owl Eyes burst from the brush and hurled themselves at her.

"That's not fair." Sparrow Fur wriggled from under them and stood at the edge of the clearing. She puffed out her tortoiseshell fur. "You have to give me a chance to hide."

Owl Eyes sat down. "Why can't we play Jump the Bird?"

Pebble Heart rubbed his nose with his brown tabby paw. "There's not enough space to play a bird game under the brush."

"We could play out here," Owl Eyes suggested, nodding toward the stretch of sandy earth.

Gray Wing glanced at the young gray tom. "Stay out of the way," he ordered. "Until we've finished talking."

Sparrow Fur's eyes lit excitedly. "Let's go back under the

bramble and see how far we can climb into the branches." She disappeared inside. A moment later the bramble trembled as she began to scramble through its spindly stems.

"Be careful!" Turtle Tail began to cross the clearing, her eyes round with worry as her kits disappeared into the tangle of branches.

Gray Wing gently blocked her way. "Their claws are sharp enough to cling on," he promised. Pebble Heart, Sparrow Fur, and Owl Eyes were still small but they were already as strong as young rabbits. The bramble rocked under their weight, making the flowery stems tremble on Rainswept Flower's spine.

The she-cat padded clear. "How can we even think of fighting?" she fretted. "We have kits to raise. We should be hunting, not arguing over borders."

Jagged Peak limped forward. His hind leg, injured in a fall from a tree, scraped the sandy earth behind him. "If Clear Sky wants to waste time creating borders, let him."

Gorse Fur frowned, the spiky fur on his forehead rippling. "But he's killing cats to do it."

Gray Wing turned on his old friend, anger flaring. "We don't *know* that."

Turtle Tail's ears flattened. "He killed Bumble."

"And Misty!" Shattered Ice spoke up. His gray-and-white pelt rippled.

Gray Wing shifted paws uneasily. "No one *saw* him kill Misty."

"We smelled Clear Sky's scent on her body when we found

her." Gorse Fur glanced at Wind Runner for confirmation. The two cats had discovered the rogue's dead body while out hunting.

Wind Runner nodded solemnly. "It's true."

"But he took in Misty's kits," Gray Wing pointed out hopefully. "A killer wouldn't show such kindness."

Turtle Tail hissed. "Guilty conscience!"

Wind Runner narrowed her eyes. "He wouldn't *have* to take them in if he hadn't killed their mother."

Gray Wing's thoughts began to whirl. How could Clear Sky be a murderer? He gazed at the moor cats. Anger sparked in their eyes. The rage in Turtle Tail's worried him most. *I can't let this argument over Clear Sky drive us apart.* He blinked at Cloud Spots. The tom seemed relaxed despite the accusations flying across the clearing; his black fur was unruffled, his gaze calm.

"What do you think?" Gray Wing appealed to him. Cloud Spots was smart enough to know how to heal sickness and injury with herbs. Perhaps he knew how to heal this rift opening among the moor cats.

"I think there is no prey on the prey heap." He nodded toward the empty patch of earth beside the flat rock jutting at the edge of the clearing. The moor cats had begun storing their prey there, where shadow protected it from the putrefying warmth of the midday sun. "The kits will be hungry soon and so will we." He glanced around at the other cats. "And empty bellies never soothed frayed tempers."

Gray Wing felt a wave of gratitude for the tom's common sense. Full bellies would calm them all. "Jackdaw's Cry." He nodded to the young black tom. "Will you go with Shattered Ice and Gorse Fur and bring back prey?"

"*Prey?*" Sparrow Fur was scrambling down the bramble stem. "Is it time to eat?" As she popped her head through the trailing branches, Turtle Tail padded toward her. "Soon, dear. Shattered Ice is going hunting."

Gray Wing looked hopefully at the green-eyed tom. "Okay?"

Shattered Ice nodded.

"I'll go with them," Hawk Swoop announced. Jackdaw's Cry was already heading for the gap in the heather that led onto the moorside, and she hurried after him. Gorse Fur followed, Shattered Ice falling in behind.

Wind Runner paced around Gray Wing. "We still haven't decided what to do about Clear Sky."

Gray Wing felt a flash of irritation. Wind Runner had only joined the group recently. Who was she to insist they make decisions about a cat who had come all the way from the mountains with them?

Turtle Tail shooed Sparrow Fur back beneath the brush and turned toward Gray Wing. "What's your plan?"

Tall Shadow padded closer, stopping a muzzle-length from Gray Wing. "You agreed that some cat has to stop Clear Sky, before more damage is done."

Gray Wing blinked. After he'd confronted Clear Sky over Bumble's deadly injuries, he'd asked Tall Shadow for advice.

He trusted Tall Shadow to know what to do. The strong, black she-cat had led them from the mountains, confident in her ability to guide her tribe mates safely to their new home. Gray Wing had been unnerved when her confidence had ebbed away after their arrival on the moor. He could hardly believe it when she'd asked him to take over as leader. But with the death of her brother, Moon Shadow, her old energy seemed to have returned. Faced with Clear Sky's hostility, Gray Wing had been so unsure about what to do that he'd offered to pass the leadership back to her, but she had refused. Instead, they'd agreed to work together and, with the help of Wind Runner—a cat more courageous and intelligent than Gray Wing had imagined a rogue could ever be—they'd agreed to face this problem together.

He stiffened his shoulders. "If Clear Sky's moving boundaries we need to know where he'll expand next."

Tall Shadow tipped her head. "How?"

Wind Runner's ears twitched. "We could send spies."

"Too dangerous." Gray Wing traced an arc in the sandy earth with a claw.

Wind Runner and Tall Shadow hopped backward to give him room. Turtle Tail paced a wide circle, her gaze curious.

"This is where the forest ends," Gray Wing explained. He traced a fresh line with his paw, expanding the arc out in a bulge. "You found Misty here, right?" He pointed to the fresh line, and then traced another bulge. "And Bumble here."

Tall Shadow was nodding. The two bulges stuck out like ears on a cat.

"This space—" Gray Wing scuffed the earth between and drew a fresh arc farther out with a sweep of his paw. "*This* area will probably be his next target."

Wind Runner's eyes lit. "Until he's pushed his boundary clear to the edge of the moorslope."

Gray Wing nodded. "If he's determined to take more territory, he might use the same strategy again and again, until"—Gray Wing traced two more bulges from the fresh arc, then scuffed the earth between—"he's pushed right up—"

"Thunder!" Rainswept Flower's mew interrupted him.

Gray Wing glanced across the clearing. The she-cat's nose was high. Her whiskers twitched excitedly.

Cloud Spots padded forward, tasting the air. "She's right."

Gray Wing looked up. The sky was clear, growing purple as the sun set. "Thunder?" He frowned. "Can you smell rain?"

"Not rain! *Thunder!*" Rainswept Flower raced toward the gap in the heather and peered through.

She hopped backward as Hawk Swoop swept past, her amber eyes glowing with joy.

Gray Wing frowned as he saw her, confused. "You went hunting." He stopped as he caught a glimpse of a familiar pelt behind her.

"Thunder!" Joy surged through his pelt as he recognized the young tom. Thunder's paws, which had been so huge when he was a kit, didn't seem big anymore. "You've grown!" His shoulders were broader, muscles rippling beneath his sleek orange-and-white pelt. Hawk Swoop had raised him in the moor cats' camp after his mother and littermates had been killed. When he'd left to be with his father in the forest, Gray Wing had missed him but he'd understood why the young cat had wanted to go. He hurried to greet him, ears twitching with curiosity. "What are you doing back on the moor?"

Thunder glanced nervously around the camp. "I hope you don't mind me coming here."

Gray Wing slowed. Thunder hadn't answered his question. Strange forest scents clung to his pelt. Doubt pricked in his paws. Why had Thunder appeared *now*—so soon after Bumble's death and Gray Wing's quarrel with Clear Sky? Had his brother sent the young tom to spy?

Hawk Swoop puffed out her chest. "He's come home," she mewed, her voice cracking.

Beside the gap in the heather, Rainswept Flower stiffened. "Who's that?"

A white tom had limped into camp after Thunder.

Gray Wing narrowed his eyes.

"That's Frost," Hawk Swoop told them, her words tumbling out. "He's been banished by Clear Sky. Thunder left with him. We found them trekking from the border." Her eyes were fixed on Thunder, shining as fondly as if he were her own kit.

Thunder was staring at Gray Wing, his gaze sharp with worry. "Frost needs help and we had nowhere else to go."

That's why they've come! Gray Wing's pelt smoothed. Thunder was helping a friend.

Hawk Swoop went on. "Jackdaw's Cry and the others went on with the hunt, but I wanted to bring Thunder home as soon as possible." Her tail flicked with anxiety and she lowered her voice. "Banished cats should not be wandering the moors alone. And Frost is injured. Clear Sky wouldn't tolerate a cat not pulling its weight!"

Cloud Spots went to circle the white tom, his nose twitching.

Frost backed away, pelt bristling.

"It's okay," Cloud Spots murmured distractedly, his eyes searching Frost's pelt. "I'm just checking to see how badly you're hurt."

"It's a burn on my leg," Frost mumbled. He held still, watching warily as Cloud Spots padded around him.

"Thunder!"

Frost whirled in surprise as excited mewls burst from the bramble and small paws thrummed over the sandy clearing. The kits were racing to greet their old friend.

Gray Wing swished his tail. "Wait," he told them. "You can greet him in a moment."

"Your wound has gone sour." Cloud Spots's nose wrinkled as he sniffed at Frost's hind leg.

"Is that why it hurts so much?" Frost's face twisted with pain.

"Yes." Cloud Spots crouched and sniffed the wide, raw wound, which showed near the top of the leg where fur should have been. Yellow pus welled on swollen red flesh.

"It's a burn from the fire that won't heal," Thunder explained.

"Come with me." Cloud Spots beckoned to Frost with a nod and led him toward a gorse bush. Its branches jutted over the clearing and Cloud Spots gently nosed Frost into the space beneath. Gray Wing saw the white tom's face soften with relief as he sank down into its shade.

"I'll fetch some herbs to ease the pain." Cloud Spots ducked out from beneath the gorse and trotted toward the gap in the heather.

"What happened, Thunder?" Gray Wing leaned closer to the young tom. "Why did Clear Sky banish you?"

Thunder shifted his paws uneasily.

Gray Wing was suddenly aware of Rainswept Flower's breath at his ear. Hawk Swoop was leaning close to Thunder. Tall Shadow and Wind Runner padded nearer, their ears twitching. Turtle Tail stood a tail-length away while the kits lined up beside her, fidgeting with impatience.

"Can we greet him yet?" Sparrow Fur begged.

Gray Wing stared into Thunder's eyes. He saw grief darkening his amber gaze. What had happened between the young tom and his father? "Come with me." Gently, he nudged Thunder through the gap in the heather and crossed the smooth grass, golden in the setting sun. As he sat down, he noticed Thunder glance over his shoulder, swapping looks with Turtle Tail. He was touched by the warmth in their gazes. He loved both cats and he was glad they were fond of each other. "I'm so pleased you've come back." He purred loudly.

Thunder nosed his shoulder fondly. "It's good to see you." He began to pace around Gray Wing.

Gray Wing's ear twitched. He had to know why Thunder was so tense. "Hawk Swoop said Clear Sky had banished you."

Thunder halted. "He banished Frost, not me," he muttered. "I *chose* to leave."

"You chose to leave your father?" *But you were so eager to join
him!*

Thunder growled. "I *have* no father!"

Gray Wing gasped. "Has something happened to Clear
Sky?" If his brother had been injured, or worse . . .

"No. He's fine." Thunder stared angrily at his paws.

"Then why—"

"He wanted me to take Frost somewhere and leave him to
die alone!" Thunder jerked up his head and stared straight at
Gray Wing. "All the forest cats are scared of him. He hurts
anyone who stands up to him. I can't stay in the forest if I
don't agree with him."

Gray Wing felt a flash of pride at Thunder's outrage. But
sadness tugged at his belly. Was Clear Sky going to drive away
every cat who loved him? He remembered his recent quarrel
with his brother over Bumble's death. *He hurts any cat who stands
up to him.* Perhaps Thunder knew Clear Sky had killed her. It
could be another reason he'd left.

"Did he mention anything about a kittypet who died?"
Gray Wing ventured.

"No." Thunder's eyes narrowed. "Why?"

"We found a body near Clear Sky's new border," Gray
Wing explained. "It was Bumble, a friend of Turtle Tail from
her time with the Twolegs. Clear Sky said he'd fought with
the kittypet, but told me it was a fox who'd killed her."

Thunder's gaze glistened. "Clear Sky did return to camp

yesterday smelling of fox," he admitted. "And I fought a fox earlier today."

Hope soared like a bird in Gray Wing's chest. "So it *could* have been a fox?"

Thunder stiffened. "Why? Do you think it could have been Clear Sky?"

Gray Wing caught his eye. "Do *you*?"

They stared at each other for a moment that seemed to last forever. Gray Wing felt his heart beating in his throat. If Clear Sky's own son thought him capable of murder . . . Gray Wing couldn't bear to finish the thought.

"He's angry." Thunder avoided the question. "And he's determined to claim as much territory as he can. He fears the coming cold season as though he was still in the mountains, and fear can bring out the worst in any creature."

Gray Wing was impressed by how much Thunder had matured. The young cat seemed to spot danger with the clarity of a hawk's gaze. He began to pace, nervous energy fizzing in his paws. "I don't want forest cats fighting moor cats. Not over something as dumb as territory." He swept his tail toward the rolling moor. "There's more land here than we could ever need."

"So long as old cats die as fast as kits are born." Thunder's mew was grim. "But what if our numbers grow? Won't our borders need to grow too?"

Gray Wing flattened his ears. "Do you agree with Clear Sky?"

"No!" Thunder growled. "But we must defend the borders

we have now or Clear Sky will take everything."

There will be war. Stoneteller's prophecy rang in Gray Wing's ears. He mustn't let it come true. Panic welled in his chest. "If only I could talk to Clear Sky," he murmured. "We could straighten everything out. We could set borders we both agree on. We could live in peace."

"Then talk to him." Thunder's clear amber eyes glowed as the sun slid behind the moortop. "You're the only cat he'd ever listen to."

Gray Wing blinked. Thunder knew his father better than any of the moor cats. If he thought that talk might be enough to settle their differences, there was a chance for peace. "You agree?"

"Yes."

"Then I'll do it!"

Thunder turned and headed for the camp. "Can Frost stay?" he called over his shoulder.

Gray Wing caught him up. "I wouldn't turn away an injured cat."

"You're not Clear Sky," Thunder muttered.

As they padded into camp, the other cats turned, their gazes curious. The kits, who had been charging up and down the clearing, stopped and turned.

"Go and make yourself a nest," Gray Wing told Thunder.

"Can we say hi to him now?" Owl Eyes called.

"Yes." Gray Wing nodded.

As Thunder padded to the edge of the camp where long grass sprouted beside the heather, the kits tore after him.

"You're back!" Sparrow Fur squeaked.

"Are you staying?" Owl Eyes asked excitedly.

"For good?" Pebble Eyes added.

Gray Wing caught Tall Shadow's eye. "I must speak with you."

Turtle Tail was watching, her gaze sharp, as Tall Shadow padded to meet Gray Wing.

He ignored it, focusing on Tall Shadow. "I want to speak to Clear Sky and see if we can set borders we both agree on with words instead of claws."

Tall Shadow's ear twitched nervously. "Alone? Is that safe?"

Gray Wing hesitated. Would Clear Sky actually harm him?

Tall Shadow dipped her head. "Take others with you, just in case."

As she spoke, paw steps sounded beyond the heather. Jackdaw's Cry, Shattered Ice, and Gorse Fur had returned, all three carrying prey. Jackdaw's Cry dropped a dead rabbit beside the flat rock. Shattered Ice placed the limp body of a lapwing beside it. Gorse Fur carried a shrew to Wind Runner and laid it at her paws. She touched his cheek with her muzzle, then sniffed the prey.

No wonder she's getting plump. Gray Wing leaped onto the flat rock. "I must speak," he called.

Turtle Tail turned to her kits as they came hurtling from Thunder's side. She shooed them back with a flick of her nose.

"Why can't we hear?" Owl Eyes complained.

"A cat who can't hunt for himself is not old enough to hear

everything," Turtle Tail told him briskly.

Sparrow Fur lifted her chin. "I caught a butterfly yesterday."

Turtle Tail gazed fondly at her daughter. "I know, dear. But, for now, take Owl Eyes and Pebble Heart back under the bramble. Play there, out of the way."

Sparrow Fur turned sullenly and began to march away. Pebble Heart and Owl Eyes followed, dragging their paws.

As Gray Wing waited for them to disappear behind the trailing branches, Gorse Fur moved closer to Wind Runner. Jackdaw's Cry sat down and swept his long black tail over his paws. Thunder padded from the grassy patch he'd been kneading into a nest. Hawk Swoop settled beside Shattered Ice while Tall Shadow and Rainswept Flower watched from the sandy clearing, Jagged Peak beside them.

Cloud Spots padded into camp, a bunch of green leaves clamped between his jaws.

Gray Wing acknowledged him with a nod and waited for him to drop his leaves beside the gorse and take his place among the others. Then he began. "Bumble's death has unsettled us all, coming so soon after Misty's."

A growl rumbled in Turtle Tail's throat.

Gray Wing silenced her with a sharp look. "Clear Sky is moving borders daily so that no cat knows where he may hunt or roam." He pressed on before anyone could yowl accusations. "I have decided I must talk with him. If I can find out what he's thinking and what he wants, then we might find a way to live peacefully side by side." *And you might sheathe your claws next time you meet a forest cat.* He glanced anxiously around the moor cats. Could he stop their anger from spiraling into revenge?

Gorse Fur snorted. "We were already living peacefully until Clear Sky started causing trouble."

"And we'll do so again," Gray Wing promised. "If I can only speak with him." He paused and looked round. "Will anyone come with me?"

"I will!" Jackdaw's Cry stepped forward.

Gorse Fur lifted his tail. "Me too."

Cloud Spots wove between them and looked up at Gray Wing. "We should wait," he meowed softly.

"Wait?" Shattered Ice jerked around to look at the black-and-white tom.

"We accused Clear Sky of murder yesterday," Cloud Spots reasoned. "He will still be angry. We should let that anger pass before we confront him."

"I don't want to confront him," Gray Wing argued. "I only want to talk."

Thunder shouldered his way between Tall Shadow and Rainswept Flower. "Cloud Spots is right. Clear Sky will see it as a confrontation," he warned. "My father has a quick temper. I've tried to reason with him but he won't listen. It's better to wait till he cools down." His gaze betrayed a flicker of grief.

Sympathy flooded Gray Wing's heart. *He's lost his father today.* "Okay," Gray Wing agreed. "Any cat who wishes to come with me to Clear Sky's camp will meet me here, at the flat rock, in two dawns' time."

Wind Runner puffed out her fur. "I'll be there."

Murmurs rippled around the cats as Gray Wing jumped down beside Turtle Tail.

"Do you really think talking will help?" Her gaze was disbelieving.

Gray Wing padded toward the dark opening of the tunnel where he and Turtle Tail made their nest. "I have to try it, Turtle Tail," he sighed. "He's my brother."

She didn't say a word in response, which felt like a greater punishment than if she'd protested. "I'll fetch the kits," she meowed eventually.

"Turtle Tail, I . . ." he began.

"I need to keep them safe!" she snapped, cutting him off.

He watched her pad away; then he climbed into their nest. Around him, night enfolded the camp. Gorse Fur and Jagged Peak were tearing apart the prey the hunting party had brought back, giving pieces to each of the cats.

Jagged Peak carried a haunch of rabbit across the clearing. "You must be hungry." He dropped it beside Gray Wing's nest.

Its warm scent filled Gray Wing's nose. "Not really." Anxiety was churning in his belly. He stared past Jagged Peak at Thunder, who was nipping sprigs of heather from the camp wall and laying them in his new nest. He was pleased to have him back. The hollow felt like Thunder's rightful home.

No.

He pushed the thought away. *He's not my kit. I have no right to claim him.* But Clear Sky had let him go twice. Was it possible to negotiate with any cat cruel enough to drive away his own son?

Jagged Peak followed his gaze. "Are you glad he's back?"

Gray Wing nodded. "Of course."

"I guess Clear Sky doesn't want *any* kin near him," Jagged Peak murmured.

Gray Wing's belly tightened more.

Small paws thrummed across the clearing. The kits were racing for the nest.

"I'm sleeping closest to Gray Wing tonight!" Sparrow Fur leaped in first.

Gray Wing felt a rush of joy. These kits weren't his own any more than Thunder was, yet they treated him like their father.

Owl Eyes stopped beside the rabbit haunch and sniffed it.

"Hungry?" Purring, Jagged Peak nudged the gray kit's cheek softly.

"Yes!" Owl Eye tore away a tiny mouthful.

Turtle Tail stopped beside the nest as Jagged Peak headed away. "Are you hungry, Pebble Heart?" She tipped her head to one side as Pebble Heart blinked solemnly up at her.

"A bit."

She leaned past Owl Eyes and, hooking the juicy haunch toward her, tore it into pieces, giving a morsel to each of her kits.

Sparrow Fur purred loudly as she chewed and snuggled closer to Gray Wing.

Gray Wing wrapped his tail over her and tugged her back to make room for Turtle Tail.

Turtle Tail hopped into the nest, her back to him, and sat stiffly, watching Owl Eyes and Pebble Heart eat.

Gray Wing eyed her. "Please don't be angry," he whispered.

"Angry?" Sparrow Fur glanced at her mother. "About what?"

Turtle Tail leaned down and nuzzled Sparrow Fur's ear. "It's nothing to worry about." Circling around in the heather, she settled beside Gray Wing. He relaxed as she rested into him, her fur warm against his flank. As Owl Eyes and Pebble Heart finished their meal, she beckoned them into the nest. "Come on, you two."

They scrambled in and pushed their way between Gray Wing and Turtle Tail.

"Ow!" Sparrow Fur wriggled. "You stood on my tail."

"You should keep it tucked in!" Owl Eyes retorted.

"Now, now," Turtle Tail chided softly. "It's time to go to sleep."

Gradually, the kits quieted down. Gray Wing watched through the darkness as the rest of the moor cats padded to their nests and settled around the clearing until they were as still as stone in the shadows.

Turtle Tail's eyes slowly closed as she drifted into sleep.

Gray Wing felt suddenly weary. What was he going to say to Clear Sky? What if talking made things worse? Tiredness dragged at his paws and he closed his eyes. His thoughts began to swirl toward sleep.

"No! No! Don't! Please!" Pebble Heart's tiny cry jolted him awake. The kit was struggling in his sleep, kicking out against his littermates, his eyes closed, clearly dreaming.

"It's okay." Gray Wing leaned forward and nosed the kit's

twitching flanks. "It's just a dream." He didn't want Pebble Heart to wake the others.

Pebble Heart blinked awake and stared in horror at Gray Wing as though he were a badger in the nest.

"You're safe," Gray Wing ran his tail softly along the kit's spine.

Pebble Heart sat up straight, his fur on end. "So much blood!" he breathed. "So *much*! It's not right for kin to fight!"

"What do you mean?" Gray Wing's breath caught in his throat.

Pebble Heart blinked at him blindly. "Kin mustn't fight," he murmured hazily.

Is he even properly awake? Gray Wing touched his nose to the kit's ear.

Pebble Heart flinched.

Why was he so scared? Who were the kin? He'd wondered before if Pebble Heart had Stoneteller's powers. The kit had described more than one vivid dream and he'd already learned the herbs that Cloud Spots used, as though he was born to heal. Could this nightmare have meaning? Gray Wing remembered his own dream of Stoneteller. *There will be war.*

But Pebble Heart was trembling and it seemed cruel to make him dwell on the dream. Gray Wing pushed away the dark thoughts crowding his mind and scooped the kit closer with a paw, so that he was pressed against his flank. "It'll be okay," he promised. He lapped the kit's pelt with long, soothing strokes until Pebble Heart's eyes began to droop.

"The worst bit of the dream," Pebble Heart murmured as

his breathing slowed. "Was that *you* were gone."

"Hush." Gray Wing's belly tightened.

"Turtle Tail was gone too. We were alone. Just me and Sparrow Fur and Owl Eyes. We were all alone."

"It was just a dream," Gray Wing promised. *Let it just be a dream!* He stretched his tail around all three kits, his heart aching as he listened to Turtle Tail breathing softly beside him. *Turtle Tail was gone too.* "We will always be close," he whispered to Pebble Heart, trying to ignore the dread, heavy as rock in his chest. *I must make Clear Sky understand. We cannot risk war! Not after coming so far.*

CHAPTER 3

Thunder narrowed his eyes against the rising sun as he padded back
into camp. He'd left to hunt before dawn, after a fitful night.
His new nest had felt strange, its heather sprigs sharp. The
scents of moor and forest had haunted his dreams. And his
heart had ached with memories of his father.

He brushed past the wall of the camp and crossed the clearing. A mouse dangled from his jaws. Its warm musk made his
belly growl. He used to believe that he hunted better in the
forest. Now he realized how much he'd missed the wide-open
spaces and the feel of the wind in his tail fur. Perhaps Clear
Sky's territory wasn't home after all.

The other cats were out of their nests. Rainswept Flower
was tugging stale heather from her nest. Dappled Pelt was
sorting through the prey pile, tossing out old prey while Jackdaw's Cry sat nearby, washing pollen from Hawk Swoop's
ears. Tall Shadow was squeezing out of the gorse den where
Cloud Spots had led Frost. Jagged Peak rubbed the sleep from
his eyes beside the long grass.

Thunder blinked. Where were Acorn Fur and Lightning
Tail? Had they gone hunting? A pang jabbed his belly. He'd

missed the cats he'd grown up with and he'd been looking forward to catching up with them. Hawk Swoop had kitted them soon after Gray Wing had brought him to live on the moor. They'd shared the same nest and played as kits. Yesterday, he'd felt too dazed, his mind too filled with thoughts of Clear Sky and the unease of returning to the moor cats' camp, to seek out their company. Although he'd glimpsed Acorn Fur and Lightning Tail among the others, he hadn't felt ready to speak with them. And they hadn't approached him. Were they scared he'd changed? He shook out his fur. He was eager to show them he was still the same cat they used to tumble around the clearing with.

Thunder scanned the clearing. He caught Jagged Peak's eye. Did he want to share the mouse? But Jagged Peak dropped his gaze quickly. Thunder's paws pricked. Jackdaw's Cry was staring at him. Thunder stared back hopefully but the tom turned away.

Uneasy, Thunder headed for the gorse den. Perhaps Frost would appreciate his mouse. He pushed under the low branches. They scraped his spine as he ducked inside. It was cool out of the sun.

Frost lay in a dip scooped from the sandy earth and lined with moss. "Thunder." The white tom seemed pleased to see him.

Thunder stopped beside his nest and dropped the mouse beside it. "This is for you."

"Thanks." Frost purred gratefully.

Thunder nudged it closer with a paw. "How are you?"

"He's got a fever." Cloud Spots's mew surprised him. The black tom was hardly visible in the shadows at the back of the den. But now that he'd spoken, Thunder could make out his white ears, chest, and paws.

Thunder blinked at Cloud Spots, his eyes adjusting to the gloom. "Can you heal his wound?"

"I've been applying poultices." Cloud Spots padded forward and sniffed Frost's hind leg. "They should work eventually. But it's been left to fester a long time. The infection's gone pretty deep. He should have been treated earlier."

Frost's eyes rounded with worry. Thunder stared at Cloud Spots. Was he accusing him, or Clear Sky, of negligence?

"That's not how things work in the forest," he mumbled uncomfortably.

"I can see that." Cloud Spots turned his attention back to Frost. "Just be patient," he reassured the injured cat. "The poultice I put on earlier will be working now and I asked Acorn Fur to bring more herbs back from her hunting trip."

"I'm going to be okay, aren't I?" Frost asked in a tremulous voice.

Cloud Spots nudged the moss closer around his body. "You'll be fine. The journey from the forest has taken a toll on you and you need to rest."

Small paws scuffed the earth outside and the gorse branches trembled. "Which herbs is Acorn Fur collecting?" Pebble Heart padded in.

"Marigold and dock," Cloud Spots told the young kit.

"Are you giving him borage?" Pebble Heart asked. "For his fever?"

Thunder was surprised by the young cat's knowledge. He hardly knew the names of any herbs; he had no idea which ones could cure infections. When had Pebble Heart learned all this?

"I would, but there's not much on the moor. It's a forest herb and I can't gather herbs there now." Cloud Spots nodded at Frost. "Do forest cats collect it for wounds?"

Frost frowned. "We don't collect herbs. Only prey."

Cloud Spots blinked. "But what if you're injured?"

"We either recover or Clear Sky banishes us," Frost muttered bitterly. "He's more interested in moving borders than protecting the cats who hunt and fight for him." He glanced at Thunder.

Thunder stiffened. Was that reproach in his eyes? *I'm not my father!* "You seem busy," he meowed quickly to Cloud Spots. "I'll go." He backed out of the gorse, ignoring Pebble Heart's curious stare.

Outside, Turtle Tail was sunning herself beside the tunnel entrance while Owl Eyes clambered over her, mewing happily.

Wind Runner and Gorse Fur were sharing a thrush, lying languidly beside the flat rock.

Thunder padded past them, wondering whether to greet them. He glanced toward them, conscious that Wind Runner stopped purring as soon as she saw him. His throat tightened. He swallowed back hurt and took a deep breath. *I'll prove myself* to them. *I'll protect them from Clear Sky. From* any *danger.*

"Great attack, Sparrow Fur!"

Jagged Peak's enthusiastic mew jerked him from his thoughts. The lame tom was urging Sparrow Fur on with a wave of his tail. "Attack it again!"

The body of a rabbit, its scent still warm, lay in the clearing. Sparrow Fur crouched a badger-length away, her short tail flicking. Her eyes were narrowed, focused on the prey.

Owl Eyes watched beside Jagged Peak. "Can I have the next turn?"

"Yes." Jagged Peak's eyes shone.

Thunder padded closer. Was he teaching them hunting moves?

Sparrow Fur shot forward, hissing. She leaped and landed on the rabbit, her small claws sinking deep into its fur. Jabbing her teeth at the back of its limp neck, she growled as she tried to shake it between her jaws.

"Your aim is great!" Jagged Peak enthused. "Perhaps you should try attacking me. You'll need to be ready to face an enemy who fights back."

Thunder's hackles rose. He was teaching the kits *battle* moves! "What are you doing?" He strode toward Jagged Peak.

Jagged Peak jerked his gaze toward Thunder, his pelt bristling. "What do you mean?"

"Why are you teaching them how to fight?" Weren't they trying to *avoid* battle with Clear Sky?

Owl Eyes looked from Jagged Peak to Thunder, blinking with confusion. "What's wrong with that?"

Jagged Peak ignored the kit. "It's none of your business, Thunder!"

Thunder flexed his claws. "I've lived with forest cats *and* moor cats. It *is* my business. I don't want to see you fight."

Sparrow Fur leaped off the rabbit. "But we *have* to learn."

Thunder turned on her. "You're too young to fight battles!"

She backed away, eyes wide.

"Don't take it out on the kits." Jagged Peak limped past him and stood in front of Sparrow Fur.

Thunder forced his fur to lie flat. "I'm not taking it out on the kits," he growled softly. "I just don't think you should be preparing such young cats for a battle that might never come."

Jagged Peak glanced at the kits. "Go and find Pebble Heart," he ordered. "Play with him. Thunder and I want to talk."

Owl Eyes frowned. "You want to *argue*."

"Don't argue over us," Sparrow Fur pleaded.

Thunder dipped his head, softening his gaze. "We won't," he promised. "Do as Jagged Peak says."

Shoulders drooping, she padded away. Owl Eyes followed.

Thunder turned to Jagged Peak, surprised by the rage burning in the tom's eyes. He hadn't meant to upset him. "I'm sorry I interfered," he meowed slowly. "I just don't think we should be—"

Jagged Peak stepped forward, curling his lip. "Who *cares* what you think? I've lived more moons than you. I came from the mountains with your father."

Thunder lifted his chin. *That doesn't mean you know more than me.* "I was here when those kits were born!"

"But you left, didn't you?"

"I wanted to live with my father!" Thunder objected. "What's wrong with that?"

Jagged Peak didn't seem to hear. "Clear Sky didn't *want* you, did he? Just like he didn't want *me*!" Triumph edged his mew. "He kicked you out too!"

Thunder's claws itched. "Clear Sky didn't kick me out," he growled. "I *left.*"

Jagged Peak hesitated, grief flashing in his eyes. "You *left?*"

"I don't agree with Clear Sky."

Jagged Peak's gaze dropped suddenly. "So Clear Sky didn't make you leave."

Thunder shifted his paws impatiently. What did it matter whether he'd left or been banished? "I came back to help my old friends!"

"And we're supposed to be *grateful?*" Jagged Peak snorted.

"No! I just—"

Jagged Peak cut him off. "You wander from moor to forest and back again, depending how you feel. Those kits—" he flicked his muzzle toward Sparrow Fur and Owl Eyes who had flushed Pebble Heart out from beneath the gorse and were chasing him around the flat rock. "*Those* kits were born here. They belong here and if I want to teach them how to defend what's theirs, then they should be allowed to learn!"

Thunder scowled at him. "Thanks for making me so welcome!" He turned away. It was pointless to argue. Jagged Peak seemed determined to hate him. Thunder padded across the clearing, sadness pressing like a stone in his belly. As he reached the soft grass edging the hollow, he spotted Gorse Fur watching him from beside the flat rock, his gaze cold.

Thunder's pelt burned. Did no one want him back?

"Is everything okay, Thunder?" Hawk Swoop was crossing the clearing toward him, her orange pelt pricking with worry. "I saw you arguing with Jagged Peak."

"It was nothing." Thunder touched his muzzle to her cheek as she reached him.

She purred. "Jagged Peak's a good cat," she assured him. "He's just a bit misunderstood. It must be hard relying on others for prey. We mountain cats are used to feeling independent." Her eyes were sympathetic. She broke into a loud purr and pushed her muzzle along his jaw. "It's great to have you back! I've missed you so much. I know how desperate Acorn Fur and Lightning Tail are to share news." She glanced at the gap in the heather. "They'll be back soon."

At least someone's glad to see me.

Hawk Swoop's gaze flashed quickly toward Gorse Fur. The thin, gray tabby tom was still watching. "Give them time," she soothed. "We've seen so much change. I guess some of us have grown wary of it. They'll adjust."

Thunder pressed his cheek against hers gratefully, hoping she was right and that he'd be accepted soon. These were good cats. They'd helped to raise him. "Perhaps I shouldn't have left," he whispered. A wave of shame washed over his pelt. Had he been disloyal to go to his father?

"You wanted to be with your kin." Hawk Swoop sat back on

her haunches. "That's the most natural feeling in the world."

Thunder felt a purr welling in his throat. "Thanks, Hawk Swoop."

"Come on." She stood and headed for the bramble. "I've got some spare moss you can have for your nest."

As he followed her across the clearing, paw steps thrummed the earth behind him.

Stiffening, he began to turn.

Before he could see who approached, paws slammed into his side.

With a yelp of surprise he tumbled to the ground.

Pelt spiking, he tried to struggle to his paws.

"Thunder!" Lightning Tail's happy mew sounded above him.

Chestnut fur flashed on the edge of his vision. Acorn Fur was circling him, her thick tail swishing with delight.

He leaped up. "It's you!" He blinked in surprise. "You've *grown!*" Acorn Fur and Lightning Tail were adult cats now—not as big as him, but far bigger than the kits he'd played with before he'd left the moor. He felt a sudden pang as he saw Lightning Tail. He looked like a hunter, his forehead and shoulders broad. Not the sort of cat who'd trail after Thunder like a shadow as he'd done as a kit. "How are you?" He butted Lightning Tail's shoulder with his head.

"I'm the best stalker on the moor." Lightning Tail's eyes shone with pride.

Acorn Fur nodded. "He can stalk a hare from the moortop

to the gorge without it scenting him."

"And Acorn Fur can kill snakes!" Lightning Tail gazed proudly at his sister.

"I only killed one," Acorn Fur protested.

"That's one more than me!"

Thunder purred, pleased to see that, even though they'd grown, Acorn Fur and Lightning Tail still felt like kin.

Acorn Fur's gaze flitted across Thunder's pelt. "You look strong." Her eyes flashed admiringly. "And *sleek*."

Heat flooded beneath Thunder's fur. "Thanks." He glanced self-consciously at his big paws. "You look great too." Her dark chestnut fur was thick and short and shone in the sun. And her squashed kit's nose had lengthened into a smooth, straight muzzle.

Lightning Tail wove around him. "So what was it like in the forest? How was Clear Sky? Are you glad you went to live there?"

"Stop interrogating him!" Acorn Fur flashed a stern look at her brother before softening her gaze for Thunder. "You came back because you missed us, didn't you?"

Thunder blinked at her gratefully. She was sparing him from explaining the real reasons he'd returned. But part of him wanted to share what he'd seen: Clear Sky's deadly fight with Misty, the kittens needlessly made orphans by his father's greed for territory, Frost's heartless banishment.

Acorn Fur's amber gaze darkened. "Is everything okay, Thunder?"

I never want you to see any of the things I've witnessed. "Everything's fine," he lied.

"We're not kits anymore." Lightning Tail must have seen his pelt pricking. "You don't have to protect us."

But I do. Thunder shook out his fur.

"We hear what the other cats are saying about Clear Sky," Acorn Fur told him.

Lightning Tail leaned closer. "Are we going to go to battle?"

Thunder gazed past them, past the heather, across the rising moor. Would they have to fight to keep all this?

"Are we?" Acorn Fur's gaze sharpened.

"I hope not," he breathed.

"Lightning Tail!" Wind Runner's mew sounded across the camp.

Lightning Tail turned.

The rogue she-cat was striding across the clearing, Gorse Fur and Jackdaw's Cry at her heels. "You and Acorn Fur can come and practice battle moves with us."

"*Battle* moves?" Lightning Tail stared at her.

"We only know how to hunt," Acorn Fur chipped in.

"Then it's time you learned some fighting skills." Wind Runner stopped at the edge of the clearing while Gorse Fur and Jackdaw's Cry took up positions in front of her.

Thunder stiffened. It wasn't just Jagged Peak! *All* the cats were preparing to fight. Did they believe battle was unavoidable?

Lightning Tail padded toward them. "I suppose we could

adapt some hunting moves," he suggested.

Acorn Fur followed. "We could turn a hunting crouch into an attack crouch."

A chill ran along Thunder's spine. This was the sort of thing Clear Sky would do. Not the moor cats. He scanned the clearing. Where was Gray Wing? Had he approved this? There was no sign of the gray tom. His nest was empty.

Tall Shadow was lying on the flat rock. She was watching the cats, her eyes round with interest.

Gray Wing wouldn't want this. Thunder hurried after Acorn Fur. "Wait. There's no need to practice fighting. Gray Wing's going to speak with Clear—"

Wind Runner darted forward and blocked his way. "Did I ask *you* to join us?"

Jackdaw's Cry and Gorse Fur backed away. Acorn Fur and Lightning Tail turned and gazed uneasily at Thunder. Wind Runner was glaring at him challengingly.

Thunder halted. "I'm just saying you don't need to practice battle moves yet."

Wind Runner narrowed her eyes and padded slowly toward him, her plump belly swinging. "You've just arrived. Don't start telling us what to do."

I was only trying to help. "Why don't we just forget the fighting," he urged. "At least until after Gray Wing's met with Clear Sky. You might find you've got nothing to fight about."

Wind Runner curled her lip. "Are you really that dumb?"

Anger flashed beneath Thunder's pelt. "It's not dumb to

try and avoid battle!" he spat. "But what do *you* know? Last time I was here you were called plain Wind—nothing but a rogue with a rogue's name."

Wind Runner glanced triumphantly over her shoulder at Gorse Fur. "See? He's only come back to cause trouble. Just like his father."

"Leave him alone!" Acorn Fur pushed between them.

"Why?" Wind Runner flattened an ear. "No one wants him here."

Thunder glanced around at the moor cats. Lightning Tail's eyes were clouded with worry. Acorn Fur's tail was twitching anxiously. Gorse Fur and Jackdaw's Cry stared at him coldly. Finally, Thunder looked to Tall Shadow.

She sat up on the flat rock, her gaze giving nothing away. "Wind Runner."

Hope pricked in Thunder's paws. Was she going to stand up for him?

Tall Shadow's eyes were shining. "I've decided that today is the day to formally welcome you into our camp. You too, Gorse Fur! You are one of us now."

Thunder swallowed. So Tall Shadow was aligning herself with Wind Runner—a rogue who was training the moor cats to *fight*! What about Gray Wing's decision to find a peaceful solution? Had Tall Shadow—had *every cat*—decided that battle couldn't be avoided?

"Thunder." Turtle Tail's mew sounded softly in his ear.

He spun around.

She was gazing at him gently. "Follow me." Beckoning him with a flick of her tail, she led him to a patch of warm grass beside the tunnel entrance where she and Gray Wing made their nest. The moss still smelled of the kits. Its warm scent drifted over his muzzle and he let his hackles fall.

"I know you're angry," she began.

"They just want to fight!" He glanced back at Wind Runner and Gorse Fur as their camp mates wove around them murmuring congratulations. "Jagged Peak was training the *kits*!" He searched her gaze, waiting to see shock, but she looked back steadily, her pelt unruffled.

"I know," she admitted. "But we're worried. We don't know what Clear Sky will do next and we want to be ready." Her gaze flicked toward Sparrow Fur and Owl Eyes. "You know I'd never let them fight. But I want them to be able to defend themselves if they have to."

"You think Clear Sky will attack kits?" Thunder's breath quickened. How could she believe that? Even Clear Sky wouldn't be that cruel.

"We'll know more once Gray Wing's spoken to him."

"Why can't they wait before they start practicing?"

"Do you really think they should?" She leaned closer. "Our home is at stake."

Thunder narrowed his eyes.

Turtle Tail pressed on. "What if Gray Wing *can't* persuade Clear Sky to stop expanding his borders?"

I couldn't. Thunder's belly tightened as he remembered

trying to reason with his father. Clear Sky had turned on him. He hadn't even tried to listen. He met Turtle Tail's gaze. "Then they'll *have* to fight."

Turtle Tail nodded. "It's better we're prepared for the worst."

Thunder dipped his head. "Okay," he conceded grimly. "If we must prepare for battle, then I'll help." If they *had* to fight, he was going to make sure they knew how to fight properly.

CHAPTER 4

✿

Gray Wing slid through a gap in the heather, shaking soil from his paws. He blinked as he saw Jackdaw's Cry, Shattered Ice, and Dappled Pelt heading for the flat rock where Hawk Swoop, Turtle Tail, and the others were already gathered.

What's going on? He pricked his ears.

Tall Shadow was standing on the rock, tail high.

Only Thunder hung back in the clearing, his gaze dark.

"Gray Wing! There you are!" Tall Shadow leaped from the rock and padded past the young tom. "I'm making Wind Runner and Gorse Fur part of our group, like we agreed."

Pleased, Gray Wing flicked his tail. "It's about time," he purred. "They already feel like they belong here." Behind Tall Shadow, he could see Thunder's pelt pricking. Something was wrong. He dipped his head. "I'll join you on the rock in a moment." He waited for Tall Shadow to leave, then crossed the sandy earth to Thunder. "Is something wrong?"

Thunder was frowning. "Wind Runner wants to teach the kits battle moves."

"So?" Gray Wing tipped his head, confused. "She's a natural leader. I trust her judgment. It's one of the reasons we want her to join us. She knows that we must be prepared."

Thunder dropped his gaze. "That's what Turtle Tail said."

"Then what's the problem?"

"No one seems to believe we can find a *peaceful* solution," Thunder muttered. "I thought talking to Clear Sky would be enough."

"Hopefully, it will be." Gray Wing felt a surge of affection for the young cat. He might be clear-sighted about his father's ambition, but he still had faith enough to believe that all would be well if only they could reason with Clear Sky. *Life is never so simple,* he thought with a pang. "I'll do my best but, if talking doesn't work, we may have to fight to keep what's ours."

"Gray Wing." Tall Shadow called from the far side of the clearing, a few tail-lengths from the flat rock. Wind Runner paced at her side while Gorse Fur watched anxiously. "We must talk."

Gray Wing touched Thunder's cheek with his nose. "Join the others." He nodded toward the cats gathered beside the rock. They were murmuring, heads bowed, casting curious glances at Tall Shadow, Wind Runner, and Gorse Fur.

"What's the delay?" Rainswept Flower called.

Tall Shadow's gaze grew more urgent. "Gray Wing!"

He bounded toward her. "Is something wrong?" he asked as he stopped at her side. Wind Runner and Gorse Fur were exchanging nervous glances. Had they changed their mind about joining the moor cats?

Tall Shadow frowned. "Wind Runner and Gorse Fur are expecting kits."

"Kits?" Gray Wing blinked. Joy warmed his pelt. "That's great news."

"Is it?" Wind Runner moved closer to her mate. "Kits will mean extra mouths to feed." She glanced at the moor cats. "Our kits will be safer if they're raised in the camp. But it'll be a burden for every cat." She held her chin high. "They should know what they're taking on before we join the group."

Gorse Fur puffed out his chest. "We don't want the mountain cats to *resent* them."

Gray Wing's ear twitched. "Why would they do that?" Pebble Heart, Sparrow Fur, and Owl Eyes were always hungry and always getting underpaw, but no one resented them. "New life brings hope and joy."

"And extra hunting," Wind Runner reminded him.

Gray Wing swept his tail toward the distant horizon. "There's enough prey out there for us all."

He suddenly realized that Tall Shadow's gaze was lingering on Wind Runner's bulging flank.

"It's a bad time for kits to be born," the black she-cat muttered. "Clear Sky's spoiling for a fight. Wind Runner won't be able to join in the battle and we'll have more kits to defend."

Gray Wing met her gaze. "*If* it comes to battle, more kits will make us fight harder. We'll have more to fight for."

Tall Shadow looked unconvinced.

"We should leave," Wind Runner growled.

"No!" Gray Wing stepped forward. Memory swept him back to Storm's den. He'd fought through dust and rubble to try to save her and her kits. She'd tried to raise them alone and it had killed her and two of her kits. Only Thunder had survived. "It's our duty to help Wind Runner and Gorse Fur raise their litter," he told Tall Shadow firmly.

The black she-cat dipped her head. "I guess they have earned their place with us," she conceded.

"*Many* times." Gray Wing nodded to Wind Runner. "Your kits will be raised as though they are our own." A purr escaped him. Suddenly he could picture tiny kits hurtling across the clearing after Pebble Heart, Sparrow Fur, and Owl Eyes. For a moment, all his fears of battle disappeared. These kits would grow up safe in their moorland home.

He strode across the clearing, pushing between Jackdaw's Cry and Rainswept Flower, and leaped onto the flat rock. Tall Shadow jumped up beside him. He beckoned Wind Runner and Gorse Fur forward with a flick of his tail.

Hawk Swoop and Shattered Ice moved to let them pass. Jackdaw's Cry and Rainswept Flower backed away to open a circle for the two rogues to stand in. Cloud Spots slid out from the gorse where Frost peeked out, his white face half-hidden in shadow. Dappled Pelt stepped aside to let the black-and-white tom in next to her. Pebble Heart, Sparrow Fur, and Owl Eyes lined up beside Turtle Tail, as neat as owlets on a branch. Jagged Peak stood beside them, eyes shining.

Where's Thunder? Gray Wing's heart lurched as he scanned the cats for the young tom. He must show support for Wind

Runner and Gorse Fur if he was to be accepted fully back into the camp. Didn't he realize how much they'd grown to be part of the group while he'd been in the forest with Clear Sky? This was an important moment; it was the first time the mountain cats had formally accepted new cats into their ranks. *Every cat* had to approve if they were to stay united. Relief flooded him as he spotted Thunder's orange-and-white pelt, half hidden between Acorn Fur and Lightning Tail. He caught the young tom's eyes. Thunder stared back, his gaze unreadable.

Tall Shadow began. "Wind and Gorse welcomed us to the moor when we first arrived."

Purrs rumbled around the circle.

"They have been loyal allies as we've adjusted from mountain life to moor life," she went on. "It is an honor to invite them to make their home with us permanently."

Wind Runner looked up at the black she-cat, her eyes questioning. Gray Wing guessed what the expectant queen was thinking. *Is Tall Shadow going to mention the kits?*

He stepped forward. This needed to be spoken now. If there were objections, they must be heard. "Wind Runner is expecting kits." He gazed around the moor cats. Warmth glowed in Hawk Swoop's eyes. Jagged Peak purred loudly.

"Congratulations!" Rainswept Flower darted forward and touched noses with Wind Runner.

Jackdaw's Cry's tail twitched uneasily. "Can we feed extra mouths?"

Acorn Fur stared at him. "Of course we can!"

Lightning Tail pricked his ears. "Our hunting skills get better every season."

Murmurs of agreement rippled around him.

"What about when the cold season comes?" Cloud Spots reasoned. "Prey will go to ground."

Shattered Ice raised his voice. "Then we'll hunt in the tunnels that Wind Runner and Gorse Fur showed us when we arrived."

Tall Shadow stepped to the edge of the rock. Gray Wing saw with relief that her eyes were shining, all doubt gone.

"Wind Runner and Gorse Fur have done so much for us," she called. "They have earned prey for their kits, and their kits' kits!"

Jagged Peak nodded enthusiastically. "They rescued me from a collapsed tunnel," he reminded them. "When every other cat thought I was dead, Wind Runner cleared my nose and throat so I could breathe."

"When we were kits, Gorse Fur taught me and Acorn Fur how to stalk rabbits," Lightning Tail chimed in. "He spent a whole afternoon showing us how to lie flat and still and let the rabbit come to us."

Acorn Fur purred loudly. "He was so patient, even when we got bored and started stalking his tail instead!"

Turtle Tail stepped forward. "Wind Runner showed me the best places to hunt after I returned from Twolegplace."

Gray Wing swallowed back a purr. Turtle Tail had often complained that Wind Runner was too bossy, holding her responsible for turning Bumble away from the camp. He was relieved to see that she had accepted the rogue at last.

He stiffened as Jackdaw's Cry flicked his tail. Was he still worried there wasn't enough prey to share?

"We would never have dared explore the tunnels if Wind Runner and Gorse Fur hadn't showed us how." The black tom glanced at them approvingly. "Now we have shelter in the worst of the cold season."

"And escape routes from dogs!" Dappled Pelt added.

Happily, Gray Wing kneaded the rock. "We are lucky to have such strong, loyal cats join us." He gazed at Wind Runner. She stared back unblinking. How long before she was the one up here, leading the moor cats while he and Tall Shadow watched from below? He welcomed the thought. It was tough having to know all the answers. Wind Runner seemed to relish the challenge of decision making far more than he ever would.

Tall Shadow's mew jerked his thoughts back to the moment. "Wind and Gorse took new names to be like us and it is with these new names that we shall welcome them." She jumped from the rock and touched noses with Wind Runner. "Welcome, Wind Runner."

Gray Wing felt the expectant gaze of the moor cats and jumped down beside her. "Welcome, Gorse Fur." He touched noses with the gray tabby tom.

"Gorse Fur!"

"Wind Runner!"

The moor cats lifted their voices to the sky as, chanting the names of their new denmates, they welcomed them warmly.

Jagged Peak broke from the circle and hopped around Wind Runner, his eyes bright with excitement. Gray Wing lifted his tail happily. The young cat had always admired the rogue. He must be delighted she'd been made part of the group.

Tall Shadow padded to the prey heap. "Let's celebrate with a feast." She tossed a mouse toward Gorse Fur. "We will eat this meal like mountain cats." She carried a thrush to Wind Runner and dropped it. Then she bent and took a bite and pushed it toward the brown she-cat. Wind Runner dipped her head in thanks and took a bite, then nudged it toward Gorse Fur. Purring, he tore off a mouthful and passed it to Jagged Peak.

Gray Wing padded to the prey heap, waiting for Shattered Ice to take a mouse before grabbing a small rabbit. Joy flooded beneath his pelt. The moor cats settled and shared prey, mewing contentedly. *We are one.* The thought sent hope surging through him. Whatever happened when he visited Clear Sky's camp, the moor cats would survive. They were united, and together they could weather any storm. He glanced at Wind Runner, chewing contentedly as she lay between Tall Shadow and Gorse Fur. *With her on our side, we'll be strong for a long time.*

A soft murmuring woke Gray Wing out of a light sleep. He blinked open his eyes and peered over the edge of his nest. He could see no one, but soft mews sounded beside the tunnel entrance.

"We can't talk here." He recognized Rainswept Flower's anxious voice. "We'll wake Gray Wing."

"Come outside."

Jagged Peak? What were the two cats up to?

Gray Wing lifted his head, unease moving in his belly, and watched them move like shadows across the camp and slip out through the gap in the heather.

Slowly, he untangled himself from the kits and tipped them toward Turtle Tail.

"Gray Wing?" Pebble Heart mewed sleepily, his eyes closed.

"I'll be back in a moment," he whispered. He hopped from his nest and padded noiselessly around the edge of the clearing, keeping to the shadows until he reached the gap in the heather. He halted and pricked his ears.

Rainswept Flower and Jagged Peak were talking beyond the thick wall.

"We've got to make Clear Sky see reason!" Rainswept Flower hissed.

"Talking to him won't work," Jagged Peak whispered. "Gray Wing still thinks of him as the brother he knew in the mountains. But Clear Sky's changed. I've seen how heartless he's become." Bitterness hardened the young tom's mew.

Gray Wing swallowed back a sigh. Would Jagged Peak never forgive their brother for sending him away?

Jagged Peak went on. "If Gray Wing turns up in Clear Sky's camp and challenges his authority, he'll just make things worse. Clear Sky will be furious. I don't think Gray Wing understands the danger he's putting himself in."

"The danger he's putting us *all* in," Rainswept Flower added. "The angrier Clear Sky is, the more dangerous he'll become."

Gray Wing stiffened. Why hadn't they come to him to share these worries? Should he step from the shadows and confront them? *No.* He had to hear what they truly thought, not what they guessed he wanted to hear. He leaned deeper into the heather.

"Gray Wing's the last cat who should try to talk with Clear Sky," Jagged Peak fretted. "So much has happened between them. Clear Sky will never see past his anger."

"But we have to do something," Rainswept Flower argued. "Or Clear Sky will keep taking territory until there's nothing left."

"Clear Sky needs to speak to a cat who can remind him who he *used* to be," Jagged Peak murmured. "Someone who can show him how much he's changed. And what he's become."

"Someone like you?" Rainswept Flower suggested hopefully.

"No," Jagged Peak answered sharply. "I'm lame now. Clear Sky thinks I'm no better than prey."

"Then *who?*"

Gray Wing held his breath. *Why don't they trust me? I know I can change Clear Sky's mind!*

Jagged Peak's hushed mew sounded through the heather. "What about you?"

Rainswept Flower gasped. *"Me?"*

"Clear Sky has always respected you," Jagged peak pressed. "You've known each other all your lives but you've hardly spoken since he's changed. Talking to you might remind him of his old self." He paused for a moment, then added, "You were a friend of Bright Stream."

Grief stabbed Gray Wing's heart at the name. Bright Stream had been Clear Sky's first love. She'd been carrying Clear Sky's kits when she'd died. Memories flooded Gray Wing so powerfully that he could hardly breathe. Guilt seared his pelt. She had been killed by an eagle while she'd been hunting with him and Clear Sky. Between them, they'd let her die.

"I don't know, Jagged Peak." Rainswept Flower sounded doubtful. "I don't think he'll care what I have to say."

"But you'll think about it?" Jagged Peak coaxed.

"I'll think about it," Rainswept Flower conceded.

Their paw steps brushed the grass. Gray Wing pressed himself into the heather, until shadow swallowed him. Holding his breath, he stood like a stone while Jagged Peak and Rainswept Flower padded into camp. He waited until they'd settled in their nests, then waited some more. His thoughts whirled. Was Jagged Peak right? Had too much happened between him and Clear Sky for words to make any difference?

No! We are brothers! Nothing can change that. Surely, everything they'd been through must bind them tighter, not push them apart?

Gray Wing slid from the heather. *Jagged Peak's wrong . . . Clear Sky* will *listen to me.*

CHAPTER 5

❧

"Hurry up, Alder!" Clear Sky pounded down the slope. He leaped the ditch at the bottom and, landing smoothly, glanced over his shoulder.

Birch was galloping toward him, his small paws sending leaf litter flying. Alder raced behind, half-running, half-slithering down the slope, no bigger than a baby rabbit. She looked more like prey than a hunter.

She has to grow up sometime.

Clear Sky pushed on, climbing the rise beyond, pleasure pulsing beneath his fur. Petal had begged him not to take the kits out to train. *Worry-worm!* He had told her that, in the mountains, kits were fighting snowstorms by the time they were two moons old. He couldn't let the forest make his cats soft.

"Birch! Help!" A small thud made Clear Sky turn.

Alder had disappeared.

Birch was leaning into the ditch, tugging something. With a grunt, he heaved his littermate out by her scruff and let go. "Are you okay?"

Alder scrambled to her paws and shook out her short, fluffy fur. "I'm fine."

"Hurry up, you two!" Clear Sky rolled his eyes. Were they going to fall into every ditch between here and the big beech tree?

"Can we go slower?" Birch called up the slope.

Is that possible? "Slow cats get caught!" Clear Sky called back. He wasn't going to indulge them. They'd have to toughen up. He turned and ran.

He was hardly out of breath by the time he reached the big beech. It towered above the other trees in this part of the forest. He stopped at its thick roots and waited for the kits to catch up. Above him, birds twittered in the bright green canopy. Beyond, sunlight glimmered.

Clear Sky pricked his ears impatiently. At last he heard small paws thrumming over the dry earth. A moment later, Birch and Alder hurtled from a clump of ferns and began scrambling up the slope toward him. Their pelts were slick against their bodies, scraped flat by ferns and brambles, their ears pressed to their head.

"We made it!" Birch stumbled, puffing, to a halt in front of Clear Sky.

Alder stopped a tail-length behind, her flanks heaving.

"You took your time."

"We couldn't run any faster," Alder panted.

"Our legs aren't as long as yours," Birch pointed out.

"But you're not carrying much weight," Clear Sky countered. He padded around the kits as they struggled to get their breath back. "Not yet, anyway." Was he being too hard on them? "If you keep training, one day you might be as strong as me."

"Or stronger!" Birch stared at him, eyes bright.

Clear Sky grunted. "I doubt it." He stopped and lifted his gaze. The warm season had wrapped the forest in a green haze. He flicked Birch's spine with his tail-tip. "Wait here."

"By *himself?*" Alder nosed past her brother.

"Of course!" Clear Sky thrust his muzzle close to hers, stifling a purr of amusement as she leaped back in surprise. "You're coming with me. We're going to play hide-and-seek."

Alder blinked. "Hide-and-seek?"

Birch frowned. "I thought you were going to teach us fighting skills."

"You think seeking isn't a fighting skill?" Clear Sky dropped his mew to a whisper. "One day your enemies will hide when they hear you coming. You'll need to know how to find them."

Alder's eyes grew round. "Are we going to hide while Birch waits here?"

"You're a smart young kit." Clear Sky lifted his nose to point at the sun where it dazzled through the branches. "Birch." With a jerk of his muzzle, he motioned the young tom kit to follow his gaze. "When the sun has lifted to the next branch, come and look for us."

Birch drew himself up. "Okay."

"Come on, Alder." Clear Sky bounded down the slope. "Let's find somewhere he'll never think of looking."

"Do you already know somewhere?" Her paws pattered over the leaves.

"Hush! We mustn't give him clues." He slowed his pace. She'd need some energy left for the next part of the training session. He crossed a dry streambed, followed a swath of brambles, and headed into a dip crowded with ferns. Climbing out the other side, he zigzagged among the trees until he reached a ridge. A clearing lay beyond. He'd picked it out the day before for training. The ground was clear; the slender birch trees that encircled it were widely spaced.

"There's nowhere to hide here!" Alder caught him up and stared around the bare clearing. "Why didn't we stop in the ferns?"

"Pick a tree, and crouch behind it," Clear Sky ordered. "When Birch comes, you'll need space to attack him."

Alder blinked at him. "*Attack* him? I thought we were playing hide-and-seek."

"We're *training*, remember?" *Why is she arguing?*

"I won't do it." Alder dug her paws into the crumbly earth. "You didn't warn Birch."

"He needs to learn!" Clear Sky snapped, swallowing back an angry hiss.

"It's not fair." Alder stared with round eyes. "He won't be ready for it." Was she trembling? "It feels *wrong*."

She's brave. He couldn't help feeling a prick of admiration for the kit. It took courage to argue with her leader. But she had a lot of growing up to do. "I know your instinct tells you that cats stalk their enemy, that they don't hide and jump out at them. But times are changing. We must learn to outgrow instincts that don't help us anymore." He padded around her. "In battles, it won't always be the strongest cats with the sharpest claws who survive."

Alder glanced down at her small paws.

Clear Sky went on. "The smartest cats with the fastest moves will have the best chance at victory. Your instincts might tell you that these tactics aren't honorable. But, if there's one thing I've learned since I came down from the mountains, honor means nothing to the dead." He stopped and leaned closer. "We must stay ahead of our enemies."

Alder swallowed. "Do we *have* enemies?"

Clear Sky swished his tail and padded toward a birch trunk. "Every cat who wants to take prey from our land is an enemy. Learn what I teach you and you'll be safe." He climbed onto a root, and sat down. "Birch will be on his way soon. You'd better pick a tree to hide behind. But first—" He scanned the forest floor until he spotted a dip in the earth still wet with morning dew. "Roll yourself in that mud." He jerked his nose toward it."

Alder sniffed. "Why?"

"To disguise your scent." Couldn't she guess? "Otherwise Birch will smell you the moment he reaches the clearing."

Alder stopped beside the muddy dip and wrinkled her nose. "It smells of rotting leaves."

"Good." Clear Sky idly scraped a strip of bark from the root. "Get rolling."

Screwing up her eyes, Alder padded into the mud and lay down. She wriggled on her back, flopping from side to side like a stranded fish, then leaped to her paws. "I stink!"

"But you've lost your scent," Clear Sky reminded her. "Now pick a tree to hide behind." He glanced at the sky. The sun had moved. Would Birch be on his way yet? Training kits was slow work. But it would be worth it. "Hurry up!" Alder was turning in circles behind a birch stem, her ears flicking. "You should be in position by now."

Her fur rippled along her mud-slicked spine. She padded uneasily to the next truck and sniffed the roots, then twisted suddenly and dug her nose into her flank as though she were chasing a flea.

"What's wrong?" Clear Sky bit back anger. "Just *hide*, will you?"

"But my pelt feels weird with all this gunk on it."

Clenching his teeth, Clear Sky hopped from the root and padded toward her. "Crouch here." He jabbed a claw into a gap between two roots. "Stay low so Birch won't see you."

She squirmed onto her belly between the roots. "It still feels wrong," she muttered. "He thinks we're playing hide-and-seek and you want me to attack him."

"I want to see if you can *surprise* him." Irritation itched beneath Clear Sky's pelt.

"I could surprise him without smelling like rotten leaves." She pressed her belly to the floor until she looked like another muddy root sticking up from the earth.

"If Birch was a real enemy, smelling like rotten leaves might be the best weapon you have."

"But he's *not* a real enemy." She sat up straight, destroying her camouflage.

Clear Sky stiffened with frustration.

"Why can't all the cats just be friends?" Alder asked. "Just because we live in different places doesn't mean we have to fight."

Stop arguing! Before he could stop himself, Clear Sky swiped a paw at her. He sheathed his claws a moment before he struck her ear, but she staggered from the fierceness of the blow and tripped over a root. "No cat wants to fight," he growled. "But we have to survive! It's better to train for a battle that never comes, than to die in one you aren't prepared for." Rage churned in his belly. "All I'm trying to do is make sure you can win if you have to fight!"

Alder scrambled to her paws and backed away. Her ear twitched where he'd hit it.

"Don't look so scared!" Clear Sky forced his hackles smooth. He hopped over the root and landed in front of her. She froze like a rabbit and stared up at him, trembling as he touched his muzzle to her head. "I'm sorry, okay? But you'll understand when you grow up and have kits of your own to protect. A good leader will do whatever it takes to keep his cats safe."

As he spoke, a dog's bark rang through the trees. Alder ducked out from beneath him, her ears swiveling as the dog barked again. "It's coming from the big beech!" Her eyes glittered with terror. "Birch is there by himself!"

She hared away from Clear Sky and hurtled across the forest floor.

Clear Sky pelted after her, showering leaves behind as he pounded between the trees. He pulled past Alder, thundering up the slope as the forest rose ahead.

"Save him!" Alder's squeal rang behind.

Through the ferns, past the bramble and over the dry streamed, Clear Sky ran, ears flattened against the dog's barking. It was frenzied now, as though it had spotted prey.

Clear Sky's heart seemed to burst as he pelted on. The ground trembled beneath his paws. A flash of brown fur showed on the slope ahead. *The dog!*

Large and broad shouldered, it thumped toward the big beech. Its teeth glistened as it barked with excitement.

"Birch!" Clear Sky hissed the kit's name. *Where is he?*

The dog was circling the beech now, its wild eyes staring up. It gave a long, full-throated bark that rose into a gleeful howl.

Clear Sky slowed, following the dog's excited gaze.

Clinging to the trunk, a few tail-lengths above the dog's muzzle, was Birch. Brown-and-white pelt bushed, eyes wide with terror, the kit pressed himself hard against the bark.

Clear Sky stopped, his heart lurching as the dog leaped, drool flying as it clamped its teeth shut a whisker beneath Birch's tail.

"It'll kill him!" Alder's horrified shriek took Clear Sky by surprise. She skidded to a halt at his side. "You have to save him."

Clear Sky hesitated. He couldn't fight the dog head-on. He'd be killed. It was bigger than a badger. As he stared, his mind whirling, a desperate yowl sounded through the trees. Pale fur flashed at the edge of his vision.

Petal!

The yellow she-cat was racing up the slope. She was heading

straight for the dog. She ran harder as she neared it.

What's she doing? Clear Sky stared. *Is she mad? She'll get herself killed.*

"Petal!" Alder wailed beside him.

Suddenly, Petal veered.

She's going to distract it! Clear Sky understood in a flash that Petal was planning to lead the dog away from Birch. "I'm coming!" Energy surging, he dived forward. Two cats would be harder to chase. Surging up the slope, he neared the dog as its gaze flicked toward Petal. Delight flared in its eyes. Its paws scrambled to find a grip on the leaf-strewn earth as it lunged for her.

She swerved, swooping past it like a snow eagle.

The dog pelted after her.

Clear Sky yowled. The dog slowed, glancing over its shoulder. Confusion shadowed its gaze as it saw him, then it turned back to Petal and pounded on. Clear Sky pushed hard against the forest floor. Petal was streaking ahead, the dog at her tail. But Clear Sky was gaining. Chest burning, he fixed his eyes on the dog. Pulling close, he leaped, raking his claws along the dog's flank, before landing beside its shoulder without missing a paw step. As the dog stumbled, yelping with pain, he raced past it and caught up with Petal. "This way!" He swerved. Brambles crowded the forest ahead, better for prey than for hunters—and they were prey now.

Petal's paws thrummed beside him. The dog's foul breath washed over them.

The brambles loomed closer.

Petal glanced at him. "Through or around?"

Clear Sky nodded to the fox trail he knew cut through the middle. They could squeeze through it easily. The dog would have to go around.

Petal's eyes lit as she saw the small gap in the prickly branches. Clear Sky slowed to let her dive through first and followed. Thorns scraped his pelt. Tendrils whipped his nose. He pressed on, Petal's tail flicking a muzzle-length ahead. Swiveling his ears, he listened for the dog.

Big paws slewed to a halt at the bramble's edge. The dog whined angrily before taking off again.

"It's going around," Petal warned.

"We'll make it to the other side before it does," Clear Sky promised.

"There are Twolegs on the moorside!" Petal screeched. "Let's lead it there. They might distract it."

"Okay." He burst from the bramble a moment after Petal. They charged between the trees, the dog some way behind. It had been slowed by the detour around the bramble, but it was not giving up easily.

Ahead, light showed as the woods thinned. Another rise and they'd break cover from the trees.

Petal's fur streamed in the wind as she ran. Clear Sky fought for breath, relief surging as they crested the rise and surged down the slope. Bursting from the trees, he saw a small pack of Twolegs.

In brightly colored pelts, they moved through the ferns on the moor slope.

"Let's get as close to them as we can!" Clear Sky yowled. He plunged into the ferns as the dog exploded from the forest behind them.

The Twolegs spun, their pink faces reddening with surprise. One began to bellow; another put its paw to its lips and shrilled a piercing alarm call.

The dog's head jerked toward the Twolegs. Its ears pricked, surprise lighting its gaze.

The Twolegs called louder.

With a rush of joy, Clear Sky saw the dog swerve. Paws skidding over the grass, it dived through the ferns and headed for the Twolegs.

"Let's get out of here," Petal puffed. She turned and raced back toward the forest. Clear Sky chased after her, relief pulsing so fiercely that he hardly heard the wind in his ears. She didn't stop running until she reached the big beech.

Clear Sky stumbled to a halt behind her, heart pounding.

"Where are they?" Petal was darting back and forth across the slope, her pelt bristling. "Alder! Birch!"

A mournful squeak sounded from above. "Petal!"

Clear Sky looked up and saw Birch and Alder huddled in the crook of the lowest branch. Eyes wide, trembling, they were pressed together like fledglings.

"It's safe to come down," he told them.

Petal stopped beside him. "The dog's gone," she called gently.

Birch stretched his forepaws down the trunk and, clinging like a squirrel, slithered down headfirst. Alder lowered herself more gracefully tail-first, still trembling as she reached the ground.

"You're safe." Petal licked her roughly while Birch pressed hard against her.

"Can we go home now?" Birch begged.

Alder shook out her fur. The mud had dried into crumbs and she shuddered as they sprinkled onto the forest floor. "I've had enough of training."

"Of course you have." Petal wrapped her tail over the young kit's spine. "Let's get you home for a rest."

As she led them downslope toward the camp, one on either side, Clear Sky caught his breath. "You've learned a lot for one day," he called after them.

Birch glanced over his shoulder. "We learned how to climb trees."

Alder pressed closer against Petal. "We were supposed to be learning how to attack other cats," she told the she-cat shakily.

"Really?" Petal slowed and licked some of the mud from Alder's pelt.

Alder nodded. "Clear Sky wanted me to jump out at Birch when he came looking for me."

Clear Sky caught them up. "It's important to know how to sneak up on an enemy."

Petal glanced at him accusingly. "It might have been better to teach them how not to get snuck up on." She scooped the kits closer with her tail. "They're too young for battle training."

Birch pulled away from her, chin high. "I'm not."

Clear Sky purred. "Of course you're not." He shook out his pelt, his paws still sparking with exhilaration from the chase. He'd saved the kits, and protected his group—just as he had promised he would.

They're too young for battle training. Petal's words echoed in his ears. A growl rumbled in his throat. *No cat's too young to fight.* Clear Sky paused, unease rippling beneath his pelt. Would Gray Wing agree? Or Quiet Rain? Or his beloved Bright Stream?

A sudden chill pierced his fur. He shivered and hurried to catch up with Petal and the kits.

Anxious yowls rang between the trees.

Clear Sky jerked up his head. Blinking away sleep, he scrambled to his paws. "What's going on?" He scanned the camp from his nest in the hollow of the slope. His heart lurched. He'd only closed his eyes for an afternoon nap; now the clearing was golden in the setting sun. He screwed up his eyes as shafts of light sliced between the trees.

"Clear Sky!" Falling Feather was pacing near the brambles that edged the far end of the camp. Quick Water had climbed the slope above his nest and was peering into the trees. Fircone and Nettle stood in the middle of the clearing, square on, facing the gap where the brambles opened into forest.

Beside them, Leaf showed his teeth, a growl rumbling in his throat.

Beyond the brambles, paw steps scuffed the earth. The scent of strange cats rolled into the clearing.

Clear Sky leaped from his nest and crossed it. Pushing between Fircone and Leaf, he glared at the opening.

Falling Feather stopped pacing, her hackles rising. Nettle hissed as two cats padded into camp.

A she-cat with short gray fur blinked at them with bright blue eyes.

Beside her, a mangy tom lifted his tail. "We've found you."

Clear Sky marched forward. "Found us?"

"I'm Dew," the gray she-cat told him. "This is Thorn." She nodded to the tom.

He dipped his head, tufts of fur hanging from his brown pelt. "We were hoping you'd have space in your camp for two more rogues."

Surprise pulsed through Clear Sky. "You want to join us?" Pride edged his mew. His reputation was clearly spreading.

Leaf narrowed his eyes. "We don't need more cats."

Quick Water scrambled down from the slope and stopped beside Falling Feather. "We have enough rogues, thanks."

Nettle stared at Thorn. "He looks like he's sick."

Thorn lifted his head and shook out his pelt. Fur clouded around him. "I'm just molting."

Clear Sky stood still. His thoughts whirled. New cats would mean more fighters. Of course, the tom would have to smarten himself up. The forest cats weren't going to take in sickly strays.

Fircone paced around the two strangers, his gaze flitting over them. "We don't need more mouths to feed."

"We can feed ourselves, thanks," Dew told him.

Clear Sky narrowed his eyes. *We'll need more territory if we have more cats.* He swallowed back a purr.

Falling Feather padded to his side. "Shall I chase them off?" she asked quietly.

Clear Sky looked at her, rounding his eyes with surprise. "Why would I want you to chase them off? We need allies, and these cats look like they can take care of themselves."

Falling Feather backed away, pelt pricking. "But I thought—"

"Let *me* do the thinking." Clear Sky swished his tail. "I think we should consider their request."

Leaf tipped his head. "Why?"

Clear Sky gazed slowly around at the cats. He knew he must appear reasonable, and not let Dew and Thorn think that they could just walk in and find a soft place to sleep. "Leaf's question is a good one." He turned to the strangers. "Why should we take you in?"

"We can hunt prey for you as well as ourselves," Thorn told him.

Dew nodded. "Thorn looks scrawny, but he's wily, and as fast as a ferret."

"Dew's a good fighter," Thorn offered. "No cat's taken prey from her since she was a kit."

Clear Sky nodded slowly. They sounded promising. "Anything else?" He wasn't going to make this easy.

Dew and Thorn glanced at each other.

"We have information you might find useful," Dew meowed softly.

Clear Sky pricked his ears. "About what?"

Thorn's whiskers twitched. "We've been watching your rivals."

Clear Sky snorted. "We have no rivals."

Dew's eyes glittered. "Really? What about the cats who live on the moor? The one they call Gray Wing?"

"And the orange tom with the big white paws?" Thorn added.

"*Thunder?*" Quick Water darted forward, ears pricking. "How is he?"

"Is he okay?" Falling Feather padded to her friend's side, eyes bright.

Thunder has gone back to Gray Wing? Clear Sky glared at Falling Feather. "Be quiet." He snapped his gaze back to Dew. "What have you seen?"

"We've watched their kits practicing battle skills." Dew stared at Clear Sky, unblinking.

"They've learned how to attack a dead rabbit," Thorn sneered. "And the older cats were discussing how to turn hunting moves into battle moves."

Clear Sky forced the fur along his spine to stay flat. What was Gray Wing up to?

Thorn went on. "They were about to practice fighting,

but a black cat interrupted."

"Do you mean Tall Shadow?" Falling Feather padded closer.

Thorn shrugged. "Maybe."

Clear Sky narrowed his eyes. "Why did the black cat interrupt?"

Dew shrugged. "She and Gray Wing made some kind of speech from a rock. Then the rest of the cats started cheering."

Thorn frowned with distaste. "They were chanting names. Then every cat ate."

"*Every* cat?" Clear Sky curled his lip. "Was there enough prey?"

"More than enough," Dew told him. "They had a heap of it and they gobbled it up like a pack of dogs."

Clear Sky's belly tightened. "It sounds like they're preparing for battle."

"Gray Wing wouldn't start a battle!" Quiet Water gasped.

Wouldn't he? Clear Sky narrowed his eyes. Gray Wing might be soft, but he was no fool. He'd fight if he thought it was the right thing to do. And yet, the last time they'd spoken, Gray Wing had backed away from challenging Clear Sky directly over Bumble's death. Why show hostility now?

Thunder!

Clear Sky stiffened. Was that why his son had left? Had he gone to warn Gray Wing that Clear Sky was planning to expand his borders?

Jealousy burned beneath his pelt. Had Thunder only come to the forest in the first place to spy for Gray Wing?

Traitor!

He'd been Gray Wing's cat all along! *I trusted him because he was my son!* Hackles rising, Clear Sky felt a growl rise in his throat. *I'm a fool!*

"Can we join you then?" Dew's calm mew jolted him from his thoughts.

"Yes!" Pulsing with rage, Clear Sky barged past the rogues and headed into the woods. *I was right to set boundaries. I'm right to train my cats for battle.* War was coming. He could feel it. Gray Wing was on the move.

Clear Sky's claws spiked leaves as he marched through the woods. *If Gray Wing thinks he's going to take us by surprise, then he can think again! We'll be ready.* He halted and stared between the trees. Beyond, the moor rose like a spine arching against the setting sun. *You want battle?* He pictured Gray Wing training his cats to fight. *I'll give you war.*

CHAPTER 6

Where is everyone? Thunder strained to see through the mist. Dawn light filtered weakly through the thick fog, which shrouded the moor. *Am I early?*

He was waiting to join Gray Wing's expedition to Clear Sky's camp. Gorse Fur had promised to come. Jackdaw's Cry had volunteered too. But Thunder was the only one outside the hollow.

Paw steps scuffed behind him.

Thunder whipped around. "Gray Wing?"

A dark shape showed through the mist. "It's me." Jackdaw's Cry's mew was hushed. "Where are the others?" His black face emerged from the fog, a muzzle-length away.

Thunder shrugged. "I'm the only one here." He stretched his ears. The fog muffled the sounds of the camp. "Is anyone else out of their nest?"

"It was too foggy to tell." Jackdaw's Cry shook out his pelt with a shiver and sat down.

Thunder faced the moor stiffly as silence descended between them, thicker than the fog. He remembered the black tom's hostile gaze yesterday. Jackdaw's Cry had never wanted him to join the cats on the moor, even as a kit. He hunched against the chill of the fog, the memory of his early loss echoing painfully in his chest. In one day, he'd lost his mother, been rejected by his father, and then had to stand and listen while Gray Wing pleaded with the moor cats to allow him to stay in their camp. Jackdaw's Cry had argued that they couldn't take in another mouth to feed. He'd backed down when Gray Wing had threatened to leave if Thunder was sent away, but Thunder still carried the memory of the black tom's resentful gaze.

He pictured it now, its sharpness boring deeper and deeper until Thunder couldn't stay quiet. "Are you hoping I'll go back to my father?"

Jackdaw's Cry jerked around, blinking. "Why would you say that?" He sounded confused.

"I've seen how you've been watching me since I returned," Thunder growled bitterly. "You didn't want me back. You never wanted me to begin with."

"You were Clear Sky's son." Jackdaw's Cry shifted his paws. "Not our responsibility."

"I had nowhere else to go," Thunder murmured.

Jackdaw's Cry didn't answer.

"Where did you think I'd end up?" Anger pricked at Thunder's paws. "I wasn't old enough to hunt for myself."

"Hawk Swoop had her own kits to take care of. I had to put them first."

"Was that a good enough reason to turn a kit out alone onto the moor?" Thunder hissed.

Jackdaw's Cry's fur lifted uncomfortably along his spine. "Clear Sky would have taken you in if you had nowhere else to go." He stared into the mist. "He'd never let his own kit die."

"Do you still believe that?"

Jackdaw's Cry didn't answer.

"What about now?" Thunder pressed. "Would you rather I went back to Clear Sky? Or lived as a rogue?"

Jackdaw's Cry swished his tail, sending the fog swirling about him. "You're here," he meowed matter-of-factly. "Why worry about it?"

Thunder stared at the black tom. Would this stubborn cat ever accept him? He padded forward a few paces and tasted the damp air. It was rich with the peaty musk of the moor. Then a fishy tang touched his nose. He stiffened as paws brushed the grass ahead and a shape showed through the mist.

Thunder hissed. "Who's that?" He didn't recognize the scent.

A purr echoed from the fog and Thunder recognized the sleek, silver-furred rogue who lived beside the water, River Ripple. A scrap of prey dangled from the newcomer's jaws.

Thunder stiffened as River Ripple dropped a dead lizard onto the grass. *Is that prey?* He gagged.

"Calm your waters," River Ripple mewed. "It's only me."

"What are you doing here?" Jackdaw's Cry stepped forward.

"You're a long way from the river," Thunder pointed out.

"I wanted to see how far the fog stretched." He peered across the hollow. "It's swallowed your camp, I see."

"Is that a gift?" Jackdaw's Cry reached forward tentatively and poked the lizard.

"I caught it earlier," River Ripple explained. "But I'd just eaten a couple of minnows. I thought I'd save the lizard for later." His belly rumbled. "I guess it's later now. Do you want some?"

"No thanks." Thunder wrinkled his nose. He couldn't imagine chewing through the gristly skin of such an ugly-looking creature. He didn't even want to guess what it tasted like.

River Ripple settled onto his belly and grabbed the lizard between his forepaws. "It's quiet up here." He nibbled one of the lizard's webbed feet.

Thunder looked away. "How can you eat that?"

"I eat what I can catch," River Ripple told him, chewing. "And with Clear Sky hogging all the good prey, I have to make do with what I can find."

Jackdaw's Cry flattened his ears. "We're planning to visit Clear Sky today."

"Is that why your fur's pricking?" River Ripple flipped the lizard around and began gnawing at its tail.

Jackdaw's Cry shook out his pelt. "It's just damp, that's all," he grunted.

River Ripple stared up at him, still chewing. "What are you going to see him for?"

Thunder lifted his chin. "We will tell him that he can't keep claiming more territory."

"Really?" River Ripple ripped off the lizard's hind leg,

chewed for a moment, then swallowed. "Good luck with that."
He hooked the lizard carcass with a claw and held it out. "Are
you sure you don't want a bite?"

Thunder backed away.

Jackdaw's Cry dipped his head. "Thanks, but no."

River Ripple got to his paws. "Then I'll use the scraps to
see if I can attract something bigger."

Thunder narrowed his eyes. "What do you mean?"

River Ripple looked over his shoulder into the mist. "Small
prey attracts big prey," he meowed absently. "You just have to
lay it down and wait to see what comes sniffing."

Jackdaw's Cry huffed. "That might work with fish, but on
the moor you need to be careful what you attract." He glanced
up, as though scanning the sky for buzzards.

"I guess." River Ripple began to amble away. "Take care
in the forest. If you manage to get Clear Sky to stop claiming
every piece of land as his own, let me know." As he disappeared into the fog, his voice echoed back. "Though I don't
expect I'll be hearing from you."

Thunder glanced nervously at Jackdaw's Cry. "Do you
think we're wasting our time with this expedition?"

Jackdaw's Cry shifted his paws. "Take no notice of River
Ripple. He's been living on his island too long. He's turned
fish-brained."

"Where are the others?" Thunder couldn't banish the
queasy feeling in his belly. "I thought Shattered Ice was coming with us."

"So did I."

"And where's Gray Wing?" Thunder's tail twitched nervously. "He's supposed to be leading the party."

"I'm here." Gray Wing's mew sounded from behind. Paws ruffled grass as he padded out of camp. He stopped beside them. "I told the others not to come."

"Not to come?" Jackdaw's Cry blinked. "Have you changed your mind about talking to Clear Sky?"

"No." Gray Wing's gaze shone gravely through the mist. "I want you two to go alone."

"Just us?" Jackdaw's Cry stiffened. "But it was your idea."

"You're his brother." Thunder stared at Gray Wing. "He'll listen to you."

"Maybe later." Gray Wing's mew was low. "But the blood between us has soured. I'm not sure he wants me walking into his camp. It might just make him angry." He met Thunder's gaze. "You're his son. That's the strongest blood tie of all."

Thunder blinked. "We quarreled too, remember? I left."

Gray Wing meowed. "I think you still have a better chance than I do. Clear Sky and I parted ways moons ago. His bond with you remains fresh."

Thunder's queasiness deepened. What had changed Gray Wing's mind? He glanced sideways at the black tom. "Why send Jackdaw's Cry?" If Thunder was going into hostile territory, he didn't want to rely on a cat who wished he'd never come to live on the moor.

"To protect you." Gray Wing's gaze hardened. "Jackdaw's Cry fought by your side during the fire. I watched you work together. You make a good team. You're strong and brave and

Jackdaw's Cry is fast and smart. Plus, he has kin in Clear Sky's camp. Falling Feather's his sister, remember? If you both have kin there, you might be safer."

Jackdaw's Cry circled Gray Wing. "What do you want us to say to Clear Sky?"

"Tell him I want to meet him at the four trees in a few days' time and discuss territory."

"Why not just meet him now?" Thunder argued. "You can get it over with."

"If he's given time to prepare, he won't see it as an attack. And the four trees belong to no one. We'll be talking on neutral ground."

Jackdaw's Cry dipped his head. "That sounds fair."

Gray Wing's eyes darkened. "Be careful," he warned. "Once you've crossed the border, if it looks too dangerous, turn back and come home. We can find another way to send this message."

Thunder lifted his chin. "We'll be okay." He wasn't going to let Gray Wing down.

The mist behind Gray Wing swirled as Turtle Tail padded out of the camp. "Have they agreed?" Was that disapproval sharpening her gaze? Did she disagree with Gray Wing's plan?

Gray Wing's gaze fixed on Thunder and Jackdaw's Cry. "Have you?"

"Yes." Thunder answered first.

Jackdaw's Cry nodded. His gaze flicked to Turtle Tail. "We'll be back before the sun's burned away the mist."

Turtle Tail didn't answer.

"Come on." Thunder turned and bounded toward the forest. He was running blind, using memory to follow the trail toward the moor's edge. He ignored the foreboding gnawing in his belly.

Don't be dumb. He won't hurt you. He's your father.

Jackdaw's Cry caught up to him. "I can smell your fear-scent."

Thunder bristled. "So?"

"You're right to be scared." The black tom fell in step. "Clear Sky has killed at least one cat, maybe two."

"I can handle him." Thunder hoped it was true.

"If there's sign of trouble, we're backing off, okay?" Jackdaw's Cry turned his head and stared at Thunder. There was no fear in the tom's gaze, only determination.

"Okay."

The moor began to slope downward, steepening until they emerged from the fog. Thunder blinked, surprised by the sudden light. Behind, mist still hid the moor. Ahead, it swallowed the treetops, but the undergrowth was clear and he could see deep into the shadows of the forest.

His nose twitched as he picked up a border scent. He slowed to a halt. It was his own scent, left only a few days ago as he'd marked out this border with Clear Sky. How strange to be an intruder now.

Jackdaw's Cry stopped beside him, his tongue showing as he tasted the air. A thick swath of ferns edged the trees. "Are you ready?"

"Yes," Thunder murmured. He felt suddenly exposed

Why had Gray Wing sent them alone? *Small prey attracts big prey.* River Ripple's words echoed in his mind.

"Come on, then." Jackdaw's Cry strode across the boundary line, tail flicking.

Thunder scanned the ferns for movement as he followed Jackdaw's Cry. Anger growled in his belly. Why couldn't they walk where they pleased without fear? Clear Sky had ruined everything with his fox-hearted boundaries.

The forest floor rose toward a familiar strip of bracken. An old rabbit trail cut through it. He knew it well. It led straight to the camp. "Follow me." He slid past Jackdaw's Cry and headed up the slope.

A hiss pierced his ear fur.

He halted, hackles lifting.

Yellow fur flashed from behind a tree.

"What are you doing here?" Petal faced him, lips drawn back.

Thunder flinched, shocked by her hostility. A few days ago, he'd watched her playing tail-chase with Alder and Birch, as gentle and loving as any mother. Now she looked as vicious as a cornered rogue. "Petal?" He spoke gently. She couldn't have forgotten they'd been denmates. "How are the kits?"

She spat, every hair bristling. "What's that to do with you? Why are you on Clear Sky's land?"

"Jackdaw's Cry!" A happy mew sounded from the bracken. Falling Feather burst out. "Relax, Petal. It's my brother!" She raced down the slope and stopped, her eyes shining.

"Falling Feather!" Jackdaw's Cry stepped forward.

A growl rumbled in Petal's throat.

Falling Feather stiffened, guilt clouding her gaze. She backed away from her brother, ducking behind Petal. "This isn't your land," she murmured stiffly. "You have to leave."

Jackdaw's Cry objected. "But I haven't seen you for—"

Petal cut him off. "Falling Feather doesn't belong with you anymore," she snarled.

"She's still my littermate!"

Littermate. Thunder felt a pang of grief for Jackdaw's Cry. Longing echoed deep within him. He blinked, surprised at the pain.

"Falling Feather chose to live in the forest with Clear Sky," Petal growled. "Which means you live on opposite sides of the border. You shouldn't be here."

Thunder hissed. "I've come to speak to my father." He dug his claws into the earth. "We may have borders now, but he can't forget that we come from the same place and share the same ancestors."

Petal padded closer, eyes slitted. "We don't *all* come from the same place." She circled Thunder, looking him up and down menacingly.

He unsheathed the tips of his claws. If she wanted a fight, he was ready.

Petal went on. "I've lived here my whole life, just like your *mother*. Clear Sky and these two might come from the mountains"—she scowled at Falling Feather and Jackdaw's Cry—"but they chose different leaders. The only things we have in common with one another now are the boundaries

Clear Sky set for us."

"That's no reason we can't live in peace," Thunder pressed. "All cats have the same needs and the same instincts."

"*Peace?*" Petal snorted. "Ever since I was a kit, I've seen nothing but fights. Boundaries will put an end to that."

"Which is why we must speak to Clear Sky," Thunder put in quickly. "We want to make sure that his boundaries bring peace, not conflict."

Falling Feather lifted her tail. "I'll take you to him." She ignored Petal's growl. "But I can't promise he'll be pleased to see you."

Thunder snorted. *I can't promise I'll be pleased to see* him. "Let me worry about that," he told her. "Just take us to the camp." He knew he'd never forgive his father for the cruelty he'd shown. He glared at Petal. "Do you want to fight first or can we go?" Unsheathing his claws, an image flashed in his mind—him sinking them into her neck. He pushed it away as Petal backed off, her eyes glittering with unease. *Am I as vicious as my father?* His chest tightened.

"Follow me." Falling Feather ducked along the rabbit trail.

Jackdaw's Cry followed, Thunder falling in behind. He felt Petal's breath at his heels and heard the bracken swish against her pelt.

Falling Feather led them along a winding trail past hawthorns and ferns. Thunder could smell his own paws-scents, still faint along the route. His heart pounded harder as he recognized the bramble ahead. The camp lay beyond and, as he followed Jackdaw's Cry past the prickly stems, he stiffened, his gaze quickly scanning the hollow.

Prey-scent filled his nose. A pile lay at one side of the clearing. Another was heaped beside the roots of the oak. A few half-eaten carcasses were scattered along the bottom of the steep slope below the hawthorn, flies buzzing over them. Leaf, the black-and-white tom, lay dozing beside the yew. Fircone and Nettle groomed each other in the clearing. A skinny brown tom sat beside the brambles, his head bowed close to a sleek gray she-cat. *They're new.* Thunder tasted the air, gathering their scent. They both had the notched ears of seasoned fighters. Was Clear Sky recruiting more cats?

Movement above caught his eye.

He jerked up his head.

Clear Sky was watching him from a low oak branch, which hung across the clearing. His tail drooped over the side, its tip twitching as he glowered at Thunder. His gaze slid to Jackdaw's Cry, narrowing, then flicked back. "I thought I'd seen the last of you, *son.*"

CHAPTER 7

Clear Sky curled his claws into the bark of the jutting oak branch, fighting to keep his pelt smooth. *What's Thunder doing here?* He kept his gaze fixed on his son, giving nothing away as he steadied his breath.

I trusted you, and you betrayed me.

Clenching his teeth, he pushed himself slowly to his paws and jumped down into the clearing. Thunder faced him. Jackdaw's Cry hung back, staying close to Falling Feather. *Trust her to be mixed up in this.*

"She brought them here, not me." Petal darted forward, ears flat as she jerked her muzzle toward the white she-cat.

Falling Feather lifted her muzzle. "Do you want to hear what they have to say?" She stared at Clear Sky, unflinching.

"It depends what it is." Clear Sky slowly circled Thunder and Jackdaw's Cry. These cats should be afraid of him. They'd crossed the border. They walked into his camp. *Let them know they aren't safe here.* He tightened his circle, nudging Jackdaw's Cry with his shoulder as he passed.

The black tom leaped back, hissing. "Don't touch me!"

He's spooked. Satisfaction surged through Clear Sky as he

thrust his muzzle close, one eye on Jackdaw's Cry's unsheathed claws. "Attack me if you want," he challenged. He flicked his tail around the forest cats. Nettle and Fircone had padded closer. Thorn and Dew watched, their bristling pelts showing they were ready to fight if necessary. "You'll die if you do."

Jackdaw's Cry's eyes sparked with fear.

"Stop trying to scare him." Thunder's mew was sharp. "If you don't want to hear why we came, then we'll leave."

"If I let you." Clear Sky turned on his son. Was that *disappointment* darkening Thunder's gaze? Pain gripped his heart like claws. *Does he actually think* I've *let* him *down?* He squared his shoulders. "Okay," he growled. "Let's talk. But not here. I know somewhere we won't be overheard."

Dew pricked her ears.

Clear Sky growled at her. "Earn your place with us, and I might show it to you." He turned, lashing his tail, and climbed the slope past his nest. "Falling Feather, you come too," he called, not looking back. She needed to see he was in charge. Pushing under the hawthorn, he broke into open woodland. Ferns lined a ditch ahead. He leaped over them, landing lightly on the other side, and padded across the dusty forest floor.

Paws thudded behind as, one at a time, the others leaped the ditch. He glanced over his shoulder. Thunder and Jackdaw's Cry were flanking Falling Feather like an escort. *They are the intruders!* A chill ran along his spine. Should he have brought more forest cats to stand guard while they talked?

Don't be flea-brained. They wouldn't dare harm you here.

Clear Sky led them over a rise and followed a dry streambed

until it reached a wide oak. It was tall and ancient, its gnarled branches bare. A few leaves sprouted defiantly at the tips, but the tree would soon be dead. Its crooked roots snaked into the dusty bank. Water hadn't flowed here since the end of the cold season, but when it had, it had hollowed a passage beneath the trunk. Clear Sky ducked into it and squeezed up through a hole into the hollow center of the rotting tree. He stayed near the hole, his tail touching the trunk, and waited for the others to worm their way after him.

Thunder's head popped up first. The young tom glanced around, eyes wide. Light from knotholes striped his head with gold. He scrambled onto the smooth earth that floored the hollow and faced Clear Sky.

With a jolt, Clear Sky noticed that Thunder was bigger than he was now. He straightened, puffing out his fur while Falling Feather and Jackdaw's Cry wriggled inside.

Clear Sky felt safe in the confines of the tree. There was enough room for the four cats to sit, spines pressed against the trunk, a tail-length between their muzzles. But it would be hard for any cat to fight skillfully here. And being closest to the hole in the bottom would ensure him an easy escape route.

Jackdaw's Cry glanced warily up. A circle of light showed far above. His black pelt was pricking. Thunder shifted his paws as though he couldn't get comfortable.

Clear Sky watched them with satisfaction. *I don't want you to get comfortable.*

"What have you come to say?" he asked them bluntly.

Thunder returned his gaze. "Gray Wing wants to meet you

by the four trees in a few days."

Clear Sky's ears twitched. "Why?"

"To talk," Jackdaw's Cry grunted.

Anger pressed in Clear Sky's throat. Did they think he was such a mouse-brain? He knew Gray Wing was preparing for battle. Why go through the pretense of talking?

"Gray Wing is worried about the borders," Jackdaw's Cry went on. "It's not what we planned when we left the mountains. We've never lived with borders before. It's making the cats nervous."

Clear Sky swallowed back frustration. If they wanted to pretend, he'd pretend. "Doesn't Gray Wing realize yet that borders keep cats safe? This isn't the mountain. The land stretches forever. Borders help us know where to roam and where to hunt. It's the best way to avoid quarrels over prey."

Thunder frowned. "It would be if you didn't keep shifting them."

"I only want my cats to flourish," Clear Sky told him. "Just as Gray Wing wants his own cats to thrive."

"Flourish?" Jackdaw's Cry curled his lip. "You sent Frost away to die. You trained Jagged Peak until you crippled him. You have orphan kits because you killed their mother. Do you call that 'flourishing'?"

Clear Sky thrust his muzzle toward the black tom, ignoring the guilt jabbing at his belly. "You know *nothing*! You listen to gossip like an old queen with nothing better to do."

Jackdaw's Cry gazed back, unflinching. "I know what I see and what I hear. And none of the news from the forest has been good since you claimed it as your own."

Clear Sky stiffened against the fury pulsing through his blood. How dare this cat judge him? *News?* He flashed Thunder an accusing glare. *It was you who spread it!*

His own son had betrayed him!

Falling Feather turned to her brother. "We *are* flourishing," she told him earnestly. "Our tribe grows bigger by the day."

"You're no *tribe*!" Jackdaw's Cry flashed back, shock showing in his eyes. "You're a band of strays and rogues!"

Falling Feather bristled. "We joined together to help each other," she meowed fiercely. "We share prey and protect each other. We're safer that way!"

Thunder's tail swished against the trunk. "We didn't come here to argue," he growled. "We came only to tell you that Gray Wing wants to talk by the four trees."

Clear Sky frowned, angry at the bold way Thunder stared straight at him.

"Will you meet him or not?"

"I'll meet him." Clear Sky tipped his head. If Gray Wing was preparing for battle, it would be interesting to hear what he had to say. "But what we decide on that day will be final. No changing minds. No going back." Would Gray Wing admit that he was preparing to fight? Clear Sky's whiskers quivered. How far was his brother prepared to carry his lie? Was the meeting intended as a distraction or would it bring an open declaration of conflict?

Either way, he'd be ready. And he was going to make sure Gray Wing kept his word. He eyed Jackdaw's Cry, a plan flashing in his mind. If Gray Wing did try to trick him, he'd pay with the life of a camp mate.

"Let's get back to the camp." He dived down through the hole and squeezed out onto the dry streambed.

Trekking through the woods, he signaled Falling Feather to walk beside him. "You spoke well." He praised her. He'd been impressed that she'd stood up for her new tribe. Perhaps she was loyal after all.

As he pushed beneath the hawthorn and leaped down the bank, Nettle hurried across the clearing.

"Is everything okay?" The young tom searched his gaze.

"It's fine." Clear Sky glanced back as Thunder and Jackdaw's Cry followed Falling Feather into the clearing.

Fircone limped from the oak tree.

Clear Sky noticed Thunder staring anxiously at the tom's swollen paw. "It's just a scratch," he growled. "My cats fight hard to defend our borders from passing strays. No cat makes the mistake of crossing our scent lines twice."

Thunder's gaze moved to Dew and Thorn, still sitting beside the bramble. "How did *they* make it across?" he asked.

"They asked permission." Clear Sky padded toward them. "They wanted to join us." Pleasure rippled though his pelt. "As did Snake." He nodded toward the striped tabby tom, camouflaged in the shadows of the bramble.

Snake got to his paws and padded out. He was lean and sleek and had the sharp eye of a hunter. Clear Sky had been pleased when he'd come to the border, asking to join shortly after Dew and Thorn. The forest cats *were* flourishing, no matter what Jackdaw's Cry claimed. He turned to the black moor cat. "Snake was a rogue in Twolegplace. But he preferred to join us," he boasted. "He knew he'd be well fed here."

Jackdaw's Cry's gaze strayed toward the piles of prey. "A little too well fed," he grunted.

Clear Sky's tail twitched irritably. Okay, so there was more prey here than they could eat. It'd start rotting soon and fill the camp with stench. But they weren't dumb. They could bury carrion. Jackdaw's Cry was missing the point. "Isn't it better to have too much prey than not enough?"

Jackdaw's Cry didn't answer.

What was it about Gray Wing's cats that made them so smug? Clear Sky scanned his own cats. At least *they* understood that life was harsh. "I've decided to meet with Gray Wing," he told them.

"When?" Fircone's eyes narrowed to slits.

Clear Sky paced. He realized they hadn't discussed a specific time. "At full moon," he decided. "In two days." He stopped and stared at Jackdaw's Cry. There was something else they hadn't discussed. "This moor cat will remain here in the forest camp until after the meeting," he growled. "If you must risk your leader, then *they* should risk something too."

"No!" Thunder flattened his ears.

"It's okay." Jackdaw's Cry stepped forward, his glance flicking toward Falling Feather. "I'll stay if that's what it takes."

Clear Sky's paws pricked with satisfaction. "Good." He flicked his tail toward his camp mates. "If anything does happen to me at the meeting, you can decide what to do with

Jackdaw's Cry." He noticed Thunder's pelt ripple uneasily and his satisfaction deepened. "Don't worry," he purred to his son. "I'm sure they'll be fair." He dipped his head. The meeting had gone better than he'd hoped. "Thank you for coming. You can leave now. And Jackdaw's Cry—" He turned his head toward the young black tom. Jackdaw's Cry lifted his chin defiantly, but unease glittered in his gaze. "We appreciate your staying with us. We'll make sure you're well fed and safe. And we'll only keep you until after I come home from the meeting." There was no harm in making sure that Thunder understood the importance of his returning from the four trees safely.

Thunder curled his lip. "You can trust *Gray Wing*." There was insolence in his mew.

Clear Sky watched him head out of camp. "Tell my brother that next time he should bring his message himself!" he called as Thunder disappeared behind the brambles. "Only kits hide."

Clear Sky padded to the oak, clawing his way up the trunk, past the low branch he'd been sitting on earlier and up to the next. He leaned back and gazed to the top. This was the highest tree around, thick with leaves. Jumping to the next branch, then the next, he climbed higher and higher, his long claws hooking easily into the rugged bark. As the thick branches gave way to slender stems, he paused and peered through the leaves. From here, he could see the forest stretch to Twolegplace and beyond, the land curve toward the rolling horizon. There was more territory than he could ever have imagined while he lived among the craggy peaks of the mountains. And every tail-length teemed with prey. Here he could build a tribe of healthy, strong cats. No kit need ever go hungry; no mother need starve until her milk dried up. His heart quickened. Why did no cat seem to understand that this was all he wanted? He'd never *wanted* to do harm.

But he would do whatever it took to keep his cats safe.

If I'd known Misty had been fighting to protect Alder and Birch, I'd have gone easier on her. Agonizing emptiness opened in Clear Sky's chest. Instead he'd killed her, and now Gray Wing and the other cats on the moor believed he'd killed Bumble too. How could he make peace with cats who believed he was a murderer? He closed his eyes, his thoughts spinning.

All I can do now is protect my own cats. He clung tight to the tree. There was no hope now of peacefully sharing this land. Determination surged through him. Unhooking his claws, he dropped onto the branch beneath. Slithering down the trunk, he called to Petal. She was sitting near the yew, Alder and Birch at her side. "Gather every cat!" She leaped to her paws. "We must prepare for battle!"

"Are you sure?" Petal stared as he leaped from the trunk and landed heavily on the ground. Her eyes were wide.

Clear Sky strode across the clearing, not even meeting her gaze. "Just do it."

CHAPTER 8

♣

The sun had burned the mist from the moor by the time Thunder reached the boundary between Clear Sky and Gray Wing's territory. He leaped up the slope, swishing through the ferns. At the top, he paused. Heather stretched toward the wide, blue sky. He relished the sun's warmth on his pelt after the extended shade of the forest. What would Jackdaw's Cry be doing? Would Falling Feather help him build a temporary nest? He glanced back at the trees uneasily.

Should I have left him?

I had no choice. Jackdaw's Cry had volunteered. His sister was with him. And Clear Sky had promised to keep the tom safe until the meeting at the four trees. Thunder quickened his pace. He pushed through a patch of heather, following a sheep trail that cut between the springy branches. It led out onto a smooth stretch of grass. He breathed the sweet scent of heather blossom and broke into a run.

As Thunder was lost in his own thoughts, paws slammed hard into his flank.

Yowling with surprise, Thunder flew sprawling onto the grass. The stench of tom filled his nose. Thunder unsheathed his claws and twisted to face his attacker, whose copper fur blotted out the sky. The tom crashed into him again, heavier than a badger. Claws latched onto his pelt as the cat rolled him over in the grass. Blood pounded in Thunder's ears as he struggled to bend his hind legs and rake the tom's belly. But paws held him too tight. The world spun. Panic rising, Thunder dragged a forepaw free and slashed the tom's nose. His claws ripped flesh. The tom screeched and let go. Thunder was suddenly rolling alone across the grass. He dug his wide paws in and leaped up, turning on his attacker.

The copper-colored tom was sitting back on his haunches a tail-length away, rubbing his nose. "What did you do that for?" he demanded ruefully. "I was just playing!"

"Playing?" Thunder glared at him. "You sheathe claws when you're playing!"

The tom licked his paw and ran it over his face, cleaning the blood from his dark moleskin muzzle. He sat up straight and met Thunder's gaze. A fresh drop of blood welled on his wound.

Thunder snorted. The wound might teach him some manners. The tom was as big as Thunder, but there was no sign of muscle rippling under his pelt. His wide flanks bulged and his belly sagged around his paws. His pelt looked as silky as kit fur. Thunder narrowed his eyes. He hadn't seen him on the moor before. "Who are you?"

"Tom."

"I know you're a *tom*." This cat really was dumb. "What's your *name*?" Thunder paused as he noticed something shiny glinting at the tom's throat. A twine was caught around his neck.

"What's that?" Thunder jerked his muzzle toward the band digging into the tom's fur.

The tom frowned. "What's *what*?"

"The thing around your neck?" Hadn't he noticed?

"It's my collar." Now the tom stared at Thunder as though he were stupid.

Thunder grunted. Of course! *I'm the dumb one!* This soft, fat cat with no manners was a kittypet. *I should have guessed.* "Your *name* is Tom."

Tom shrugged. "That's what my housefolk call me."

Housefolk? He must mean Twolegs. Thunder knew that Turtle Tail had stayed with Twolegs for a while. Had they named her *She-cat?*

Tom delicately flicked a grass seed from his ear with a paw. Then he stuck out his tongue and licked his nose, the tip touching the blood still welling there. "Did you *have* to scratch me?" he mewed irritably. "I hope it doesn't leave a scar. My housefolk will be sad."

"Why?" Thunder frowned. "It's not *their* nose that's scratched."

"They like me to look handsome." Tom stared across the heather. "Do you live around here?" His mew was casual, but his gaze was taking in every flickering stem and trembling sprig of heather.

Thunder's paws pricked with unease. This cat was after something. "Why are you here?"

Tom blinked at him slowly. "I'm looking for a friend."

Thunder's fur began to lift along his spine.

"Someone I used to know." Tom gave a long sigh and stretched his forepaws out, bending his back till his round belly touched the earth. A shiver ran along his tail. "Her name's Bumble. We used to play together."

Thunder stiffened. "Bumble?" He realized this cat had no idea that his friend was dead.

"I'm bored without her," Tom meowed absently. "I thought it might be nice to find her and play with her again."

Thunder dropped his gaze. How could he tell this cat that Bumble had been killed? "I—I'm sorry," he began awkwardly.

Tom's gaze snapped toward him. "Sorry? About what?"

"Your friend, Bumble." Thunder shifted his weight from paw to paw. "She's dead."

"*Dead?*" Tom jabbed his muzzle forward. "How can she be dead? What happened?"

Thunder's thoughts whirled. "We don't really know." He glanced down the slope to where they'd found Bumble dying. "Do you want to see her grave?"

"Her grave?" Tom's sleek fur was fluffed out now, his eyes sparking with disbelief.

"They buried her," Thunder explained. "Gray Wing and the others. They were the ones who found her."

"*Found* her?"

"I'll show you." Thunder headed for the heather and pushed through, following a rabbit trail toward the patch of land where Bumble had been killed. He heard branches swish behind as Tom followed. "Here." He stopped as he reached the grassy clearing. The grass was still stained with blood. A mound of freshly dug earth marked Bumble's grave. Thunder shuddered at the lingering scent of death.

Tom paced around the bloody markings, his nose trailing over the grass.

Thunder watched him sadly. "When they found her it was too late to save her."

The tom didn't seem to hear. He was murmuring to himself. "I can make out . . ." He darted to another patch. "I can make out . . ." He lifted his head, his eyes lighting. "Badger! Is that what killed her?"

Thunder shook his head, sorrow for this poor dumb cat welling in his chest. "It's fox scent," he corrected. "It attacked her. She couldn't—"

Tom interrupted. "There's another smell." He was sniffing a fresh patch of grass. "A cat, right? A tom?" He stared at Thunder.

Thunder's tail twitched. Should he mention Clear Sky? He'd been here after she'd died. And *before*.

Tom sniffed the grass again. "I *know* this smell. It's that vicious rogue, right? The one that's been making borders everywhere. The one the other kittypets have been talking about."

Pain clawed Thunder's heart. *My father, a vicious rogue?* "Maybe."

Tom padded closer. "Why did you mountain cats have to come here? You've been nothing but trouble. Even Turtle

Tail! She came to live with us, then ran away, carrying *my* kits."
A sneer twisted his lip.

Thunder showed his teeth as the tom's stinking breath
bathed his muzzle. "She didn't just 'run away.' Turtle Tail
came *home*. Where she belonged!"

Tom growled. "She stole what was mine." He began to pace,
shoulders low, tail twitching angrily. "And Bumble followed
her, the mouse-brain!" He glanced angrily at Bumble's grave.
"She was *worried* about her. And it got her killed." He halted.
His agitated gaze suddenly softened.

Thunder watched him warily. This cat was forcing himself
to appear calm. *Why?*

"You sound like you know Turtle Tail." His mew was suddenly as sweet as blossom scent.

Thunder nodded cautiously.

"Will you take me to meet her?"

Thunder hesitated.

"Bumble was so worried about her," Tom pleaded, rounding his eyes. "She died trying to find out if she and the kits
were okay. The kits *are* okay, aren't they?"

"They're fine." Thunder swallowed. He should leave before
this tom asked any more questions. Something wasn't right. "I
have to go."

"Then you know where they are?" Tom pressed. "And Turtle Tail?"

"Someone's waiting for me." Gray Wing would want to
hear how the meeting with Clear Sky had gone.

"Will you take me to her?" Tom didn't blink. "She was very

fond of me. I know she'd like to see me again."

"I'll tell her I saw you." Thunder backed away.

Tom's eyes lit up. "Tell her I'm here." He sat down on Bumble's grave. "Tell her I'm not going anywhere till I've seen her. Tell her I'll wait for as long as it takes."

A chill rippled through Thunder's fur. "Okay." He glanced up the slope. He could see the hollow in the hillside where the camp nestled, and felt relieved that swaths of heather shielded it from view. A dark sense of foreboding told him that this tom shouldn't know where Turtle Tail lived. "I'll tell her." He raced up the hill, plunging through the heather. He zigzagged, following the freshest rabbit tracks, hoping their dung would put Tom off his scent trail if he tried to track him later.

As he neared the hollow, he imagined Gray Wing waiting. Excitement began to prick in his paws. Clear Sky had agreed to a meeting. There was going to be peace after all.

CHAPTER 9

Gray Wing shook Sparrow Fur from his shoulders, and the kit tumbled to the ground with a wail. "You promised me a *long* badger ride!"

"Sorry, Sparrow Fur." Gray Wing was out of breath. "Maybe later."

"But you carried Owl Eyes around the hollow *twice!*"

Turtle Tail padded forward and nuzzled the tortoiseshell she-kit. "Once is enough for now," she murmured. "Let Gray Wing rest." She nosed the kit gently away. Owl Eyes was play fighting with Jagged Peak in the long grass beside the heather. "Go and join those two. Owl Eyes looks like he needs help." Jagged Peak was squashing Owl Eyes beneath his belly while the gray kit flailed his paws and squealed with frustration.

Sparrow Fur gasped. "Owl Eyes!" She charged toward him. "I'll save you!"

Jagged Peak's whiskers twitched as he spotted her. "Hurry up!" he teased. "I'm going to squash him flat!"

"Where's Pebble Heart?" Gray Wing hardly listened for an answer. He stared toward the distant moor, scanning the horizon for movement while worry spiraled in his belly.

"He's helping Cloud Spots make ointment for Frost." Turtle Tail nudged his cheek with her muzzle. "Can you see them?"

Gray Wing knew she was talking about Thunder and Jackdaw's Cry. They should be home by now. He remembered Jackdaw's Cry's parting words. *We'll be back before the sun's burned away the mist.* The sun was high. The fog had melted away long ago.

"Are you wheezing again?" Turtle Tail pressed closer.

"A little." His chest was tight. He'd been trying to ignore it. Since breathing smoke from the forest fire, Gray Wing sometimes struggled to find breath. Especially when he was anxious.

Turtle Tail touched her flank to his. "They'll be fine," she promised. "They're both strong, brave cats."

He wanted to believe her, but knew she was just trying to soothe him. Fear edged her mew. She thought that Clear Sky had murdered her friend Bumble. Why would she believe he would spare two intruders from the moor?

I should have gone with them. Gray Wing shivered, cold despite the scorching sunshine. He dragged his gaze from the far slopes and glanced around the camp, taking comfort from the familiar faces.

Lightning Tail and Acorn Fur sat beside the gap in the heather, watching for their father's return. Hawk Swoop paced beside the flat rock where Tall Shadow was sitting. The black she-cat was staring across the moor, ears pricked.

Wind Runner lay at the edge of the clearing, her bulging

belly rising and falling. Her eyes were closed against the bright sunshine but her ears twitched each time grass swished beyond the heather wall.

Rainswept Flower crouched beside her, nudging a ball of soaked moss closer. "Have a drink," she urged. "You must be thirsty."

As Wind Runner lapped at the moss, Gorse Fur paced behind them, his long tail twitching. "Shall I go hunting?" he called to Tall Shadow. "I could head for the forest border and see if there's any sign of them."

"Don't go alone," Tall Shadow answered.

Hawk Swoop crossed the clearing toward Gorse Fur. "I'll come with you."

"Me too." Shattered Ice ducked out from beneath the bramble, his green eyes sharp with worry.

"Wait!" Tall Shadow suddenly stretched onto her hind legs, eyes fixed on the moor. "I can see Thunder!"

Gray Wing darted across the clearing, Turtle Tail at his heels, and rushed through the gap in the heather.

Lightning Tail called after him. "Is Jackdaw's Cry there too?"

Gray Wing didn't answer. There was no sign of the black tom. But Thunder was racing toward the hollow.

Gray Wing met him on the grassy clearing outside, scrambling to a halt as Thunder reached him. "What did Clear Sky say? Will he meet me?"

"Yes." Thunder skidded on the grass.

Gray Wing saw the young tom's gaze flick nervously toward

Turtle Tail. *Something's wrong.* Before he could ask, Hawk Swoop barged past.

"Where's Jackdaw's Cry?" She scanned the heather.

Gray Wing tasted the air. No scent of the black tom. Thunder had returned alone.

Thunder stared at Gray Wing. "Clear Sky will meet you at full moon by the four trees."

Gray Wing's heart quickened. "That's great news!" Dare he hope that battle could be avoided? His mind started to whirl. What if he couldn't find the right words to persuade Clear Sky to see reason and stop moving his boundaries? What if he made battle come sooner by saying the wrong thing?

"Where is Jackdaw's Cry?" Hawk Swoop's mew was urgent. She paced past Thunder.

Thunder dipped his head. "Clear Sky asked him to stay in the forest camp until after the meeting at the four trees."

"What?" Hawk Swoop's eyes widened in shock.

Turtle Tail's fur spiked. "How dare he keep one of our cats!"

Gray Wing forced his fur to stay flat, though fear sparked through it like lightning. "Is he safe?" He searched Thunder's gaze.

Thunder swallowed. "He promised that Jackdaw's Cry would be fine until after the meeting." His gaze slid toward Hawk Swoop.

"And then what?" she demanded.

"He'll let him return to the moor." Thunder's ears twitched nervously

"Is that what he said?" Hawk Swoop glared at him.

Thunder stiffened. "He just said he'd be safe until after the meeting."

Turtle Tail hissed. "We must fetch him. Now!"

Gray Wing met her gaze. "But Clear Sky's agreed to meet," he protested. "We have to tread carefully."

Turtle Tail growled. "That's what he wants!" she spat. "He wants us to slink around like mouse-hearts while he does what he wants. He's a bully and you know it!" She headed for the camp.

Gray Wing closed his eyes. He could understand her anger. Why hadn't Clear Sky just agreed to meet? *Doesn't he trust me?* Or was Turtle Tail right about him enjoying having power over other cats?

Hawk Swoop growled as though in pain. "What should we do, Gray Wing?"

Gray Wing looked at her. "Let's ask Tall Shadow." He led the cats back into the hollow where Tall Shadow, Acorn Fur, and Lightning Tail waited.

Turtle Tail was already at Tall Shadow's side. Wind Runner was on her paws, Rainswept Flower beside her. Gorse Fur stood, tail lashing, while Shattered Ice paced around him.

In the long grass Jagged Peak looked up. Owl Eyes and Sparrow Fur tumbled around him, play fighting. They hadn't even noticed Thunder was back. He slid from between them and crossed the clearing.

"Has Turtle Tail told you everything?" Gray Wing looked at Tall Shadow.

"Clear Sky's holding Jackdaw's Cry." Her gaze flitted around the others.

"But he's agreed to the meeting," Gray Wing told her.

Hawk Swoop padded forward. "Turtle Tail thinks we should get Jackdaw's Cry back."

"I know," Tall Shadow told her calmly.

Gray Wing flattened his ears. "If we do that, Clear Sky will call off the meeting."

Wind Runner lashed her tail. "We can't let him bully us."

"Avoiding battle is more important!" Gray Wing felt frustration flash beneath his pelt.

Gorse Fur growled. "Is it more important than Jackdaw's Cry's life?"

"He's not in danger!" Gray Wing turned on the gray tabby. Did *every* cat believe Clear Sky was a monster?

Tall Shadow stepped between them and lifted her muzzle. "Jackdaw's Cry can take care of himself," she meowed calmly. "He will stay in the forest if that's what it takes to get Clear Sky to agree to talk. We must do everything in our power to make sure we can live in peace."

Acorn Fur padded forward. "Falling Feather is with him." Her mew trembled but she kept going. "Jackdaw's Cry isn't alone. He'll be okay." She glanced at her brother.

Lightning Tail nodded. "Jackdaw's Cry would never forgive us if we tried to bring him home."

Hawk Swoop's shoulders drooped. "You're right," she conceded.

Relief seeped beneath Gray Wing's pelt. The meeting

would go ahead. There would be peace. He gazed gratefully at Hawk Swoop, not daring to look at Turtle Tail. He wasn't sure she'd be so easily convinced that they were making the right decision.

Fur brushed his flank.

"Lightning Tail is right." Turtle Tail pressed against him. "Jackdaw's Cry would never forgive us if we sent a rescue party. He's a proud cat."

Gray Wing blinked at her gratefully. "It'll be fine, you'll see," he promised.

Thunder was fidgeting at the edge of the clearing, his gaze uneasy.

"Is there something else?" Gray Wing looked at him.

Thunder's tail quivered. "I met a cat on the way back to the camp." He glanced at Turtle Tail. "He's called Tom. He came looking for Bumble. I told him she was dead and showed her his grave but he wants to meet with Turtle Tail."

"No!" Gray Wing stepped in front of his mate. He'd heard plenty about Tom, the kittypet who'd made Turtle Tail's life miserable when she'd lived with the Twolegs. And the first time he'd met Bumble, the poor cat had been covered in scratches and bruises. Tom was a bully. He glanced at the long grass where Sparrow Fur and Owl Eyes were trying to outpounce each other. He could hear Pebble Heart beneath the gorse, asking Cloud Spots endless questions. He didn't care that they were Tom's kits. They must never meet him. Nor should Turtle Tail. His fur lifted along his spine. How had she ever loved such a cruel cat?

Thunder glanced at him nervously. "He said he'd wait at Bumble's grave until she came."

"He said *what*?" Rage surged through Gray Wing. How dare he make such demands?

Thunder backed away. "He said he'd wait for as long as it took."

"Gray Wing." Turtle Tail slid in front of him, her green eyes soft. "It's not Thunder's fault."

"I know." Gray Wing let his hackles fall. "But we don't want that kittypet on our moor. I'm going to chase him back to Twolegplace." He began to head for the gap in the heather but Turtle Tail blocked his way.

"No." Her mew was firm.

He blinked. "Why?"

"I must meet him." She was trembling.

Gray Wing could hardly believe his ears. "You can't!"

Turtle Tail lifted her head. "I know him, Gray Wing. If I don't meet with him, he'll find me. He'll come to the hollow." She glanced over her shoulder toward Owl Eyes and Sparrow Fur. "And then he'll know where his kits are." Fear edged her mew.

Gray Wing understood. She must face him or live in fear. "I'm coming with you."

"So am I." Tall Shadow's mew took him by surprise. The black she-cat was gazing at him, eyes round. "If this Tom can frighten Turtle Tail, you may need an extra set of claws." She nodded to Thunder. "Show us where he is."

* * *

Gray Wing let Thunder lead the way through the heather. Bumble's grave was no secret, but he thought Thunder deserved to head the party. He felt guilty that he'd reacted so angrily to news of Tom's arrival. Thunder had shown true courage today, traveling to Clear Sky's camp, returning with news that he'd left Jackdaw's Cry there. Did Clear Sky realize what a fine son he'd given up?

It's his loss.

Gray Wing ducked as heather branches arched over their heads. He could feel Turtle Tail's quick breath on his tail-tip. She was scared, though she was doing her best to hide it. Tall Shadow brought up the rear. Hopefully, her calm clear-sightedness would ease any tensions in the meeting.

Gray Wing's pelt itched with sudden curiosity. He'd often wondered what the father of Turtle Tail's kits was like. Guilt gnawed at the edge of his thoughts. She'd never have turned to such a cruel cat if he'd realized earlier that he loved her. She'd loved him since they were kits, but he'd been blinded by his own love for others, first for Bright Stream and then for Storm. Turtle Tail had always come last, but with quiet perseverance she'd won his heart and now he couldn't think of life with any other mate.

As he pictured Tom waiting for her, a growl rumbled in his throat. He'd make sure the kittypet left the moor and didn't come back.

"He's still waiting," Thunder called over his shoulder. "I can smell him."

Gray Wing tasted the air, his nose wrinkling as sweet, sour, sickly smells filled it. They'd clung to Bumble's pelt too, and Turtle Tail's when she'd first returned from Twolegplace. It must be the scent of Twoleg nests.

Bright light showed ahead and Gray Wing blinked. He slid out of the tunnel into sunshine. Thunder already waited on the grass. Turtle Tail and Tall Shadow padded out behind him.

Screwing up his eyes, he looked down the slope. Lying at one end of Bumble's grave was a glossy tom, his thick pelt colored like autumn leaves. He stretched in the sun, rolling over as Thunder padded toward him.

Gray Wing glanced at Turtle Tail. "Ready?"

She squared her shoulders. "Yes." Striding forward, she followed Thunder.

"Don't worry." Tall Shadow stopped beside Gray Wing. "We'll make sure that he knows he's not welcome here."

Gray Wing lashed his tail. "I'd like to send him home with a nick in his ear."

"Let's not antagonize him unnecessarily." Tall Shadow padded down the slope and Gray Wing followed.

Tom was climbing to his paws. His wide flanks rippled. Gray Wing curled his lip. Soft fur coated soft flesh. Wasn't he ashamed to be so fat?

Tom's gaze fixed on Turtle Tail. "You kept me waiting." He yawned, showing yellow teeth.

Turtle Tail shrugged. "It looks like you didn't have anything better to do." She padded to the edge of Bumble's grave and began smoothing the earth he'd disturbed with her paw.

Tom narrowed his eyes. "Why did you bring them?" He flicked his tail toward Tall Shadow and Gray Wing.

Thunder padded forward. "She travels with who she likes."

Tom padded around Turtle Tail, letting his thick tail run along her spine.

She shuddered. Gray Wing growled and glared threateningly at Tom.

Tom ignored him. He was staring at Tall Shadow, his silky muzzle wrinkling in disgust. "Are all you rogues fleabags?" He nudged Turtle Tail roughly with his shoulder. "How many times did the housefolk have to comb you to clean your pelt?" His gaze flicked over Tall Shadow's. "I don't think there'd be enough combs in the world to scrape the fleas from *her*."

Tall Shadow held his gaze.

Gray Wing flexed his claws. Did this cat *want* to fight?

"Thunder told us that you've come to pay your respects to Bumble," Tall Shadow meowed diplomatically.

Tom sniffed. "Something like that." He turned, his feathery tail swishing past Turtle Tail's muzzle. "I really wanted to see my old mate." His eyes lingered on her pelt. "The nest is too quiet without you now that Bumble's gone." He stopped, his muzzle a whisker from hers. "Won't you come back? I miss our play fights."

"*Play* fights?" Turtle Tail hissed. "You were the only one who was ever playing!" She reared, spitting with fury.

Gray Wing darted forward.

Tall Shadow leaped in front of him. "Let her stand up for herself."

He scrambled to a halt, staring past Tall Shadow as Turtle Tail lunged for Tom. Her claws raked his snout. Snarling, she battered his muzzle with a flurry of claws.

Tom backed away, his broad, sleek face twisting into a snarl. "Rogue!" he roared and flung himself at her.

His weight knocked her backward. Paws crumpling, she collapsed onto Bumble's grave. Tom slashed her flank, sinking his claws deep and pressing her shoulders into the earth. She writhed, hind legs scattering the loose soil as she struggled to reach his belly. He let his fat body drop, smothering her.

Tall Shadow stepped aside. "Stop him," she growled to Gray Wing.

But Gray Wing had already leaped past her.

Thunder dived from the other side. He hooked his claws into Tom's flanks while Gray Wing sunk his teeth into the kittypet's scruff. Heaving, they dragged Tom off Turtle Tail.

She screeched in pain as he tore fur from her belly.

"Dungheart!" Gray Wing swung a hefty blow at Tom's ear. The kittypet's eyes widened as it struck him. He yowled in fury and flung a blow back. Gray Wing reeled at its force. As he struggled to regain his balance, Thunder dived beneath the kittypet's belly and knocked his hind legs from beneath him. Tom twisted, reaching out a forepaw and clawing Gray Wing's flank.

Wincing in pain, Gray Wing kicked out with a hind leg, catching Tom beneath the chin.

Turtle Tail struggled to her paws and dived at Tom's hind leg. Sinking in her teeth, she tugged him backward.

Gray Wing felt a surge of triumph. *We've got you now, kittypet!*

"Stop!" Tall Shadow's yowl made him freeze.

Turtle Tail backed away. Thunder stopped mid-rear and let his paws drop to the ground.

Tom collapsed on Bumble's grave.

"Show some respect!" Tall Shadow stared at the churned earth. "A dead cat lies here."

Tom heaved himself to his paws and backed away from the moor cats. Blood dripped from his cheek.

Gray Wing noticed a nick in the kittypet's ear and felt a flicker of satisfaction.

Tall Shadow marched between them, her face stern, then reached out and began to paw the scattered earth back into a mound over Bumble's grave.

Gray Wing watched Tom. He wasn't going to take his eyes off the vicious kittypet. "Are you okay?" he murmured to Turtle Tail.

"Yes," she panted.

"Thunder?" Gray Wing glimpsed the tom's golden fur from the corner of his eye.

"I'm fine."

Tom's gaze flicked from one to the other, then rested on Turtle Tail's belly. "Thunder said that you'd kitted," he grunted.

"So?" Turtle Tail's answer was guarded.

Gray Wing padded closer to her. Why was Tom interested in his kits now? Turtle Tail had told him that one of the reasons she'd left Twolegplace was because her Twolegs would take her kits from her and give them to other Twolegs to raise. Is that why he wanted them? To give them away?

Tom narrowed his eyes. "You stopped them from being kittypets and made them live like rogues," he sneered. "Do you think they'll thank you for that?"

"They're not rogues!" Gray Wing stepped forward. "They live with us. They're the best-loved cats in the hollow!"

Interest sparked in Tom's gaze. "The *hollow*?"

Gray Wing winced, realizing what he'd done. He clamped his jaws shut before he gave anything else away. Now the kittypet knew they lived in one of the hollows that dented the moor. It wouldn't take long for him to find them.

Turtle Tail moved closer. "They're scrawny little things," she sniffed. "They must have been born with your kittypet softness. I doubt they'll make it through the next cold season."

Gray Wing's heart twisted at the thought. But he knew she was lying. If Tom thought the kits weren't worth having, he might go away and leave them alone.

"I should have drowned them instead of wasting my milk on them," she added.

Thunder's eyes widened. "You don't mean—"

Tall Shadow cut him off. "Turtle Tail's right." She turned from the grave, eyeing Thunder sternly. "They're sickly and good for nothing."

Tom narrowed his eyes. "Still," he mewed smoothly, "I'd like to meet my own kits."

"*Never!*" Turtle Tail hissed. Horror sparked in her eyes as she realized that she'd given away how fiercely she loved her kits.

Tom's face lit up. "Surely they'd like to meet their father?" He sounded pleased with himself.

Pain gripped Gray Wing's chest as it tightened. He struggled to draw in breath.

Turtle Tail showed her teeth. "They will never meet you!"

Tom shrugged and, flicking his tail, scuffed his way across Bumble's grave. "Shame it was Bumble who died and not you," he called over his shoulder.

Gray Wing stared after him. How could any cat be so cruel?

"Come on." Tall Shadow was the one to break the silence as Tom slid into the heather. "Let's get back to camp."

Turtle Tail was wide-eyed. "He mustn't *ever* find my kits," she whispered.

"He won't." Gray Wing pressed against her, stiffening as his chest tightened harder. He tried to draw in breath but it was too hard. He stumbled.

"Gray Wing!" Turtle Tail pushed her shoulder under his, holding him up as his paws gave way. "Thunder! Help me!"

Thunder was already at his other side. Gray Wing fought for breath as they held him between them.

"Be calm." Tall Shadow sniffed his breath. "You're okay, Gray Wing. It's just the old smoke sickness. Cloud Spots will have some herbs for you if we just get you back to camp."

Gray Wing watched her mouth moving, hardly hearing.

"Walk." Turtle Tail's stern mew sounded in his ear.

Gasping, he dragged a paw forward, forcing another in front. Suspended between Thunder and Turtle Tail, he began the long walk back to camp.

"That's right." Turtle Tail's mew sounded through the darkness, pressing at the corners of his vision. "We're nearly there."

Gulping tiny breaths, he pushed himself on. *I'll make it. Someone has to defend the kits. Who else can reason with Clear Sky?* His mind whirled. He dragged in breath after breath until suddenly he felt soft moss beneath his paws. It was his nest.

"Cloud Spots is fetching coltsfoot." Turtle Tail's breath bathed his muzzle.

"What's wrong with Gray Wing?"

"Is he dying?"

Kit mews sounded around him.

"He's going to be fine." Cloud Spot's calm mew sounded above him. "Eat these leaves, Gray Wing."

Gray Wing smelled the tang of herbs beneath his muzzle and leaned down, lapping blindly until he felt them touch his tongue. He swallowed them, faintly aware of their bitterness.

Paws kneaded his back, easing the tightness that squeezed his chest like a snake. "He'll probably sleep." Cloud Spots's mew sounded as his thoughts swirled and darkness reached for him. "He'll be better when he wakes."

"Wake up!" Stoneteller's mew jolted him from sleep.

"What's wrong?" He leaped to his paws, staring around. He was in the cave again. Moonlight filtered through the waterfall at the cavern's mouth. His old tribe mates were curled in their nests.

"You mustn't sleep, Gray Wing." Stoneteller's eyes blazed in the half-light. "There's danger. Your loved ones are in danger!"

Heart lurching, Gray Wing jerked up his head. He blinked open his eyes, surprised to find himself in his own nest. He breathed, air filling his chest. Relief swamped him. Turtle Tail was asleep beside him, her chin resting on his flank. The kits were curled against them, warm and soft, eyes closed.

It was just a nightmare. Sighing, Gray Wing closed his eyes and drifted back into dreams.

"Gray Wing." Turtle Tail's mew woke him into a soft, gray dawn. He gazed around the shadowy camp. It was hardly light but Rainswept Flower was hurrying across the clearing. Cloud Spots was carrying herbs toward the bramble. Gorse Fur paced with Shattered Ice beside the long grass.

"What's going on?" Gray Wing pushed himself to his paws.

Turtle Tail pressed her muzzle to his cheek. "Wind Runner's begun her kitting."

CHAPTER 10

❧

Thunder watched Gorse Fur pace beside Shattered Ice. The thin gray tom stopped as another pained yowl burst from beneath the bramble.

Rainswept Flower poked her head from the trailing stems. Gorse Fur glanced fearfully toward her. "The kitting's started too soon!"

Thunder's belly tightened. *Too soon?* Were the rogue and her kits going to die?

He looked toward the bramble, bright with yellow flowers.

"Any news?" Turtle Tail called from her nest. Owl Eyes, Pebble Heart, and Sparrow Fur blinked sleepily beside her. Gray Wing was hauling himself to his paws.

Thunder headed toward her. "Cloud Spots is with her. Dappled Pelt went to fetch herbs." He stiffened as another yowl sounded from the bramble. "Rainswept Flower says the kits are coming too soon."

Turtle Tail frowned. "By the look of her belly, she wasn't due for another moon." She hopped from the nest.

Thunder glanced anxiously at Gray Wing as he remembered helping him back to camp. The gray tom looked weary, his golden eyes dull. And Thunder could still hear him wheezing with every breath. "How are you?" He leaned closer.

"Better," Gray Wing rasped.

"He's going to rest," Turtle Tail meowed briskly.

Sparrow Fur was there, looking at her mother with eager eyes. "We'll look after him."

"Thank you, dear," Turtle Tail told her fondly. "Let him be." She nudged Sparrow Fur from the nest, scooping Pebble Heart after her before swinging Owl Eyes out by his scruff. "The best thing for you three to do is to play over there in the long grass. I want to go check on Wind Runner." She leaned close to Sparrow Fur. "Come and check on Gray Wing every now and then," she whispered. "But don't wake him if he's sleeping, and if his wheezing gets worse, come and find me, okay?"

Sparrow Fur nodded earnestly, before turning and nudging her brothers away. "You heard her," she told them.

"*I* should be the one to check him," Pebble Heart complained as they scampered away. "I know more about herbs than you do."

Turtle Tail called after them. "You can take turns." She faced Gray Wing. "You will rest, won't you?"

Gray Wing nodded. He looked as though he could do little else.

"Can you sit with him for a while?" Turtle Tail begged Thunder. "I don't like leaving him—"

Wind Runner wailed again.

Turtle Tail bounded away. "I must see how she's doing,"

she called over her shoulder.

Thunder shook out his fur. The rising sun was beginning to burn away the gray mist swathing the hollow, but there was still an early-morning chill. "Lie down," he told Gray Wing. "You look exhausted."

Gray Wing didn't argue, curling into the heather with a sigh. Thunder's pelt pricked. It wasn't like Gray Wing to give in so easily. He must be really ill. "Can I get you anything?" he asked. "Are you hungry? Do you need prey?"

Gray Wing didn't answer, his gaze following Turtle Tail as she disappeared behind the screen of yellow flowers. "This is no time for kits to be born."

Thunder shivered at the darkness in his tone. "New life brings hope and joy," he argued. "You said it yourself."

"That was *before*," Gray Wing answered grimly.

"Before what?" Thunder searched his gaze, but the gray tom's eyelids were drooping.

"There's danger." Gray Wing's mew was barely a whisper as he rested his nose on his paws and closed his eyes. "But you will lead us through it, Thunder. I know you will. . . ." His mew died away.

Thunder leaned closer, relieved to hear Gray Wing's steady breath. He'd just fallen asleep. "Get better," he whispered. "We need you."

He turned, Gray Wing's words echoing in his ears. *There's danger. But you will lead us through it.* What did he mean? Was he talking about the threat from Clear Sky? *How will I lead us through it?* Surely it was Gray Wing who was going to prevent battle by meeting Clear Sky?

Another yowl sounded from beneath the bramble, louder than before.

Turtle Tail burst from drooping branches. "Thunder!" She raced toward him. "Fetch a stick."

"A stick?" Thunder blinked at her. "What for?"

"Just fetch one. It's for Wind Runner!" Turtle Tail ordered. "A sturdy one that won't snap or crumble." She nosed him toward the gap in the heather. "Hurry! I'll get someone else to sit with Gray Wing."

Thunder charged from the camp, his paws sliding on the wet grass outside. He scanned the moor. There was only heather and grass here. For a sturdy stick he'd need to go to the forest. Dare he risk crossing Clear Sky's border? He pictured Turtle Tail's anxious face. Another agonized yowl drifted from the camp. He had to.

Haring across the moor, he plunged through the heather, swerving past a thorny gorse bush and bursting onto the slope beyond. He raced to the border, not even hesitating as he crossed the scent line. The tang of it touched his tongue. Fircone had marked this part. He scanned for a sign of the mottled brown-and-white tom, but nothing moved beyond the trees.

Pushing through ferns, he crept between the trees. Ears pricked, he searched the forest floor. A long stick lay beneath a birch. He sniffed it. *A sturdy one.* He remembered Turtle Tail's orders and clamped his jaws around the gnarled bark. The old wood disintegrated between his teeth. Snorting with frustration, Thunder searched again. A thicker stick lay nearby. He darted toward it and bit down. It fell to splinters in his mouth. Spitting out wood chips, he looked up. If he wanted a stick that wasn't half rotten, he'd have to pick a fresh one.

His heart sank. Climbing trees wasn't his best skill. His heart twisted as memory flooded back. He'd practiced tree climbing with Clear Sky. His father had instructed him to leap from tree to tree. He shuddered as he recalled the branches wobbling beneath his paws, dipping with every paw step. He'd lost his balance and fallen. He'd been smaller then; how would the branches hold his weight now?

He pushed away his doubts. Wind Runner needed a stick. Hunkering down, he fixed his gaze on the trunk of an oak. The bark was old and knobby. It should be easy to get a grip. He leaped, hooking the trunk with his claws. They stung as he dangled, clinging on desperately. *How do squirrels make this look so easy?* Digging in his hind claws he pushed himself up and flung his forepaws over a low branch. It was thick and he managed to clamber onto it, relief loosing his muscles as he felt it solid beneath his paws. Catching his breath, he glanced along it. Shoots sprouted at the end. They looked thick. They'd be solid branches one day, but now were still young and pliable. They wouldn't crumble or splinter under pressure. He just hoped he had the strength to snap one off.

Padding along the branch, he stopped beside a thick green stem sprouting from a knot in the bark. He grabbed it with his forepaws and curled his claws around it. Grunting, he heaved.

The stem bent. He heaved again. The stem trembled in his claws. *Break, you dumb stick!* He whined with effort, his muscles trembling as he pulled on the stem.

Crack!

The stem snapped. Thunder lost his balance. Belly flipping, he tumbled from the branch and hurtled toward the ground. Terror surged beneath his pelt. He flailed his paws and flicked his tail, turning in the air a moment before he hit the ground. He landed heavily on his paws, gasping with surprise. The stem clattered down beside him.

I knew I wasn't cut out for tree climbing! He shook out his pelt. *But I'm great at falling.*

He inspected the stem, pleased to see that it had snapped at the base. It looked sturdy. He just hoped Turtle Tail would agree. Grabbing it between his jaws, he headed for the border.

Breathing deeply, he checked for scents, hoping the forest cats wouldn't notice his when they patrolled the border later. If they did, he hoped they'd assume it was simply lingering from yesterday's visit. He pushed through the ferns, the stick catching among the thick fronds. He sank his teeth into one end and heaved it free, then dragged it toward the border.

His jaws were aching by the time he'd hauled it up the slope. He dropped it and took a better hold, clamping the middle of it between his jaws. He ran, crossing the grass, head high. *I must look like one of those dumb dogs that carry sticks to their Twolegs.* Embarrassment heated his pelt. *I hope no one sees me.*

As he neared the hollow, he heard Wind Runner yowling. There were no gaps between her shrieks now. Had Turtle

Tail's kitting been this painful? He couldn't remember cries like this. Wind Runner was one of the bravest cats he knew. She must be suffering. He raced into camp and crossed the clearing.

As he skidded to a halt outside the bramble, Turtle Tail ducked out. She inspected the stick, sniffing and sinking her teeth into the young wood. "It's good," she told Thunder. "Thanks."

"What's it for?" he asked as she picked it up and headed back inside.

"Come and see."

Thunder hesitated as she disappeared. Did he want to see Wind Runner's suffering? He frowned. He wasn't going to let Turtle Tail think he was scared. He nosed his way gingerly through the flowery stems.

The cavern was gloomy. Wind Runner lay stretched on the cool earth. Cloud Spots and Dapple Pelt huddled near her tail while Gorse Fur crouched by her cheek, lapping it as she writhed. She gave a low yowl.

"She's exhausted by the pain." Gorse Fur stared round-eyed at Cloud Spots. "Can't you do anything else to help her?"

Turtle Tail hauled Thunder's stick across the earth and laid the thick end beside Wind Runner's head. "She could bite down on this." She searched Cloud Spots's gaze.

"Yes!" Cloud Spots's eyes shone in the gloom. "It might focus her mind away from her pain!"

Gorse Fur stared at Turtle Tail. "Will it really help?"

"Let's find out." Turtle Tail crouched beside Wind

Runner and nudged her muzzle toward the stick. Wind Runner blinked at it hazily, confusion showing through her pain.

"Bite on it," Gorse Fur whispered in her ear.

Thunder leaned closer, holding his breath as Wind Runner reached out and grabbed the stick between her jaws. As her body shuddered, convulsing, she bit down.

Thunder tensed. *Don't let it splinter!*

The stick creaked but didn't split.

"Good!" Cloud Spots nodded to Turtle Tail. "It's helping her bear down!"

Wind Runner shuddered again, biting down hard on the stick.

"The first kit!" Cloud Spots's mew was tense. Turtle Tail raced to see as the white she-kit sniffed at the tiny, wet bundle.

Thunder leaned forward, fear rising in his throat. *Is it okay?*

Gorse Fur lapped Wind Runner's head. "You're doing well."

Wind Runner convulsed again.

"Another!" Cloud Spots scooped the first bundle toward Turtle Tail, who began lapping at the glistening skin that encased it. Thunder stared wide-eyed as the skin split and a tiny gray kit flopped out, looking half drowned. It let out a tiny wail.

"It's fine!" Turtle Tail's mew was jubilant. "And it's a tom. Come and see, Thunder." She beckoned him with a flick of her tail.

Thunder padded nervously around Cloud Spots and Dappled Pelt and stopped beside Turtle Tail. The kit was mewling, its eyes closed. Its tail was short and wet like a lizard's.

"Is it supposed to look like that?" he asked, breathless.

"That's what Pebble Heart, Owl Eyes, and Sparrow Fur looked like," Turtle Tail purred. "You probably did too." She grabbed the tom by the scruff and placed it beside Wind Runner's head, next to his litter-sister.

Wind Runner grunted as a spasm gripped her.

"Two more toms!" Cloud Spots called.

"*Four* kits!" Gorse Fur broke into a purr.

"Three toms and a she-kit," Dappled Pelt announced proudly. "Small, but perfect."

Wind Runner let the stick fall away and turned to her firstborn. Gently she lapped the scraps of membrane clinging to its wet fur. It flailed blindly, mewling, and she scooped it closer to her muzzle with a paw.

Thunder watched, his heart swelling, as one at a time, Dappled Pelt placed the other newborn kits beside Wind Runner's muzzle. He stared, his throat tightening with emotion. He wanted to congratulate Wind Runner and Gorse Fur, but words didn't seem enough.

Wind Runner began purring, as though she could no longer feel the pain. Gorse Fur lapped her head even more fiercely.

"That's all," Cloud Spots announced.

Turtle Tail's whiskers twitched with amusement. "That's *plenty.*"

Wind Runner curled around her kits. Thunder watched as they wriggled blindly toward her belly, mewling with frustration as they struggled to get close. He fought the urge to lean in and scoop them toward their mother. Wind Runner seemed to know instinctively what to do and wriggled closer until they were pressed against her. One by one, they sought her belly and latched on, purring as they began to gulp down her milk.

Thunder backed away, blinking. He felt Turtle Tail's pelt press against his.

"Isn't it wonderful?" she breathed.

Thunder gazed at the kits. "It's the best thing I ever saw," he admitted.

Turtle Tail purred with pleasure. "Toms will never know how it feels to bring kits into the world."

"I don't think they want to!" Thunder remembered Wind Runner's agonized yowls. But, watching her nursing her kits, it was like it never happened.

Gorse Fur looked up at Turtle Tail. "Thanks for fetching the stick."

"Thunder found it," she told him. "It was perfect. I was worried he'd bring a rotten . . ." Her voice trailed away and she pricked her ears. "Where are Sparrow Fur and Owl Eyes?" She stiffened. "And Pebble Heart."

"They'll still be playing in the long grass," Thunder told her. Unease pricked his pelt. Had he seen them there when he left camp to fetch the stick? He couldn't remember.

"I can't hear them." Panic edged Turtle Tail's mew.

Thunder pricked his ears. Beyond the trailing branches, the only sound was the murmur of the moor cats. He darted past Wind Runner and stuck his head out. The long grass was quiet. No stems trembled. He pushed his way forward.

Turtle Tail barged past him. "Where are they?" She raced to the long grass and began sniffing it desperately. "Sparrow Fur!" She lifted her muzzle and called across the camp. "Pebble Heart! Owl Eyes!"

Lightning Tail bounded from the flat rock. Shattered Ice leaped to his paws beside the heather.

"What's wrong?" Rainswept Flower hurried toward Turtle Tail.

"Has anyone seen my kits?" Turtle Tail called.

The cats exchanged glances.

Hawk Swoop padded forward. "I saw them playing on the grass outside camp a while ago."

"They were supposed to stay *here*!" Anger flared in Turtle Tail's mew. "They shouldn't be outside the hollow." She glared accusingly around the moor cats. "Why didn't anyone stop them?"

Tall Shadow slid from beside the flat rock. "We didn't know you wanted them to stay inside," she meowed calmly.

"But anything might have happened to them!" She glanced at the sky. "Have you seen any buzzards?"

"No," Tall Shadow soothed. "And there's no scent of foxes. I'm sure the kits are fine."

Jagged Peak limped across the clearing. "They're probably just having fun."

Turtle Tail stared at him hopefully. "Do you think so?"

"I'll search for them on the moor," Jagged Peak offered. "I know where they like to play."

"Good idea," Tall Shadow agreed.

Thunder narrowed his eyes. Anxiety edged the black she-cat's mew.

"What's going on?" Gray Wing's wheezing mew sounded from his nest. He was hauling himself to his paws.

Tall Shadow looked at him. "Have you seen the kits?"

"Wind Runner's?" Gray Wing looked confused. "Has she had them?"

"Yes!" Turtle Tail began pacing, eyes glistening. "But *my* kits are missing."

"Have you *seen* them?" Tall Shadow asked Gray Wing firmly.

He shook his head, his paw slipping as he tried to climb out of his nest. "Let me look. I know I'll find them."

Thunder bounded toward him. "Stay there." Gray Wing was not in a fit state to search the moor. He glanced at Jagged Peak. "Are you going to search for them or not?" he snapped.

Jagged Peak flattened his ears. "I said I would."

"Then go." Thunder nudged Gray Wing back into his nest as Jagged Peak headed out of the camp. "I'll make sure he stays here." Turtle Tail blinked at him gratefully, then bounded after Jagged Peak. Shattered Ice and Hawk Swoop followed.

"I'll search the moortop," Shattered Ice volunteered.

"I'll look by the gorge," Hawk Swoop offered.

Thunder watched them go, frustration tugging at his belly. Part of him wished he hadn't offered to watch over Gray Wing. He felt helpless stuck in the hollow.

Gray Wing moved beside him. He was struggling to climb out of the nest again.

"Shhhh, just rest." As he nosed Gray Wing back into the moss, Tall Shadow padded closer.

"Sit on him if you have to. He must be fit by full moon." She stared sternly at Gray Wing. "We're depending on you to make a peace with Clear Sky that will last." She glanced toward the bramble, where the sound of mewling was muffled by the thick shield of flowers. "We need it now more than ever."

Gray Wing flopped down helplessly. "I just hope I can find the right words."

"You only need to be reasonable," Tall Shadow growled. "Clear Sky's no fool. Why choose bloodshed over peace?"

Thunder felt dread uncoil in his belly. He'd seen the vicious rogues Clear Sky had recruited. With them on his side, Clear Sky might settle the peace by driving the moor cats from their home forever. Should he warn them? As Thunder hesitated, Gray Wing drew in a shuddering breath. *Let him rest.* Now wasn't the time to burden anyone with more worry. He stared through the gap in the heather, straining to see the moor. *Please let them find the kits.*

A frantic yowl sounded in the distance. *Jagged Peak!* Thunder raced for the moor. He glanced over his shoulder and saw Tall Shadow pressing Gray Wing back into his nest.

She signaled to Lightning Tail with a nod. "Go with Thunder. I'll watch Gray Wing."

Thunder heard Lightning Tail's paws thrum across the clearing behind him. He leaped through the gap in the heather and tore over the grass.

Plunging through a swath of heather, he zigzagged along a rabbit trail until he burst onto smooth grass on the other side. Bumble's grave was ahead. He leaped over it, skidding as he landed. Lightning Tail exploded from the heather behind.

"Thunder!" Jagged Peak's yowl sounded beyond a wall of gorse. Thunder nosed his way under the bush, ignored the thorns scraping his spine. "What's happened?" His heart was in his throat as he squeezed out the other side, Lightning Tail bursting out at his side, and Jagged Peak limping toward him.

His eyes were sparking with fear. "The kittypet took them!"

"What kittypet?" Lightning Tail frowned.

Thunder ignored him. "Where's Turtle Tail?"

"She's gone after the kittypet," Jagged Peak puffed. "She told me to come back. She said I couldn't keep up." Anguish twisted his mouth.

"How do you know it was the kittypet?" Thunder demanded.

"The scents," Jagged Peak struggled to get his breath. "We tracked the kits' trail and it met another. The heather was drenched with Tom's scent. Turtle Tail recognized it at once."

Tom! Shock pulsed through Thunder. Turtle Tail had been right to look so afraid yesterday. "She's gone after them?" How could she stand up to Tom alone? The kits might give her the courage to fight harder, but they'd also make her vulnerable— and what if he turned his nasty temper on them?

Thunder's mind reeled. "Lightning Tail." He turned toward the black tom. "Come with me." He jerked his head toward camp. "Jagged Peak, tell Tall Shadow and Gray Wing what's happened. Don't let Gray Wing follow us. He's too ill. Tell him I won't return without Turtle Tail and the kits!"

He hurtled forward, heading for the river. What was Tom planning to do with them? "Hurry!" He heard Lightning Tail's paws pounding behind him. They had to catch up with Tom before Turtle Tail did. Who knew what he'd do to her if she tried to stop him?

CHAPTER 11

"Wait." Clear Sky nudged Snake to a halt. His nose twitched as unfamiliar cat scent touched it.

The forest here was ridged, dips opening between the ancient trees that marked the borderline. Beyond, marsh meadows lined the river.

"Follow me." Clear Sky crept up the slope toward the edge of the tree line and peered from the shade. Sunshine bathed the fields and he blinked.

"What is it?" Snake asked as he caught up.

"Can't you smell?"

Snake opened his mouth to taste the air, but Clear Sky had already spotted the cat. A sleek, broad-shouldered tom was weaving his way through the long grass beyond the border. Three kits trotted in his wake. Clear Sky narrowed his eyes. The tom's copper-colored pelt had the softness of a kittypet, but the scrappy young kits looked wild. Why were they traveling together?

Snake hissed beside him.

Clear Sky glanced at the brown tabby rogue. His back was arched and bristling like a hedgehog. "Take it easy," he soothed. "They're not on our land."

"But if I give them a scratch or two, they won't even come near it again." Snake leaned forward, showing his teeth.

Clear Sky nodded approvingly. This rogue's aggression would prove useful in the future. But not here. "It's just a kittypet and some kits," he reasoned. "Why bother fighting?" He beckoned Snake forward with a flick of his tail. "Words can be just as powerful." He padded from the trees and pushed through the grass. The hot morning sun glared down, searing his pelt. Pelt pricking with satisfaction, he stepped into the path of the kittypet and faced him, ears flat. "What are you doing here?" he snarled.

The kittypet stopped. Behind him, the kits clustered together, eyes wide. Tiny growls trembled in their throats as they pressed against his bulging flank. He glanced around as though searching for an escape route.

"Don't bother running." Clear Sky glanced at Snake as he slid from the grass. "You're too fat to outpace us."

The kittypet shifted his paws. "My name is Tom. Are we on your territory?" His mew was smooth. "I didn't realize. Please accept my apologies. We'll leave at once if you'd kindly show us the way." He blinked at Clear Sky innocently.

Clear Sky snorted. "Would you like me to fetch you food too?" Kittypets were all the same. They'd beg anyone for anything rather than fend for themselves.

"Of course not." Tom dipped his head courteously. "I have not come this way for any reason but that it is the way home. I certainly wouldn't want to challenge any cat"—he paused to let a purr rumble in his throat—"*any* cat as *impressive* as you."

Clear Sky's whiskers quivered. He was enjoying watching this kittypet ingratiate himself. And it secretly pleased him to be called *impressive*. But Snake and this trespasser mustn't know. He curled his lip. "Hurry home, kittypet. This is my forest." He nodded toward the trees. "I don't like cats in it, and I don't like cats *near* it. Ask anyone. My name's Clear Sky."

Tom's gaze strayed toward the trees. "Of course," he purred. "I realize I am trespassing near your land. Please forgive me but I am only escorting my kits back to my housefolk."

Snake leaned close. Clear Sky screwed up his face as the rogue's stinking breath washed his nose. "Those aren't his kits," Snake hissed. "Look at them. They're muscle and bone, like wild kits."

"I know that!" Clear Sky nudged Snake sharply backward, his eyes fixed on the kittypet. "They don't look like your kits. They're not fat."

Tom's face hardened and malice glinted in his gaze.

Clear Sky stiffened with surprise. He stepped closer, hackles rising. "Whose kits are they?"

"*Mine.*" Tom met his gaze squarely. "They were taken from me. I'm returning them to their proper home with my housefolk."

Clear Sky blinked, curiosity tugging in his belly. He ignored it. This was not his problem. If this kittypet wanted to steal wild kits, let him. So long as he didn't steal from the forest cats. Besides, the kits huddling at Tom's side weren't complaining. The tabby tom-kit's gaze caught his eye. It was strangely blank, as though he was observing, unimpressed.

"Go away." Clear Sky stepped out of the path, and jerked his head toward Twolegplace. "And *stay* away." The kits scurried past him, the gray tom and tortoiseshell watching him with wide, frightened eyes while the tabby tipped his head inquisitively.

"We won't be back, I promise." Tom shooed them onward, glancing at Clear Sky. "Thanks for being so understanding."

Clear Sky puffed out his chest. "You see," he growled to Snake. "That's how you patrol territory. No bloodshed, but he understood who's in charge around here. And he'll tell his kittypet friends."

He bounded toward the forest, relishing the cool shade of the trees as he slid beneath them. "Let's head to camp. The other patrols should be back. I want to do some battle training before the end of the day."

Snake hurried after him. "So you think there will be a battle?" He sounded eager.

"It sounds like my brother's preparing for one." Clear Sky lashed his tail. Why did he have to fight to keep what was his? Couldn't Gray Wing respect his boundaries? He pushed harder against the cracked earth of the forest floor. There hadn't been rain in days. The moor cats must be scorched beneath this relentless sun. Was *that* why they resented him taking the forest?

"Clear Sky!" Birch's happy mew welcomed him as he raced past the brambles into camp.

Alder scrambled from beneath the yew. "You're back!"

The kits' eyes shone happily.

Clear Sky felt warmth flood beneath his pelt. It lasted a moment before regret pricked in its place. Would Thunder have run to him like this if he'd raised him? He pushed the thought away. It was too late. Thunder was Gray Wing's cat now.

"Can we train?" Alder and Birch skipped around him while Snake padded to a prey pile and began to sift through the morning's catch.

"You can watch," Clear Sky told them. "The big cats are training today. I need you to stay out of the way. But learn as much as you can."

A body thumped the ground beside him.

Clear Sky spun around.

Dew lay in the dirt, Thorn rearing over her, claws stretched. The skinny tom pulled back his lips and lunged.

Dew rolled out of the way, her gray pelt a blur, and leaped to her paws. She faced Thorn. A purr burst from her. "You thought you'd got me!"

Thorn lashed his tail, his eyes sparked good-humoredly. "One of these days your speed will fail you."

Clear Sky padded between them. "Not if we train." He scanned the clearing. Nettle was back from border patrol with Petal and Leaf. They lay, chewing prey, in the shade of the oak. Falling Feather paced beside Quick Water while she quietly groomed herself. Fircone rested beside the bramble, his chin on his paws, half-opened eyes fixed on Jackdaw's Cry. The moor cat had hardly moved from the nest he'd built beside the

holly bush. Falling Feather had kept her distance, but Clear
Sky noticed how often her gaze strayed toward her littermate.
Don't forget the border that separates you now. Clear Sky shot her a
look and she hesitated a moment before pacing again.

He lifted his muzzle. "It's time we trained for battle!" At
his call, the forest cats scrambled to their paws.

Clear Sky traced a wide circle in the clearing with his claw
and stood at the center. "In this space, we fight with claws."

Quick Water blinked. "Why harm each other?"

"We can't risk injuries." Leaf stepped forward. "We need to
be fit and healthy in case there's a battle."

Clear Sky met his gaze, unblinking. "We have to know
what it's like to fight for our lives," he growled. "If we only
train to play fight, we'll face battle no stronger than kits."

Snake nodded. Thorn padded to join him. Their eyes lit.

"I'll fight first," Snake hissed.

Clear Sky looked around his cats, his gaze stopping on
Falling Feather. "You can be his opponent." He beckoned her
into the ring.

"No!" Jackdaw's Cry jumped up, his eyes sparking with
fear. Clear Sky glared at him.

"It's okay." Falling Feather nodded to her brother. "I'll face
him." She strode into the ring as Snake took his place opposite
her. "What are we practicing?" she asked Clear Sky, not taking
her gaze from Snake.

"Lie down," Clear Sky told her.

She jerked her muzzle around. "What?"

She's questioning me! He'd crush the arrogance from her. She had to be loyal. Her camp mates were relying on her. They must be able to trust her. "Lie on your back," he ordered. Fear glittered in her gaze. Satisfaction rippled through his pelt.

Quick Water padded to the edge of the ring. "Clear Sky, what are you doing? She'll be helpless on her back. Snake will hurt her."

"If you fall in battle, you're going to need to know how to get back on your paws," Clear Sky told the she-cat. He looked back at Falling Feather. "Are you going to lie on your back, or does Snake have to put you there himself?"

Falling Feather gave a low hiss and settled onto her side. Watching Snake warily, she wriggled onto her spine.

Clear Sky turned, addressing the watching cats. "When Snake attacks, Falling Feather must get her hind claws under his chin. He's bigger than she is, but if she uses her weight properly, she should be able to push him off." He nodded to Snake. "Ready?"

Snake unsheathed his claws. "Ready." He circled Falling Feather slowly, pacing around her with deliberate steps.

Falling Feather watched him, switching her head back and forth as he moved from one side to the other. Clear Sky could see her trembling. Fear would make her fight harder.

A low growl sounded in Jackdaw's Cry's throat. Clear Sky shot him a look. "You are here as our guest," he growled. "Keep quiet."

With a snarl, Snake lunged for Falling Feather's throat. He moved fast. Falling Feather yowled as he sunk his claws into her neck. With a strangled cry, she writhed beneath him.

Grunting, she heaved up her hindquarters, rolling her weight back onto her shoulders. Snake's hind paws slipped as she shifted beneath him and she tucked in her hind legs, drawing them up and hooking her claws beneath Snake's chin. With a snarl, she thrust him up and backward, sending him flying out of the ring. She leaped to her paws and dived after him, teeth bared.

"Stop!" Clear Sky ordered sharply.

She froze and turned.

He nodded to the line he'd drawn in the earth. Her paws were outside it. "No teeth or claws beyond the ring," he reminded her.

Blood stained her neck fur. "But he hurt me."

"And you fought like a fox to defend yourself." Pride pressed in Clear Sky's chest. "You'll remember the lesson in battle. Your enemies will meet you only once in combat; the next time they'll run when they see you."

He nodded Leaf and Thorn toward the ring. "Your turn now," he growled. "Don't forget: use your claws."

By the time each cat had trained in the ring, the earth was spattered with blood, and clumps of fur drifted across the clearing.

Clear Sky nodded approvingly to his cats. "Well done."

Quick Water rubbed a cut on her muzzle with her paw. Leaf lapped at a wound in his flank. Yet their eyes shone. Every one of the forest cats moved with pride. They had proven to themselves and to each other that, even when they seemed beaten, they could fight off an enemy, no matter how dangerous.

Clear Sky padded to the prey pile. "You must all be hungry." He plucked a thrush from the top and tossed it to Thorn, then hurled a mouse to Petal. One by one, he threw food to his cats and they took it. Nodding gratefully, they settled down to eat.

"What about me?" Jackdaw's Cry climbed from his nest.

Clear Sky narrowed his eyes. "We hunted this prey, not you." Why should they share the forest's riches with a moor cat?

Falling Feather stepped forward. "You promised Thunder you'd keep him safe and well fed."

Clear Sky grunted. "I told Thunder what he wanted to hear. It was up to him to believe me."

Jackdaw's Cry crossed the clearing and headed for the bramble opening. "I'll hunt my own food then," he snarled.

"Not on *my* territory," Clear Sky snapped.

Jackdaw's Cry spun around. "Then I'll hunt on the moor!"

"You'll stay here," Clear Sky growled, narrowing his eyes threateningly. "Or the meeting is off."

Quick Water looked up from the shrew she'd been given. "It's two more days till the meeting! He'll starve."

"No cat ever starved in two days." Clear Sky whipped his tail behind him. Cats took moons to starve. He'd seen it with his own eyes, back in the mountains.

Muttering angrily, Jackdaw's Cry slunk back to his nest.

Dumb moor cats. Anger pulsed beneath Clear Sky's pelt. *Always expecting more than they deserve.*

He stalked from the camp, furious that Jackdaw's Cry had

sullied the pleasure he'd felt from the training session. He headed instinctively for the meadow border. He felt sure the kittypet would be gone, but he wanted to check. He'd trusted cats before. He'd been wrong. As he reached the edge of the forest and felt midday heat rolling from the sun-drenched wetlands, he tasted the air. The kittypet scent was stale but a fresher smell tainted it. One he recognized.

Thunder!

Racing forward, he burst from the trees.

He could see his son's orange pelt moving through the long grass. He bounded toward him. "What are you doing, sniffing at my borders?" He stopped in front of Thunder, ears flat.

Thunder lifted his head. "I'm not on your territory." He was tasting the air, distracted.

Rage pulsed in Clear Sky's belly. "Stay away from my land!"

The grass swished beside him. A black tom slid out. "Have you found anything—" He stopped as he saw Clear Sky. "We haven't crossed the border," he snapped defensively.

"Then why are you here?"

Thunder gazed across the grass. "We're looking for someone."

Clear Sky sniffed Lightning Tail. His scent was familiar. Was this one of Jackdaw's Cry's kits? "Have you come looking for your father?" He narrowed his eyes suspiciously.

Thunder turned on him. "Turtle Tail's kits have gone missing, okay? We're looking for them. Have you seen them?"

Lightning Tail leaned forward. "Or Turtle Tail?"

Clear Sky flattened his ears and turned away from them,

muttering: "Perhaps these kits belong with their father."

"Really?" Thunder snarled. "Is that why you sent me away? *Twice?*"

Clear Sky could see Thunder's hackles rising. "I did the best for you!"

"*Thanks,*" Thunder sneered.

Lightning Tail padded through the grass, tail twitching above the long stems. "We should keep on looking." He gazed across the meadow.

Thunder was still staring at Clear Sky. "Have you *seen* them?" he repeated.

"No!" *Why should I help you and your dumb friends?* If Turtle Tail had lost her kits, it served her right. He thought of Alder and Birch waiting in the hollow and how they'd run to him, eyes shining when he arrived back at camp. They'd never wander off with a strange cat. They *wanted* to be with him. Thunder had only ever wanted to be with Gray Wing. That was clear now.

"Stay off my land!" Lashing his tail, he turned his back and stalked into the forest.

CHAPTER 12

✦

Had Clear Sky really not seen the kits? Thunder thought he had recognized something shifty in his father's gaze. But perhaps it was unease at meeting Lightning Tail; after all, he was holding Jackdaw's Cry hostage. Either way, Thunder knew that Clear Sky would not help and he wasn't going to waste his breath asking.

A maple sprouted, tall and solitary, in the middle of the meadow. "Let's try over there for scents." Lightning Tail headed toward it. "The kits might have rested in the shade."

Thunder followed as Lightning Tail wove through the grass. The stems grew thicker, the soil beneath his paws turning to marsh so that he was splashing through shallow water by the time they reached the maple. He was relieved that the ground rose above its roots so that it formed an island in the wide, wet meadow. He shook the water from his paws. "Any sign?"

Lightning Tail was sniffing the base of the tree. "Cat scent!" He whisked his tail excitedly.

Thunder darted forward to sniff the bark. Disappointment dropped like a stone in his belly. "It's a rogue she-cat." *Not kittypet, or moor cat.*

"Maybe the rogue saw them," Lightning Tail suggested hopefully. "If we can find her, we can ask her."

Thunder stretched up onto his hind legs and scanned the meadow. There was no sign of another cat, even though the scents around the tree were fresh. He sighed heavily and dropped onto all fours. "Too late. She's not around here anymore."

"Are you sure?" A mew sounded above their heads.

Thunder jerked back his muzzle and stared up into the fluttering leaves.

An orange face peered back. A tabby she-cat was crouched on a branch. "I've been watching you sniffing your way around the meadow for ages," she mocked gently. "You didn't even know I was here. I'm surprised you can find your own tails in the morning."

"Have you seen three kits?" Thunder was too worried to respond to her teasing. "They were probably with a kittypet. A tom."

The she-cat scrambled down the trunk and landed lightly beside him. "I'm Swift." She introduced herself, tail high, circling Thunder and Lightning Tail.

Thunder's pelt itched with frustration. "Have you *seen* them?"

Swift shrugged. "Yes, but why are you looking for them?"

"They've been stolen," Lightning Tail explained.

Swift blinked. "They didn't look stolen. They were following the tom quite happily. I thought he must be their father."

"He is," Thunder snapped.

"So what's the problem?" Swift blinked at him.

Thunder clawed the earth. "He's a cruel kittypet who hurt their mother and has taken them without her permission."

"Where *is* their mother?" Swift stopped circling. "Shouldn't *she* be looking for them?"

Thunder was losing patience with this nosy rogue. "She went on ahead. We're trying to catch up to her before she finds the kittypet."

"Why?" The rogue tipped her head to one side.

"Because he's vicious and he might hurt her!" Thunder thrust his muzzle close to Swift's. "Did you see where they went?"

Swift flicked her tail. "They crossed the meadow. They were heading toward the river."

"Is that the way to Twolegplace?" Lightning Tail paced, scanning the sea of grass.

"Yes." Swift sniffed. "Once he gets them there, you'll never find them. It's too noisy and smelly for any cat to pick up their trail."

Thunder's heart pounded. "We'll find them before they reach it."

"Good luck." Swift padded down the slope and headed into the long grass.

Thunder watched her disappear. How long since the kits had passed this way? At least they weren't scared. Swift had said they were following him happily. *Why?* A pang jabbed his belly. *We raised them to be too trusting!* Perhaps Clear Sky was

right. Kindness was a weakness cats couldn't allow. It made
them vulnerable.

"Come on." Lightning Tail was already heading toward the
river. He slid into the grass. Thunder hurried after him.

How would they cross the river? How did the *kits* cross
the river? A flash of hope flared in his chest. Perhaps they
couldn't! Perhaps they'd find them on the shore with Turtle
Tail.

But what about Tom? He wouldn't give them up without a
fight. Not after having made it this far.

Thunder shouldered his way through the thick grass, following Lightning Tail. The young tom's tail-tip snaked a
muzzle-length ahead. As it slid out of sight, Thunder burst
from the grass onto the pebbly shore of the river. Lightning
Tail was already pacing at the water's edge, his gaze fixed on
the other side. The river was wide, but the long hot days had
made it sluggish and it slid sleepily between the banks.

"Can you swim?" Lightning Tail looked over his shoulder.

Thunder shook his head. He crossed the pebbles and stood
at the river's edge, shuddering as water washed his paw tips.
He scanned the bank, straining to see any sign of the kits. The
shore was deserted, the far side empty. A frog croaked noisily
a little way downstream.

"I smell Turtle Tail!" Lightning Tail ducked his head and
began sniffing the stones. He padded downstream. "She defi-
nitely came this way."

Thunder joined him, his heart lifting as he detected Turtle

Tail's familiar scent. He tracked it, muzzle skimming the stones.

Lightning Tail followed. "Do you think she crossed the river?"

"If the kits crossed, then she would have found a way to follow."

"But how could the kits have got across?" Lightning Tail frowned.

"Perhaps kittypets swim." Thunder pictured Tom dragging Sparrow Fur, terrified, through the water before swimming back for Pebble Heart and Owl Eyes. He padded faster over the stones.

"Look!" Lightning Tail's cry rang through the shimmering air.

Thunder jerked up his head. "What?"

"Crossing stones!"

A line of flat stones showed above the water a little way downstream. They dotted the river, stretching from one shore to the other while the river flowed smoothly around them. The gaps between them were narrow enough for a full-grown cat to leap across easily—even one with a kit dangling from his jaws.

Thunder's heart sank. "Tom would have taken them that way."

"And Turtle Tail would have followed!" Lightning Tail streaked past Thunder, racing for the stones. He leaped from the bank onto the first and jumped from stone to stone, his eyes fixed on the far shore.

"Careful!" Thunder hurried after him, pebbles cracking beneath his paws. The crossing stones were smooth, worn by countless seasons of wind and water. "They might be slippery."

As he spoke, one of Lightning Tail's paws slid from beneath him, Thunder gasped as he heard the thud of his chin hitting the rock. "No!" Lightning Tail's eyes rolled back and, dazed, he tumbled into the water.

Silently, smoothly, the river pulled him under.

"Lightning Tail!" Thunder leaped the crossing stones, claws stretched.

Black fur swirled beneath the surface, already tail-lengths away. Lightning Tail didn't even struggle. The fall must have knocked him out. Thunder slithered to a halt in the middle. The river was stronger and faster than it looked. *I'll never reach him from here.* He teetered at the edge of a stone, preparing to dive. *I have to try and save him!* Could he swim that far? And then what? Did he have the strength to drag his dazed friend to the shore?

A splash sounded from the far bank. Thunder gasped as he saw a shape slide through the water. A tom's head surfaced, flicking water from his ear tips as he swam smoothly toward Lightning Tail.

River Ripple! As he recognized the tom's silver fur, Thunder's chest swelled with hope. He leaped the last few stones to the far bank and raced to the shore where River Ripple had dived in. The rogue was catching up with Lightning Tail as the river swirled him around. Lunging forward, River Ripple grabbed the helpless tom by the scruff. He turned and began to haul Lightning Tail back to shore.

Relief flooded Thunder's pelt. He waded into the shallows to meet River Ripple as he neared the bank. Grabbing a mouthful of Lightning Tail's pelt, he helped the rogue pull his friend from the water.

They laid him on the pebbles. Lightning Tail was as still as stone. "Is he dead?" Thunder blinked at River Ripple. Had they been too late?

River Ripple pressed his ear to Lightning Tail's chest, then began pumping him with his forepaws. "He's alive. If I can push out the water . . ." His mew trailed away as Lightning Tail twitched beneath him.

The black tom gurgled, half-opening his eyes. With a splutter, he coughed up a mouthful of water, then scrambled to his paws. He crouched, so much water falling from his mouth, Thunder began to wonder if he'd swallowed half the river.

"He'll be okay now." River Ripple's calm mew sounded in his ear.

Thunder spun. "Thank you!" He purred loudly at the rogue. "I don't know what I would have done if you hadn't saved him."

River Ripple shrugged. "You'd have either learned to swim or drowned trying."

"Thanks, River Ripple," Lightning Tail croaked.

River Ripple shook out his pelt.

Water sprayed Thunder. "Watch out!" he spluttered.

River Ripple purred. "You moor cats really don't like

getting wet." He glanced at Lightning Tail, whose dripping pelt was clinging to his wiry frame. "What do you do when it rains?"

"You can't drown in rain," Thunder muttered.

"What are you doing here anyway?" River Ripple scanned the shore behind them.

Thunder nodded. "We're looking for some kits."

"Turtle Tail's?" River Ripple narrowed his eyes.

"Have you seen them?" Thunder leaned closer.

River Ripple shook his head. "No. But I smelled Turtle Tail's scent."

"She's looking for them, too. Their kittypet father snatched them from the camp," Thunder explained. "We think he's taking them back to his housefolk."

"In Twolegplace?" River Ripple glanced across the lush meadow behind them. Huge, dark shapes showed, jagged against the horizon.

Thunder followed his gaze, anxiety pricking in his paws. "Is that it?" He nodded toward the dark shapes.

"Yes."

Lightning Tail stopped coughing and straightened. "Have you ever been there?"

River Ripple nodded. "There's a narrow river there, but it's putrid." He shivered. "It's mostly full of Thunderpaths and monsters."

Thunder flattened his ears. "I've never seen a Thunderpath up close." He'd heard the older cats talk of them and seen the one that ran below the far edge of the moor. The distant monsters that raced along it shone like beetles in the sunlight, their whining roar piercing his ear fur. "We must get there as soon as we can." Turtle Tail and the kits were in even more danger than he'd thought. He gazed intently at River Ripple. "Will you help us?" If the rogue had been to Twolegplace, he could help them find their way around.

"You say a kittypet's taken Turtle Tail's kits?"

Thunder nodded. "We have to get them back."

"Okay." River Ripple glanced at Lightning Tail, who was still dripping. "Shake out your pelt and we can leave."

Thunder backed away quickly, but not quickly enough to avoid another soaking as Lightning Tail obeyed River Ripple. The rogue snorted with amusement as Thunder screwed up his face and shook water from his whiskers, then headed into the grass.

The lush grass of the meadow thinned as the dark shapes of Twolegplace loomed ahead. Thunder's fur lifted along his spine as he heard the distant drone of monsters and felt a sour tang bathing his tongue. Before long they were crossing a stretch of short grass. Spindly trees lay ahead and Thunder felt relieved to be out of the hot sunshine as they padded beneath the branches.

River Ripple halted. "Are you ready?" He nodded toward a line of bushes ahead. "There are Twoleg nests beyond there."

Thunder exchanged glances with Lightning Tail. "I promised Gray Wing I'd bring Turtle Tail and the kits back safely." The muscles along his spine were tight with fear. "You can wait here if you prefer."

"Never!" Lightning Tail flicked his tail. "We're sticking together."

Thunder nodded to River Ripple. "I'll understand if you want to turn back."

"I'm coming," River Ripple told him firmly. "If you've never seen a Thunderpath up close before, you'll need my help." Thunder and Lightning Tail followed River Ripple through the gap in the hedge, surprised to see a wide stretch of grass on the other side. Flowery bushes edged both sides. Where were the monsters and Thunderpaths? He glanced questioningly at River Ripple.

"Follow me." The rogue scurried over the grass, keeping close to the bushes. A huge stone shape loomed at the end of the grass. It seemed to be staring at Thunder through four square shiny eyes. "Is it safe here?" He shrank beneath his pelt.

"Don't worry," River Ripple called over his shoulder. "It's just a Twoleg nest. Hurry up!"

Thunder raced after him, surprised by the softness of the grass beneath his paws. It didn't feel anything like the coarse, spiky grass on the moor.

River Ripple was heading for a narrow gorge that ran between this nest and the next. As shadows swallowed him, Thunder quickened his pace. "Are you okay?" he whispered to Lightning Tail.

"I'm fine," Lightning Tail answered. "I just hope we find Turtle Tail and the kits quickly."

Doubt nagged in Thunder's belly. "Do you really think they came this way?"

"I haven't caught their scents yet," Lightning Tail answered as he followed River Ripple into the gorge.

Thunder opened his mouth. Acrid fumes filled it. How could he smell the kits through such a stench?

River Ripple stopped at the end of the gorge and peered out into sunshine.

Thunder stopped beside him. "Where are we going?"

River Ripple shrugged. "This is the easiest way into Twolegplace for a cat. Most kittypets use it. The tom might have come this way."

"And Turtle Tail has probably followed," Lightning Tail murmured.

"Let's hope so," Thunder muttered darkly. He followed River Ripple's gaze, screwing his eyes up against the fierce sunshine. His heart lurched as he spotted a huge shiny shape on the flat ground ahead of them. "Is that a monster?" He gulped. Bigger than any stone on the moor, it sat silently on four huge black paws.

"Don't worry," River Ripple breathed. "It's asleep." He darted forward and crouched beside one of its stinking round paws.

Thunder scurried after him, Lightning Tail at his heels. "Where now?"

River Ripple nodded past the monster. More monsters crouched in front of more Twoleg nests, stretching either side of a Thunderpath. "We need to check around all the nests along this Thunderpath," he murmured.

Lightning Tail stared. "*All* of them?"

Thunder blinked. There were too many to count. "What if they're not here?"

"There are plenty more places like this that we can search," River Ripple told him.

Thunder's heart sank. *I promised Gray Wing I'd find them! But it looks like we could be searching all night.* He straightened, tasting the air.

A loud slam sounded from the monster.

"What's that?" He stared in terror at River Ripple.

The rogue's gaze flicked up. Above them, a Twoleg was sitting inside the monster. "Run!" River Ripple hurtled forward. "Get out of here!"

The monster roared into life. It shuddered against Thunder's flank. Blind with panic, he darted after River Ripple. Lightning Tail's pelt flashed beside him as the monster leaped forward with a deafening growl. As it turned, squealing, its huge black paw yanked a piece of fur from Thunder's tail. He swerved sideways, racing over the hard stone ground, then turned, skidding to a halt. "Lightning Tail!"

The young tom slammed into his flank and sent them rolling over the ground.

A few tail-lengths away, the monster leaped onto the Thunderpath and hared away, spouting hot, choking air.

Thunder watched it disappear, his breath coming in gasps. "It nearly killed us!" he panted.

Lightning Tail cowered against him, his body trembling.

River Ripple crept shakily from a bush that sprouted in

front of the Twoleg nest. "Perhaps we should stay away from monsters."

"Do you think so?" Thunder asked sarcastically. He glanced over his shoulder at the monster outside the next nest and the next. A roar sounded from the Thunderpath as another hurtled past. There were more monsters here than Twolegs! "But I don't think it's going to be very easy."

"Thunder." Lightning Tail's trembling whisper sounded in his ear.

"What?" Frazzled, Thunder turned to face his friend.

Lightning Tail was staring past him, eyes wide with horror.

Thunder followed his gaze. A white shape, splotched with orange and black, lay like abandoned prey at the side of the Thunderpath. Dread hollowed Thunder's belly as he recognized the battered tortoiseshell pelt. Horror spiked through his pelt and he froze, not wanting to look closer. But Lightning Tail was already creeping forward.

"Turtle Tail?" The young tom's mew caught in his throat. "Turtle Tail? Is that you?"

Thunder stiffened as the scent of death touched his nose.

"Turtle Tail!" He hardly heard Lightning Tail's cry as, numb with grief, he stumbled toward the lifeless body.

CHAPTER 13

❧

Thunder's throat tightened.

Lightning Tail crouched over the she-cat, desperately lapping her cheek. "Wake up, Turtle Tail. It's us! We're here!"

Thunder crept closer. Turtle Tail lay on the hard stone ground, her body strangely twisted. Her claw-tips were frayed and blood stained her mouth. Her eyes stared, dull and unseeing.

"It looks like a monster got her." River Ripple stopped behind Thunder.

"How do you know?" Thunder stared at the rogue.

"I've seen it before. Look at her claws. She'd have unsheathed them when the monster hit her, then shredded them as she skidded across the stone." River Ripple gazed sadly at Turtle Tail's body.

"Come on, Turtle Tail!" Lightning Tail shook her with his forepaws. He glanced over his shoulder at Thunder. "We have to warm her up. Quickly!"

Thunder crouched beside him. There was little heat left in Turtle Tail's body. He could see that there was nothing to do. "She's dead, Lightning Tail." He felt distant, numb with shock, his words sounding in his ears like someone else's.

"No!" Lightning Tail nudged her shoulder with his nose. "She's hurt, that's all. Cloud Spots will be able to make her better. If we get her home, she'll be okay."

The ground seemed to sway beneath Thunder's paws as his thoughts swirled back to the camp. He remembered the time when he'd pressed against Turtle Tail and watched Wind Runner's kits take their first gulps of air. Now she was dead. She'd never see the kits grow. She'd never see her own kits become full-grown cats. Grief swamped him until he could hardly breathe. "Turtle Tail." The name came as a sob.

As he spoke, a monster hared around a corner toward them. Terror flaring, Thunder leaped back, dragging Lightning Tail by the scruff. The black tom froze in his jaws as the monster swept past. Twoleg faces peered from inside, eyes wide, mouths moving as they pointed their paws at the cats. The monster's stinking wind tugged Turtle's Tail's fur, so that for a moment she seemed to be moving. But as it disappeared into the distance, she lay still once more.

"Let's get her away from the Thunderpath." River Ripple's mew sounded softly in Thunder's ear. The rogue pushed his muzzle beneath Turtle Tail's flank. "Haul her onto my shoulders."

Lightning Tail backed away, eyes wide with disbelief.

Numbly, Thunder nudged Turtle Tail's body onto River Ripple's back. As she hung there limply, he pressed his cheek to her flank, holding her clumsily in place while River Ripple staggered toward the bush outside the Twoleg nest.

The rogue dipped his head and let her slip from his shoulders. She slumped onto the earth beside the bright pink flowers.

Lightning Tail stared bleakly at her body. "She's not going to wake up, is she?"

Thunder pressed his muzzle to Lightning Tail's cheek. Pain seared his heart so ferociously he could hardly breathe. They had known Turtle Tail since they were tiny kits, just a few moons old. And now she was dead.

"No," he whispered.

"Help me push her out of sight," River Ripple murmured.

"No!" Panic lit Lightning Tail's gaze. "You can't just hide her. She deserves more than that."

Thunder met the tom's gaze, his eyes pricking. "We can't bury her here and it's too far to carry her home. And if we bring the kits back this way, they mustn't see her." He shoved his nose under Turtle Tail's shoulder and rolled her. She flopped heavily beneath the bush, her paws brushing the branches. As they quivered, petals showered over Thunder's pelt. He shook them off, his heart aching. How would he ever explain this to Gray Wing?

River Ripple caught his eye. "She'd want us to find her kits."

Thunder nodded. "It's up to us to get them home now."

"But how?" Lightning Tail jerked his head around, his gaze flashing from one Twoleg nest to another. "We don't know where they are."

"We know their scent." Thunder lifted his muzzle.

River Ripple narrowed his eyes thoughtfully. "I know a kittypet who might help us. Follow me."

Hope flashed in Thunder's belly as the rogue headed along the row of Twoleg nests, then turned down a narrow passage between the high stone walls. He followed, nudging Lightning Tail forward. The tom was stumbling, not focusing on where he was going. "You have to save your grief for later," Thunder growled. "The kits need us. They're not safe with Tom."

Lightning Tail stared bleakly at Thunder. "I can't believe she's dead."

Thunder glared at him. "I need you to be strong. The *kits* need you to be strong."

"Are you coming?" River Ripple's mew echoed from the shadows.

Lightning Tail nodded. "Yes." He hurried after the rogue.

Relieved to hear determination edge his friend's mew, Thunder followed.

"Flower lives here," River Ripple told them, padding into sunshine at the back of the Twoleg nest where bushes surrounded a wide stretch of grass. "She's a sweet little tabby and very nosy. Nothing happens without her knowing about it." He nodded toward a small hole in the back of the Twoleg nest. It looked like a tunnel entrance, screened by a sheet of ice. "I'll see if she's in."

He crept across the patterned stone outside the nest and stopped outside the tunnel. Lifting a paw, he tapped the ice sheet.

It rattled and he backed away.

Thunder blinked at him. "What now?"

"We wait." River Ripple glanced at him. "Stay out of sight. You'll scare her." He nodded toward a large shiny cylinder standing beside the nest wall.

Thunder wrinkled his nose. It smelled of carrion. He ducked behind it.

Lightning Tail slid in beside him. "I never imagined we'd hide from a kittypet."

A moment later the ice sheet rattled again and he heard a mew.

"River Ripple? Is that you?" A gentle purr sounded outside the Twoleg nest.

River Ripple purred back. "Hi, Flower."

"What are you doing here?" Flower asked. "I thought you didn't like coming to Twolegplace."

"I don't," River Ripple told her. "But I'm on an important mission."

"Really?" Flower sounded impressed. "What?"

"I'm with some friends."

"Who?" Flower's mew was guarded.

"They're from the moor."

Thunder leaned forward impatiently. *Hurry up!*

River Ripple went on. "They've never been here before, but a kittypet has stolen some of their kits and they're here to get them back."

"Stolen their kits?" Flower sounded horrified. "Where are they?"

Thunder glimpsed the plump tabby-and-white kittypet from his hiding place as she padded further into the sunshine. She scanned the bushes, nose twitching. She froze as she caught Thunder's gaze. "Is that one of them?" she hissed to River Ripple.

Thunder padded out. "We're sorry to disturb you." He lifted his tail amiably.

Flower backed away, her hackles lifting as Lightning Tail followed him out. She glanced toward her tunnel.

"Please don't go," Lightning Tail begged.

"It's important we find the kits." Thunder blinked at her. "They're in danger."

Flower tipped her head. "Really?"

Thunder nodded. "A kittypet stole them from their mother." His throat tightened as he thought of Turtle Tail, alone beneath the bush. "We want to take them home."

Flower frowned. "Which kittypet?"

"His name's Tom. He's a copper-colored cat. Very sleek."

Flower's gaze hardened. "I know Tom." There was contempt in her mew. "He's a bully."

Thunder nodded. "That's why we have to get the kits back." Hope pricked in his paws. "Can you help?"

Flower was already stalking past him, heading for the shadowy gap between the nests. "Come with me."

Thunder bounded after her. He heard Lightning Tail and River Ripple walking behind as he followed Flower along the gap and out into the sunshine. She padded to the edge of the Thunderpath, glanced both ways at the empty stone and raced across. He didn't hesitate, pushing the memory of Turtle Tail from his thoughts. Flower was leading him to the kits. He sensed it. Her head was high, her paw steps purposeful. She knew exactly where she was going.

Lightning Tail's pelt brushed his as the tom fell in beside him and they ducked into a passage beside a Twoleg nest. High wooden walls edged each side. The path was cracked. Grit jabbed Thunder's pads. He glanced over his shoulder. River Ripple was keeping up.

The passage split into two. One opened onto a wide grassy slope, the other curved away between two rows of nests. Flower chose the curving path, following it until it split again. She headed on, choosing one split after another until Thunder wondered how they would ever find their way back. His pelt bristled as strange scents touched his nose. Beyond the wooden walls, Twoleg kits shrieked. Suddenly, a dog's bark exploded a tail-length away. Claws scrabbled at the other side of the wall. Thunder froze, terror ripping though his chest.

"Don't worry," Flower called over her shoulder. "It can't get over the fence."

She quickened her pace, following another passage until it opened onto a wide stone path. A long row of low Twoleg nests lined one side. The other was walled by stone.

"Tom hangs around in one of those." Flower nodded toward the nests.

"With his Twolegs?" Thunder frowned. "Isn't it too small?" The nests they'd seen so far had been huge.

"His Twolegs live in the big nest behind it." Flower nodded

toward the larger den rising beyond the line of small ones. "The low ones are where Twolegs keep their monsters. Tom's Twolegs don't have one so he hangs out there instead." She turned and began heading back along the passage.

Thunder blinked after her. "Aren't you going to show us which one?"

Flower glanced back. "You can work it out." Unease glittered in her gaze. "If Tom knew I brought you here, he'd be very angry. Good luck." She nodded, then hurried back down the passage and disappeared around the corner.

Thunder ignored the fear sparking through his pelt as he stared at the row of dens. He lifted his muzzle. "Come on."

Padding across the stone, he swiveled his ears, listening for monsters growling. He could only hear distant rumbling from beyond the large stone dens. Lightning Tail fell in beside him. River Ripple flanked his other side.

Thunder opened his mouth. He tried to ignore the sour Twoleg fumes coating his tongue, searching for a hint of Tom's scent.

Lightning Tail froze beside him. "I smell something!"

"What?" Thunder halted.

Lightning Tail's tongue showed pink below his nose. "Kit scent!" He quickened his pace.

"Wait!" Thunder hurried to keep up. "Those are monster dens!" What if one leaped out without warning?

River Ripple caught up. "Don't worry. You'll hear them if they're awake."

Lightning Tail headed past the first monster den, picking

up speed as he reached the next. He broke into a run. Thunder bounded after, River Ripple at his heels. He opened his mouth. Tom's scent drenched his tongue.

"Here!" Lightning Tail pulled up sharply. Thunder and River Ripple scrambled to a halt at his heels.

Ahead, an open den yawned onto the wide stone path. Lightning Tail crouched beside it and peered in.

"Do you see him?" Thunder crept forward.

Lightning Tail stretched until he was peering through the wide opening. "Yes."

Thunder's heart raced.

A kit's mew echoed from inside. "I'm hungry!"

Owl Eyes! Thunder sucked back a gasp.

"Me too." Sparrow Fur joined in. "Are you going hunting soon?"

Thunder slid past Lightning Tail and stared inside. Sunlight spilled in through the wide, square entrance, glinting off the clutter that crowded the den. Strong scents wafted out. Tom was pacing around the kits near the back wall. "We don't have to hunt," he told them. "Food will come soon."

"Don't we have to catch it?" Sparrow Fur asked.

"How soon?" Owl Eyes mewed.

"We can't stay here long." Pebble Heart's eyes were round. "Turtle Tail will be worried."

"She knows you're with me," Tom told him sharply.

Liar! Thunder's blood burned beneath his pelt.

Tom went on. "Besides, you don't want to go home. This is exciting, isn't it?"

"I don't like it here." Owl Eyes was staring at the clutter, his nose wrinkling.

Tom froze. His ears swiveled toward a corner of the back wall. He'd clearly heard something.

Thunder strained to listen. Heavy paw steps were approaching the den.

Tom lifted his tail. "Why don't you three hide and see how long it takes me to find you?"

Sparrow Fur began running for the entrance. "You'll never find me!"

Thunder stiffened. "Let's snatch the kits," he hissed to Lightning Tail and River Ripple. "I'll grab Sparrow Fur. You get the others."

Sparrow Fur was hurtling closer. He hunkered down, heart racing.

"Sparrow Fur! Stop!" Tom's yowl was edged with panic. "Stay in the den!"

Sparrow Fur skidded to a halt.

Foxdung! Thunder pressed River Ripple and Lightning Tail back. "Wait."

"Why can't I go out?" Sparrow Fur turned, blinking at Tom.

"Because I said so!" Tom's glance flitted nervously toward the back of the den, where the paw steps were growing louder. "Just hide inside the den. Quickly!"

Pebble Heart scampered behind a pile of clutter. Owl Eyes squeezed under a massive stained pelt that lay crumpled on the ground. Sparrow Fur gazed quickly around before sliding behind a tall slice of wood. As her tail flicked out of view, an opening appeared in the back of the den.

A Twoleg appeared, framed by daylight, which streamed in behind.

Tom looked up. "Hi," he meowed.

The Twoleg meowed back, then mumbled as it crossed the den and started stroking Tom.

Tom lifted his tail and purred loudly.

"Yuck!" Lightning Tail shuddered beside Thunder.

River Ripple squeezed in beside him, peering around the entrance. "Why's he hiding the kits from his Twoleg?"

"He obviously doesn't want it to know he has them." Thunder narrowed his eyes. Why take them if he had to keep them secret? Had he just done it to torture Turtle Tail? Rage churned in his belly. His act had *killed* her!

Tom was weaving around the Twoleg as it bent to pour rattling berries into a small hollow stone at the end of the den.

"Is that food?" Lightning Tail asked, his nose twitching.

"Yes." River Ripple curled his lip. "I've tried kittypet food. It tastes horrible."

When the Twoleg stopped pouring, Tom yowled pitifully, reaching up to tug desperately at the Twoleg's pelt.

The Twoleg mumbled again and poured more berries into the bowl.

He's getting extra food for the kits. A growl rumbled in Thunder's throat. *He doesn't even know how to hunt for them. He has to beg!*

He watched as the Twoleg headed for its small entrance at the back and disappeared.

"You can come out now!" Tom called to the kits.

Owl Eyes ducked out from under the stained pelt. "But you didn't even look for us."

Pebble Heart padded from behind the pile of clutter. "Why was there a Twoleg here?"

"It brought us food," Tom explained. "Just like I promised."

"You were so brave!" Sparrow Fur hurried out from behind the thin wood. "You didn't even look scared!"

Tom shrugged. "Nothing scares me."

Arrogant mouseheart! Thunder exchanged glances with Lightning Tail. "Are you ready to grab them?"

"Let's go." Lightning Tail strode past him into the den.

Thunder followed, ears flat.

River Ripple padded to the center of the opening and waited, hackles up.

"Thunder!" Sparrow Fur's excited squeak echoed around the den as she spotted him. "You've come too!"

Owl Eyes blinked. "Is Turtle Tail with you?"

Thunder swallowed back the pain rising in his chest. "No," he told Owl Eyes. "We came by ourselves. Turtle Tail and Gray Wing wanted us to bring you home."

Tom stepped forward, ears flattening. "They *are* home."

Pebble Heart's gaze sharpened. "If this is home, is Turtle Tail coming to live here?"

Tom growled. "You don't need Turtle Tail. You're my kits and you're living with me."

Sparrow Fur's eyes clouded. "But Turtle Tail promised I could see Wind Runner's kits!"

"I told you!" Tom snapped. "You're *my* kits. This is where you belong!"

Thunder's pelt rippled with sudden cold. Tom had told them he was their father. He glanced at Lightning Tail. The black tom's gaze was dark. If the kits knew that Tom was their father, they couldn't snatch them back. The kits wouldn't understand.

Thunder sheathed his claws. They would have to use reason. "How are you going to look after them?" he challenged. "You can't hunt."

Tom flicked his tail toward the hollow stone filled with berries. "I got them food, didn't I?"

"But your Twoleg didn't know it was feeding three hungry kits as well as you," Thunder argued. "It doesn't know they're here, does it?"

Tom glared at him. "So?"

"You can't keep them secret forever." Lightning Tail stepped forward. "And when your Twoleg finds out, what will it do with them?"

Owl Eyes's fur spiked. "What do you mean?" He looked anxiously toward the Twoleg entrance.

Thunder forced himself to ignore the frightened kit. He had to convince Tom that keeping them here was impossible. "They're half wild." He paced around Tom, gazing at him beseechingly. "They don't belong here. They belong on the moor. With cats who love them."

"Who says *I* don't love them?" Tom puffed out his chest. "I rescued them from the moor. They were wandering around by themselves. Anything could have happened to them."

"We were practicing tracking rabbits," Pebble Heart mewed.

Tom glared at the tabby kit. "How do you know a fox wasn't practicing tracking kits at the same time?"

Pebble Heart's eyes widened.

Tom stopped Thunder's pacing by turning to face him. "They're safe here," he growled. "They have me to protect them."

By filling their heads full of horror stories about the moor? Thunder bit back a growl. *We have to get them away from him.* He glanced desperately around the den. They couldn't fight Tom. Not now the kits knew he was their father. He moved closer to Lightning Tail. "What do we do?"

"We'll have to leave them," Lightning Tail meowed calmly.

Thunder stared at him. "But—"

Lightning Tail nudged him toward the den entrance.

"We can't!" Thunder stopped as they reached River Ripple. "Those are Turtle Tail's kits! They belong on the moor." He stared desperately at Lightning Tail, pausing as he saw the black tom's eyes narrow. He dropped his mew to a whisper. "You've got a plan, haven't you?"

Lightning Tail winked at him and marched away from the den.

Hope fizzing in his paws, Thunder hurried after.

CHAPTER 14

☘

Help me!

Gray Wing jolted awake as his ears rang with Turtle Tail's desperate cry. He blinked open his eyes, heart lurching, and jerked his head around. "Turtle Tail?" The camp was quiet, the sunny clearing empty. There was no sign of his tortoise-shell mate. Relief swamped him. It had been a dream.

Where is she? He sat up, his muscles weary. Warmth drenched his pelt as the sun slid toward the horizon. It would be dusk soon and he was still in his nest. He drew in a breath. The tightness in his chest was gone at last. He could breathe easily again.

Rainswept Flower nodded to him as she crossed the clearing. Water-soaked moss dripped from between her jaws. She was heading toward the bramble den, where Gorse Fur's tail stuck out among the flowery stems. Wind Runner had kitted! He remembered Turtle Tail telling him through the haze of his sickness.

And then she'd left to search for the kits. Surely she'd found them by now? He tasted the air. Her scent bathed his tongue and his heart quickened for a moment. Then he realized it was just lingering traces of fur in their nest. He climbed out, his paws trembling. His belly rumbled.

"You're awake!" Jagged Peak trotted toward him. "How are you feeling?"

"Better." Gray Wing noticed Acorn Fur, crouching beside the heather wall. The chestnut brown she-cat was gazing anxiously through the gap. Was she watching for Turtle Tail and the kits?

Cloud Spots padded past her. He was carrying herbs between his jaws, heading for the bramble. Gray Wing frowned. Why was his gaze so dark? "Is Wind Runner okay?" he asked Jagged Peak.

"She's fine," Jagged Peak reported. "She had four kits— three toms and a she-kit."

Gray Wing purred. "Sparrow Fur will be excited," he meowed. "She'll have new friends. They all will. Kits need playmates." He paused as he saw Jagged Peak's gaze cloud. "What's wrong?" He leaned forward, alarm pulsing through him. "Has there been any news?"

"Not yet." Jagged Peak glanced toward Tall Shadow. The black she-cat was on the flat rock, looking out over the moor. Had she moved at all while Gray Wing had slept?

"Why aren't they back yet?" Gray Wing couldn't believe the kits would have wandered so far from the camp.

"We found kittypet scent near their trail," Jagged Peak told him softly. "Tall Shadow didn't want you to know until you'd recovered."

"*Kittypet* scent?" Gray Wing searched Jagged Peak's gaze.

Why did he look so worried? He stiffened, suspicion pricking in his mind. "Did Turtle Tail recognize it?" he demanded.

Jagged Peak nodded.

"It was Tom, wasn't it?"

"Yes." Jagged Peak's ear twitched. "We can't be sure they went with him. But Turtle Tail went after him, with Thunder and Lightning Tail. He won't get far."

"He took the kits?" Gray Wing could hardly believe it. What kind of sick cat would steal kits from their mother? He strode toward the gap in the heather. "I'll get them back." Strength surged through him as he left Jagged Peak, blinking, behind.

"Wait!" Tall Shadow's call surprised him.

He stopped at the flat rock and looked up at her. "I have to help Turtle Tail get the kits back."

Tall Shadow leaped down and landed lightly beside him. "Thunder and Lightning Tail are already following her. They've probably found them by now and are on their way home." She stared gravely at Gray Wing. "You need to save your strength for your meeting with Clear Sky. The safety of all of us may depend on it."

Gray Wing dipped his head. She was speaking sense. His whiskers twitched wryly. Not long ago, *he'd* led the moor cats. Now Tall Shadow was back in charge, making decisions.

"Get something to eat." Tall Shadow nodded toward the prey heap beside the rock. "You must be hungry."

"I guess." He'd rather search the moor for Turtle Tail than eat. But Tall Shadow was right. His belly was growling like a bad-tempered badger. He padded toward the pile. A fat blackbird was balanced on top of a mound of mice and shrews. Clearly the other cats had been busy hunting while he'd been recovering in his nest.

Shattered Ice lay a tail-length away, chewing hungrily on a thrush. "There's a vole near the bottom if you dig for it."

Gray Wing nodded gratefully, touched that the tom remembered how much he enjoyed sweeter flesh. He pawed through the prey until he found the vole, then carried it to Shattered Ice and settled beside him. "Do you mind if I eat here?"

"Of course not." Shattered Ice tore a mouthful of flesh from the thrush and chewed it noisily.

Gray Wing gnawed at his vole.

"We followed their trail to the river," Shattered Ice mumbled through his mouthful. "Me and Hawk Swoop." He swallowed. "It smells like Tom crossed with the kits, and then Turtle Tail, Thunder and Lightning Tail followed."

"They crossed the *river*?" Fear sparked through Gray Wing's fur. What if they'd drowned?

"They seem to have made it over safely," Shattered Ice told him, as though reading his thoughts. "We found crossing stones running from one shore to the other and we could smell cat scent all over them. Just you wait. They'll be back before sunset, full of stories about their exciting adventure."

Gray Wing blinked at the gray-and-white tom, relieved to see his green eyes shining happily. He imagined Owl Eyes strutting around the clearing, telling everyone how he crossed a river. "They'll be boasting about it for days."

Tall Shadow padded to join them. "Have you thought about your meeting with Clear Sky?" She gazed at the round, pale moon. It was just starting to show as the sun began to set, transparent against the purple sky.

Shattered Ice grunted. "Just tell him if he moves his borders again, we'll shred him."

Tall Shadow shot him a piercing look. "I understand your frustration, Shattered Ice. But talk like that will provoke war. We want peace."

"We don't want to be pushed around season after season," Shattered Ice growled.

Gray Wing's pelt rippled along his spine. "Perhaps if I can get him to explain why he *needs* so much territory, we can come to an understanding."

"He's just greedy," Shattered Ice muttered.

Gray Wing gazed at the ground. "He was *never* greedy." Memories of playing with him in the snowy peaks sent pangs of sadness through him. "It must be something else that's driving him."

Tall Shadow met his gaze. "Two things drive all creatures," she murmured. "Fear and greed. If it's not greed, it must be fear."

Shattered Ice snorted. "What's he scared of?"

"Us?" Hope twitched in Gray Wing's paws. "If I can persuade him he has nothing to fear from us—that we just want to live in peace on the moor—then he might back down."

Tall Shadow nodded slowly. "But what if it's something else he's scared of?"

"He's a coward," Shattered Ice commented.

"Clear Sky's no coward," Gray Wing snapped.

"Then why's he scared?" Shattered Ice hooked a feather from his mouth with a claw.

Gray Wing remembered all the losses his brother had suffered. Fluttering Bird, Bright Stream, and Storm. Even Thunder. Perhaps the thought of losing anyone else was more than Clear Sky could bear. *He just needs reassurance.* Gray Wing jumped to his paws, a plan flashing in his mind.

"Aren't you going to eat that?" Tall Shadow gazed in surprise at the half-chewed vole.

"When we get back."

"Back from where?" She blinked at him.

"I know what I'm going to say to Clear Sky," Gray Wing told her. "But he won't listen unless he feels at ease."

"So?" Tall Shadow frowned.

"Come with me to the four trees." Gray Wing flicked his tail. "Let's check out the valley. I want to know every tail-length. I want to feel comfortable when I meet him and I want to find somewhere Clear Sky will feel safe. Somewhere he will listen. Somewhere he'll feel at home."

Shattered Ice stood and stretched. "I think you're wasting your time," he muttered. "Sitting under the right tree isn't going to change Clear Sky."

Gray Wing met the tom's gaze. "We don't have to *change*

him, don't you see? We just have to help him remember who he was." He headed for the gap in the heather, pausing as he passed Acorn Fur. "Will you send someone to find me when Turtle Tail gets back with the kits?"

She nodded, eyes round. "I hope they're okay."

Lightning Tail's with them. "Your brother will be fine," he promised, heading out of the hollow.

"Where will you be?" Acorn Fur called after him.

"At the four trees." Gray Wing broke into a run.

Tall Shadow caught up and fell in beside him. "Is your breathing okay?"

"Fine." His chest felt clear and strong and a prickle of frustration jabbed his belly. Why had the sickness struck when Turtle Tail had needed him most?

He pushed the thought away. He had to concentrate on the four trees. Every cat in the hollow needed the meeting to be a success.

He ran across the moor, veering past heather, ducking gorse, following the slope up to where it met the rim of the hollow where the four trees stood.

The sun dipped from sight as he reached the top of the valley. Moonlight silvered the four great oaks standing at the bottom. Ferns rustled along its slopes as a light wind washed down from the moor.

Tall Shadow stopped beside him and shivered as she gazed at the branches below. "I'll never get used to trees," she murmured. "They hide the sky and stop the wind. They're unnatural."

Gray Wing glanced at her. "Perhaps I should tell that to Clear Sky. He might stop worrying about us trying to steal his forest."

She purred. "If only it were that simple."

Springing forward, she plunged down the slope. Gray Wing bounded after her. The grass here was long and brambles trailed between swaths of ferns. Trees sprouted so that Gray Wing had to swerve one way, then another, as he raced after Tall Shadow.

He slowed as he neared the bottom. A clearing opened before him, one oak at each corner and a great rock towering at one end. Tall Shadow padded toward it, craning to see its top. "It looks like it grew here," she commented as Gray Wing caught up.

"I wonder if we could climb it?" Gray Wing padded around it, scanning its smooth sides until he caught sight of a ledge halfway up. He leaped, reaching it easily, then bounded onto the gently rounded summit.

The clearing spread ahead of him. "It's like being back in the mountains up here!" As he called down to Tall Shadow, his thoughts whirled. He could suggest Clear Sky climb the rock with him. They could talk as they'd done on the mountain crags when they were younger. Perhaps then, Clear Sky would remember the cat he'd once been.

Claws scraped rock as Tall Shadow landed beside him. She circled him, staring out at the clearing. Overhead, leaves rustled and branches creaked.

Gray Wing stiffened, a thought sparking in his mind.

"He'll smell our scent and know we've been here!" It would make him suspicious.

"The meeting's not until tomorrow night," Tall Shadow soothed. "The wind and dew will have washed our scent clear." She stared up through the leaves. Thin clouds scudded across the sky. "It might even have rained."

Still, Gray Wing felt uncomfortably aware of his paws leaking scent into the rock. He scrambled down to the ledge and leaped to the ground. As Tall Shadow joined him, he turned, studying the slopes. "Every side's covered with bushes except that one." He padded toward one side of the hollow, clear of trees and brambles. Grass coated the slope from top to bottom, rippling like water in the moonlight. "That's the approach I will use. Clear Sky won't be alarmed if he can see me arrive."

Tall Shadow ducked in front of him. "You're not going alone!"

Gray Wing frowned. "I asked Clear Sky to meet *me*."

"It's too dangerous." Tall Shadow's mew was firm. "Do you think *he* will leave *his* cats behind?"

Words froze on Gray Wing's tongue. He hadn't asked Clear Sky to come alone. He'd simply assumed that they would meet as brothers. He shifted his paws, unnerved. There was a time when he could predict exactly what Clear Sky would do— when he could trust his littermate's honor. Now he wasn't so sure. Clear Sky might bring every forest cat with him. Gray Wing lifted his chin. "I will face him *alone*."

Tall Shadow narrowed her eyes. "No. Thunder and I will

come with you. I will not let you risk your life."

"You think he'd hurt me?" Gray Wing blinked.

Tall Shadow stared at him steadily, her eyes dark. "I don't know what he's capable of anymore." She leaned closer. "Would Turtle Tail let you come to the meeting alone?"

"No." Gray Wing dipped his head. "All right. You and Thunder can come too." Hearing Turtle Tail's name woke his anxiety. "We should get home." He headed for the slope. "They might be back by now."

Tall Shadow followed as Gray Wing swished through the ferns. At the top, he relished the rush of wind on his face as he bounded onto the moonlit moor. In the distance, he could see the dark dip in the moorside where the hollow nestled, heather wrapped around it like a protective tail. Was Turtle Tail in the clearing, waiting for him? Were the kits okay? *If Tom has harmed them, I'll find him and make him pay.* If Turtle Tail hadn't already.

He reached the camp first, his lungs burning as he hurtled into the clearing. He skidded to a halt, fur pricking.

It was quiet.

Shapes moved in the shadows. Rainswept Flower paced the heather, her striped tail down. Acorn Fur and Jagged Peak murmured in the long grass, heads together. Shattered Ice sat somberly beside Gorse Fur. No one turned to welcome him home.

Paws thrummed behind him as Tall Shadow caught up. "What's going on?" She blinked as she looked around the clearing. "Has something happened?"

Gray Wing's heart twisted with worry. Was there news of Turtle Tail and the kits? Had something happened to them? He tasted the air for their scents, but there was no sign.

Gorse Fur padded slowly forward, his gaze desolate. He met Gray Wing, shoulders drooping. "Wind Runner lost one of the kits."

"*Lost* one?" Gray Wing stared past him to the bramble, noticing for the first time Cloud Spots and Dappled Pelt huddled outside.

"Emberkit died." Gorse Fur's mew sounded more like a gasp of pain.

A chill swept through Gray Wing's fur. He hadn't even known Wind Runner had named her litter. *Emberkit*. His thoughts flashed to the smoldering cinders of the forest fire. "No!" He rushed to the bramble and shouldered his way through the drooping branches.

Hawk Swoop crouched beside Wind Runner, snapping her gaze toward him as he burst in. "Quiet!" she ordered.

Gray Wing crept toward the queen. She lay curled, moss and heather pressed around her, encasing her in a makeshift nest. He peered in. Three kits suckled at her belly. "Where's Emberkit?" Gray Wing whispered.

Wind Runner gave a low groan and pulled her forepaws closer to her muzzle. A tiny body hung limp in their grip, not moving as Wind Runner pressed her cheek against the kit's feather-soft fur.

"I'm so sorry." Grief stabbed Gray Wing's heart.

Hawk Swoop bent and lapped Wind Runner's shoulder.

Gray Wing noticed flecks of spittle at the corners of the kit's mouth, as though he had struggled as he died. "Did he suffer?" he whispered.

Wind Runner swung her head around, eyes blazing in the half-light. "Of course he suffered! Look at him!"

She shook Emberkit, his pelt matted, his eyes clouded.

"It's not fair," Gray Wing whispered bleakly. What could he say to comfort her? "Emberkit may have been spared future suffering. We live in the wild. Life is tough. Perhaps it's best that only the strongest kits survive."

"I thought we cared for our weak!" Wind Runner snapped. "We're not like Clear Sky."

Gray Wing flinched. "We can't save every cat," he reasoned.

Wind Runner flashed him a warning look but he pressed on hopefully.

"Perhaps Emberkit is in a better place now. Playing with other kits. It might make your loss easier if you—"

"How would *you* know?" Wind Runner hissed. "You're not a mother. You're not even a *father*!"

Gray Wing backed away, shock pulsing through him as though she'd raked his muzzle with her claws. At her belly the other kits began to mewl fretfully. But she hadn't finished.

"Just because you've borrowed Turtle Tail's kits and pretended they're your own, you think you know what it's like. I hope you never have to say good-bye to a kit. If you ever do, I'll remind you that they might be in a *better place* than at their mother's belly. I'm sure you'll find that a great comfort!" Her eyes glazed and she let her head fall back as a mournful yowl wracked her body. "Go away!" she gasped.

A paw touched his flank gently. Hawk Swoop was gazing at him with round, sympathetic eyes. "She doesn't know what she's saying," she whispered.

Gray Wing looked away. He understood grief. It made a cat hard. And yet he was breathless with the sting of her words. He slid from the den and crossed the camp. Blind to the cats crouched at the edges of the clearing, he crept to the gap in the heather and stared out across the moor. *Turtle Tail, where are you?* His heart seemed to crack in his chest. *Come home and bring the kits with you. I need you.*

CHAPTER 15

❧

"You want to distract *Tom?" Thunder* stared at Lightning Tail, his heart quivering like a captured bird in his chest. He could hear the faint mews of Tom and the kits in Tom's den. "How?"

Lightning Tail paced the passageway. "I'm not sure yet. Let me think!"

River Ripple sat and groomed his belly.

The sun was sinking behind the nests.

Lightning Tail's eyes glittered in the twilight. "We know Tom's vain, right? And selfish."

"Yes," Thunder agreed.

"We can take advantage of that."

"How?" Thunder swished his tail over the gritty stone. "It'll just make him hold on to the kits harder."

"What if they don't *want* to stay with him?" Lightning Tail argued.

"But he's their *father.*" Guilt tugged at Thunder's belly. "Their mother's dead. They might see him as their only choice now."

River Ripple lifted his head. "Why make it a choice between father and mother? Won't they really be choosing between being a kittypet and living wild?" He glanced toward Tom's den. "It can't be that hard to show the kits that hiding in a stinky Twoleg den with only rotten kittypet food is no way for a real cat to live."

Lightning Tail nodded. "They've only ever known the moor," he pointed out. "Don't you think they'll miss it?" He glanced at the stone nests crowding out the sky. "They must see how trapped they are here."

"And how ugly it is," River Ripple muttered. He went back to grooming his silver belly.

Lightning Tail stopped pacing and stared Thunder in the eye. "Do you *believe* it's the right thing to take them back to the moor, even though Turtle Tail is dead?"

Thunder didn't hesitate. "Yes." The moor cats would care for them, just as they'd cared for him. The kits would be far more loved than if they stayed here with Tom.

Lightning Tail nodded. "Good. Then all I have to do is distract Tom so you can talk to the kits and get them away from here." He circled River Ripple. "Will you help us get them home?"

River Ripple shook out his fur. "I'll do anything I have to." He flattened his ears. "That kittypet has caused nothing but grief. He deserves some grief of his own."

Lightning Tail turned to cross the wide stone path to Tom's den.

Thunder hurried after him. "What's your plan?"

"I'm going to make him jealous."

"How?" Thunder fell in beside his friend, puzzled.

"Leave it to me," Lightning Tail told him. "You just have to persuade the kits to leave while I'm keeping Tom busy." He marched to the middle of the opening of Tom's den and stopped. Darkness engulfed the nest.

"You came back!" Pebble Heart dashed from the shadows.

Tom's pelt rippled as he followed the kit into the pale evening light. "What are you doing?"

"You didn't think we'd leave without saying good-bye to the kits, did you?" Lightning Tail's mew was unruffled.

Thunder lifted his tail. "We're going to miss you on the moor." He glanced fondly at Sparrow Fur and Owl Eyes as they bounded forward.

Lightning Tail caught Thunder's eye, suddenly mischievous. "What a shame you'll never learn how to pluck a lapwing from the sky like Hawk Swoop can."

Sparrow Fur blinked at him. "Tom promised to teach us to hunt."

"I'm sure he will," Thunder meowed enthusiastically. "I'm sure there are plenty of rats around here to practice on."

River Ripple wove around Sparrow Fur and stopped beside Owl Eyes. "I wonder if the Twolegs will give you new names?"

"Names like Tom's," Lightning Tail suggested cheerfully. "You could become She-Kit instead of Sparrow Fur."

Sparrow Fur's eyes widened. "But I *like* my name."

Guilt pricked at Thunder's chest. This felt cruel. He stiffened his shoulders. It had to be done if they were to get the kits back to where they'd be safe and happy. He padded toward Pebble Heart and touched his nose to the kit's head. "Cloud

Spots will miss you," he murmured. "I know how proud he was of your skills."

Pebble Heart's eyes glistened. "I still had so much to learn."

"Stop it." A growl edged Tom's mew.

The kits turned to stare at him.

"We're just saying good-bye." Sparrow Fur blinked at Tom. "You don't mind, do you?"

Before he could answer, Lightning Tail whisked past him. "Of course he doesn't mind. Do you, Tom?"

Tom glared at him as Lightning Tail padded into the shadows at the back of the den, toward the Twoleg opening.

Hooking his paw through a narrow gap where light seeped in, Lightning Tail swung back a tall slice of wood.

Thunder blinked as yellow light streamed in. It flooded from the eyes of the Twoleg nest, illuminating a stretch of grass between the dens.

Lightning Tail padded onto the grass and began yowling loudly at the Twoleg nest.

What's he doing?

Tom chased after him. "Stop it!" He glanced anxiously back at the kits, who were staring wide-eyed.

Thunder felt a prickle of triumph. *He doesn't want to show his true self in front of the kits.*

Lightning Tail kept yowling, lifting his head toward the brightly lit eyes.

River Ripple slid close to Thunder. "What's he up to?"

"I have no idea." As he answered, a hole opened in the back of the Twoleg nest. Light flared, framing a pair of Twolegs.

They stepped onto the grass, murmuring to each other.

Lightning Tail broke into a purr, so loud that Thunder could hear it from inside Tom's den. Then he began weaving around the Twolegs.

Thunder felt River Ripple shudder.

"How's he doing that?" the rogue breathed.

Thunder swallowed. "I don't know." Lightning Tail was acting like a kittypet! Wasn't he scared? Twolegs were capable of anything. How did he know they wouldn't steal him or hurt him? He wasn't *their* kittypet, after all.

"What's Lightning Tail doing?" Sparrow Fur's squeak surprised Thunder. The young kit was standing beside him, Pebble Heart and Owl Eyes bunched beside her. They were watching the black tom anxiously.

Thunder searched for words. "I guess he's thanking the Twolegs for looking after you," he told them at last.

Tom turned and hissed at Thunder. "How dare he!" He charged across the grass. Stopping beside his Twolegs, he snarled at Lightning Tail. "Get out of here. They're mine!"

"Really?" Lightning Tail gazed back at him mildly. "They look like they'd take in any cat. They took in Turtle Tail, didn't they? Perhaps they want me to stay too. That way I can keep an eye on Turtle Tail's kits."

One of the Twolegs reached down and ran a paw along Lightning Tail's spine. He lifted his tail and arched his back with pleasure, as though he was scratching an itch on a branch.

"He's letting them touch him!" Pebble Heart sounded horrified.

Thunder looked at him gravely. "You'll have to let them touch you if you stay here."

"No way!" Pebble Heart backed away.

"I don't want Twolegs touching me!" Sparrow Fur mewed crossly.

Suddenly the Twoleg bent and scooped Lightning Tail up into its paws.

Owl Eyes pressed against Thunder, trembling. "Will they do that to us too?"

"Of course." Thunder tried to sound matter-of-fact, even though his flesh was crawling beneath his pelt at the thought. "Look." He watched the other Twoleg pick up Tom. "Your father will show you what to do, I'm sure. He'll show you how to be stroked and fussed over by Twolegs. You'll be perfect kittypets before you know it."

Tom hissed at Lightning Tail. "I'm going to shred you." His growl was dripping with malice. The Twoleg holding Lightning Tail backed away, its face creasing. It rumbled something to its mate as Lightning Tail curled deep into its embrace, like a kit hiding against its mother's belly.

The Twoleg purred and held Lightning Tail harder.

Tom lashed out a paw.

"He's trying to hurt Lightning Tail!" Owl Eyes's mew was filled with dismay.

"Why's Tom being mean?" Sparrow Fur blinked up at Thunder.

Thunder leaned closer. "Perhaps he doesn't like sharing his Twolegs," he mewed innocently.

Pebble Heart frowned. "Perhaps he won't like sharing them with us either."

"I don't *want* to share them!" Owl Eyes growled. "I want to go home where there aren't any Twolegs!"

"Really?" Joy sparked in Thunder's belly. "We can take you home if you want."

"Yes, please!" Sparrow Fur bounded around him, her short tail flicking with excitement.

Thunder touched her spine with his tail-tip. "You have to be very brave and very quiet, though," he told her gravely.

Owl Eyes blinked at him. "Why?"

"We'll be traveling through Twolegplace in the dark," Thunder told him. "It's dangerous here for moor cats." He exchanged glances with River Ripple. "River Ripple knows the way. Will you go with him while I help Lightning Tail get away from the Twolegs?"

Pebble Heart tipped his head. "Now?"

Thunder nodded. "Gray Wing is waiting for you." He ignored the pang in his heart. *But not Turtle Tail.*

"Okay." Sparrow Fur lined up beside River Ripple. "I'm ready."

"So am I." Owl Eyes fell in beside her.

"Pebble Heart?" Thunder gazed at the solemn kit. "Are *you* ready to go home?"

Pebble Heart nodded. "You'll come too, won't you?"

Thunder purred. "As soon as I've freed Lightning Tail from the Twolegs."

"Come on." River Ripple began nosing the kits toward the

wide opening of Tom's den. "I'll take them over the crossing stones," he whispered to Thunder.

"Be quick," Thunder urged. He wanted the kits as far away from here as possible before Tom noticed. If there was a fight, they mustn't see it. Tom was their father. He flexed his claws. He watched River Ripple hurry the kits onto the dusk-shadowed stone and headed for the Twoleg opening at the back of Tom's den.

Lightning Tail was still curled in the embrace of the Twoleg, while Tom struggled, hissing with rage, in the paws of the other.

The Twoleg grunted and then dropped Tom, confusion wrinkling its smooth, pink face. It glanced anxiously at the other Twoleg as Tom growled at Lightning Tail.

Thunder padded across the grass. "What's the matter, Tom? Don't you like sharing?"

Tom turned on him with a hiss and flung out a paw. His claws sliced the air a whisker from Thunder's nose.

"You don't want your Twolegs to see you in such a temper," Thunder growled. How was he going to persuade the Twoleg to let Lightning Tail go? As Tom hissed at him, the Twoleg held Lightning Tail closer, eyes flashing with alarm. It began to back toward its nest.

No! It mustn't take Lightning Tail inside!

He blinked up at the Twoleg, forcing himself to purr as Lightning Tail had done. His purr stuttered, his throat tight with fear.

The Twoleg murmured back at him.

Thunder tipped his head, pleadingly. "Let Lightning Tail go."

Tom's eyes flashed with sudden malice. "You want him back now, do you?" He glanced toward the opening in the Twoleg nest, where light flooded out. "Perhaps I should persuade my Twolegs to keep him. It'll be fun having him locked up inside with me for the night." Tom showed his teeth.

Thunder felt cold as dread hollowed his belly. The cruel kittypet would rip Lightning Tail to shreds. His breathing quickened as he saw the taller Twoleg back through the opening. It called to its mate, who was still holding Lightning Tail.

"Get me down from here!" Lightning Tail glanced toward the opening, eyes flashing with fear as the Twoleg turned toward its mate.

Tom had trotted inside, tail high. His Twoleg bent to stroke him and he purred, blinking up at Lightning Tail, his gaze wide and friendly.

He's pretending! Why were Twolegs so dumb! *Can't you see he's tricking you?* Panic sparked beneath Thunder's pelt. He dashed for the Twoleg. He had to stop it before it entered the nest. He barged past it as roughly as he could, then doubled back and knocked it from the other side. It stumbled and he nudged it again, winding forcefully around its legs, purring desperately. The Twoleg staggered. With a yelp, it dropped Lightning Tail, and grabbed the side of the opening to steady itself.

"Run!" Thunder shoved Lightning Tail forward and sprinted after him. They hurtled for Tom's den. Streaking through it, they burst out into the night. Thunder's paws skidded from under him as he swerved toward the passageway.

He scrambled to regain his balance. Lightning Tail was racing ahead. Thunder found his paws and hared after, catching up as Lightning Tail flew into the shadowy passageway.

"Can you remember how to get back?" Lightning Tail called over his shoulder.

Panic sparked through Thunder. Which way had Flower brought them? Ahead, the passage split.

"Thunder?" Lightning Tail's mew was sharp with fear as he slowed to a halt and stared one way, then the other.

Thunder stumbled into his flank, his paws burning as he skidded to a halt. He tasted the air. *The kits!* He could smell their scent clearly. "This way." Taking the closest opening, he raced along it. Lightning Tail chased after.

They zigzagged through the maze of passageways. Thunder ran, mouth open, letting the kits scents guide him until he burst out beside the Thunderpath that Flower had led them across. He felt sure he knew how to get back to camp from here.

A monster swished past, its eyes shooting light ahead of it. Thunder flinched as its glare streaked over his pelt.

Lightning Tail froze beside him. "Can you see the kits?" He squinted into the darkness as the monster hurtled away.

"Not yet." Thunder dashed across the wide stone path and ducked into a gorge between two nests. It opened onto grass and bushes and he saw, with a surge of relief, that open sky lay beyond. They'd reached the edge of Twolegplace!

He bounded across the grass, his flanks heaving.

"Tom's following us!" Lightning Tail's alarmed call shattered the air.

Thunder glanced over his shoulder and saw Tom burst into the moonlight.

"Give them back!" Rage pulsed through Tom's yowl.

Lightning Tail turned to face the kittypet. "We can't risk leading him to the kits!"

Thunder stumbled to a halt and spun around. "We'll have to fight him."

Standing shoulder to shoulder, they confronted the kittypet.

Tom stopped and stared, his narrowed eyes gleaming in the moonlight. "I suppose you think you're clever, getting them away while you distracted me."

"You're not the only one that can steal kits," Thunder snarled through gritted teeth.

"They came with me willingly," Tom snapped.

Lightning Tail took a step forward. "They belong on the moor."

"I know where your camp is." Tom lashed his tail menacingly. "I can come and take them anytime I want."

Thunder lifted his chin. "Not now they've seen what it is to be a kittypet." He glanced at Lightning Tail. "How did it feel to picked up and stroked?"

Lightning Tail shuddered. "Horrible."

Thunder's whiskers twitched. "The kits are wild," he told Tom. "They'll never choose your life. They'll always find their way back to the moor."

"Like their mother," Tom snarled in disgust.

"She had the heart of a mountain cat," Lightning Tail hissed.

"*Had* the heart of a mountain cat?" Tom tipped his head. "Has something happened to her?"

Grief seared Thunder's heart. They'd lost Turtle Tail forever. "She got killed by a monster, following you and her kits." He glared at Tom, blood roaring in his ears as he saw triumph spark in the kittypet's gaze.

"Will her kits thank you for taking them to a home with no mother?" Tom asked nastily.

Fury exploded in Thunder's chest. "You fox-hearted—"

He leaped for Tom but Lightning Tail blocked his path. "Will they thank you for leading her to her death?"

Tom blinked.

Thunder stumbled.

Lightning Tail went on. "Never come near the moor again. You'll regret it. Your kits will remember you as the cat who killed their mother. They won't follow you next time, and if any of us see you again, we'll shred you."

Thunder showed his teeth. "We'll shred you *now,* if you like."

Tom backed away, growling. "*Keep* the dumb kits," he snarled. "Let them grow up wild. I don't care." Tail flicking angrily, he turned and stalked away, the shadows swallowing him as he padded into the gorge.

"Come on." Lightning Tail turned and raced across the

grass. "Let's catch up to the kits."

Thunder hared after him as he crashed through the bushes. Beyond, he recognized the narrow strip of woodland that opened onto the marsh meadow. He opened his mouth and tasted the air. Kit scent hung fresh just ahead. He pushed into the wall of thick stems.

A mew sounded ahead. "My paws are wet!"

Owl Eyes! Quickening his pace, Thunder shouldered on until he glimpsed a short, splotchy tail snaking through the grass ahead. "Sparrow Fur!"

The tail slid from view and her face poked out between the stalks. "Thunder!" She stared at him, eyes sparkling. "Pebble Heart said we'd make it back to camp before you, but I knew you'd catch up." Her gaze flitted to Lightning Tail. "Did you bring Tom?"

Lightning Tail shook his head. "Tom didn't want to come," he mewed softly. "He wanted to stay with his Twolegs."

"Hurry up!" Pebble Heart's mew sounded from farther ahead. "I want to see Turtle Tail!"

"There's the river!" Owl Eyes called out happily, pointing with a forepaw. "We'll be on the moor soon." Sparrow Fur turned and disappeared into the grass.

Thunder caught Lightning Tail's eyes. The black tom's gaze was dark with grief. Thunder guessed what he was thinking. *How will we tell them about their mother?*

Heart aching, Thunder pushed after the kits. He stretched his head up and saw River Ripple's silver tail poking above the stems. Pebbles crunched ahead and a moment later he emerged onto the shore.

The river glimmered beneath the moon, which was rising high above the moor.

The kits raced to the water's edge and began lapping thirstily.

River Ripple dipped his head to Lightning Tail. "You were brave today," he murmured.

"So were you." Lightning Tail glanced past the rogue toward the kits. "Thanks for getting them away. We couldn't have done it without you."

Thunder nodded. "Yes, thank you, River Ripple. We can take it from here."

"I'm glad I could help." River Ripple turned to the kits. "Take care!"

Three pairs of eyes turned and flashed through the moonlight.

"Where are you going?" Owl Eyes asked the silver rogue.

"Back to my nest." He stretched. "I'm worn out. Aren't you?"

"Yes, but we'll be home soon." Pebble Heart licked droplets from around his mouth.

"I bet Turtle Tail and Gray Wing are already there waiting for us," Sparrow Fur mewed excitedly. "They'll be so surprised when they hear where we've been."

Thunder's breath caught in his throat. How was he going to tell them the truth? Turtle Tail wasn't waiting for them. *They're never going to see her again.*

CHAPTER 16

❧

Gray Wing *stared out over the* moonlit grass. Wind Runner's vicious snarl rang in his ears. *You think you know what it's like?* He didn't *want* to know what it was like to lose a kit. He strained to see through the shadows, hope sparking beneath his pelt every time the wind ruffled the heather.

The other cats were still awake. Tall Shadow paced beside the flat rock while Jagged Peak watched.

Shattered Ice's nest rustled. The tom was clearly trying to get comfortable. Eventually, he snorted and hopped out, then sat beside Cloud Spots and Dappled Pelt. "It started as such a good day," he muttered.

Cloud Spots's fur brushed the ground. "Thunder will be back soon with Turtle Tail and the kits."

Acorn Leaf called across the clearing. "What's taking them so long?"

"Hush!" Hawk Swoop chided gently. "Let Wind Runner grieve in peace." Her eyes flashed in the darkness as she looked toward the bramble.

What is taking them so long? Gray Wing began pacing. "Perhaps

I should go and look for them." He looked questioningly at Tall Shadow.

"Save your strength," Tall Shadow glanced at the round, white moon. "The meeting with Clear Sky is tomorrow night."

"They must have gone all the way to Twolegplace," Gray Wing fretted.

"Turtle Tail knows her way around there," Jagged Peak reminded him. "She'll bring them back."

Gray Wing halted beside the gray tom. "What if Tom persuades her to stay? What if he uses the kits to keep her?"

Jagged Peak met his gaze. "Do you really think Turtle Tail would let that happen?"

The heather rustled. Gray Wing pricked his ears. Was that a faint mew in the distance? He jerked his head around.

"Turtle Tail!" Owl Eyes's mew sounded from the darkness. "We're coming!"

Gray Wing dashed to the edge of the hollow as shadows emerged onto the moonlit grass. Thunder and Lightning were flanking the three kits. He raced to meet them, joy flooding his pelt. "You're back!"

"Turtle Tail!" Sparrow Fur raced past him and hurtled into the camp.

Pebble Heart chased after her. "Guess where we've been!"

Owl Eyes was on their heels. "We went to Twolegplace. We saw where you lived." He called toward the tunnel entrance where Turtle Tail's nest sat in shadow.

"Turtle Tail?" Sparrow Fur stumbled to a halt, blinking through the gloom. "Where are you?" Her head jerked around as she scanned the camp. Owl Eyes and Pebble Heart clustered beside her.

"I can't smell her." Pebble Heart's mew was tinged with worry.

Sparrow Fur lifted her tail. "She must be out looking for us."

Gray Wing snapped his gaze toward Thunder. Why were his eyes hollow with grief? Had they left her behind? "Where is she?" Perhaps they'd missed each other while they were searching for the kits. She must still be out there in Twolegplace. "I'll go and find her." He started toward the gorse, but Thunder blocked his way.

"She's dead, Gray Wing."

Gray Wing stared at the young tom. "Don't be mousebrained." *How can she be dead? She'd never leave her kits.* "She can't be. I'll find her."

Lightning Tail lowered his head. "We saw her body," he murmured. "She was killed by a monster in Twolegplace. We had to leave her behind."

"*Leave* her?" Gray Wing struggled to understand.

"Killed?" Sparrow Fur's gasp made him turn. The kit was staring from the clearing, her eyes round with horror.

Owl Eyes stared. "Isn't she coming home?"

Pebble Heart moved closer to his brother. "No." His mew cracked. "She'll never come home now."

Rage flared in Sparrow Fur's eyes. "Why did you bring us back?" She marched past Gray Wing and glared at Thunder. "You took us away from our father when you knew our mother was dead."

Thunder froze, pain glazing his eyes.

Lightning Tail leaned toward the kit. "Turtle Tail would have wanted you to grow up here with Gray Wing."

She backed away. "You brought us home to *nothing!*"

Gray Wing flinched. "You have me," he ventured softly. "You are like my own kits. *I'm* still here."

Sparrow Fur turned to meet his gaze.

His throat tightened as he saw anguish wash over her and rushed to curl himself around her as she collapsed, her body shuddering with grief. Wrapped tightly around her, he sank into the grass. Tiny paws scrambled over his back as Owl Eyes and Pebble Heart buried themselves deep in his embrace. "I'll look after you just as Turtle Tail would have," he murmured thickly. "We will never forget her." His heart broke, misery pulsing through him. "I'm glad Thunder brought you home."

"We belong on the moor." Pebble Heart's mew was muffled by Gray Wing's pelt. "This is where we're supposed to be." There was certainty in the young kit's mew that sent shivers along Gray Wing's spine. *Does he know something?* He tucked his nose beneath his tail, enfolding the trembling kits like fledglings in a nest.

"I'm so sorry." Tall Shadow's gentle mew sounded in his ear. But he didn't lift his head. He nuzzled the kits, lapping them in turn as they burrowed against his fur. Swamped by grief, he was only vaguely aware of paw steps moving around him, the shapes of the moor cats moving in the moonlight, the brush of their muzzles against his flank.

"I'm sorry." Hawk Swoop pressed her muzzle to his shoulder.

"She loved you." Acorn Fur's breath touched his pelt.

As the paw steps eventually padded away, one pelt remained pressed against his flank. Rainswept Flower had settled beside him, the warmth of her fur seeping into his as he comforted the kits.

"Turtle Tail was happy that you loved her," Rainswept Flower whispered.

"I wish I'd loved her sooner," Gray Wing murmured.

"It's enough that you loved her at all," Rainswept Flower returned.

Gray Wing felt the kits grow still against him. Exhausted by their adventure, worn out by grief, they grew limp as they drifted into sleep. He let his own eyes close. His mind whirled with memories of Turtle Tail. She'd tried to cheer him up when dark thoughts had haunted him. *Look, Thunder has caught a bird! He's going to be a great hunter.* She'd encouraged her tribe mates when they grew weary on the long journey from the mountains. *No cat said it would be easy!* Her cheerful mew rang in his mind.

How can she be gone? Emptiness opened inside him, more chilling than death. *I have her kits.* He pressed closer around them. *I will raise them and protect them just as she would have.*

"Gray Wing." Rainswept Flower's mew roused him. He blinked open his eyes. Pale light seeped over the horizon. Was it dawn already?

Wind Runner padded from the camp, her brown pelt

matted, her eyes weary. She stopped beside Gray Wing. "I'm sorry for what I said to you yesterday." Her mew was hoarse. "I should never have wished grief on you."

"It's okay." Gray Wing met her gaze, understanding the pain shadowing her gaze. The sun showed golden above the horizon, bringing the first color of the day to the moor.

"We should bury Emberkit," Rainswept Flower murmured.

Wind Runner dipped her head. "Gorse Fur has already dug a grave. Gray Wing, will you carry Emberkit to it? His burial can serve as a farewell to Turtle Tail too."

Gray Wing blinked at her. "What happened to her body?" Was she still lying alone in Twolegplace?

"Thunder says they laid her beneath a bush outside a Two-leg nest," Wind Runner told him forlornly. "Her pelt was scattered with petals when they left her."

Rainswept Flower gazed toward the distant river. "Perhaps someone will find her and give her a proper burial. Twolegs, or kittypets."

Gray Wing's throat tightened. *I hope so.* He uncurled himself from the kits and nudged them gently to their paws. "One of Wind Runner's kits died yesterday," he told them softly. "It's time to bury him."

"Should we bury Turtle Tail too?" Pebble Heart stared at him blearily.

"Her body is in Twolegplace," Gray Wing told him. "But we will remember her when we bury Emberkit. We can say good-bye to both of them." With a pang, he wished he could give Turtle Tail the burial she deserved. Would remembering her spirit be enough?

"Come on, kits." Rainswept Flower slid past him and began lapping Owl Eyes's ruffled pelt. "Let's get you cleaned up for the burial."

Gray Wing glanced at her thankfully before following Wind Runner into camp.

The wiry she-cat led him to the bramble den, sliding wordlessly through the trailing stems. He ducked in after her, surprised to see the three healthy kits scrambling clumsily over Hawk Swoop as she lay in Wind Runner's nest. They had not opened their eyes, yet they squirmed and fidgeted energetically. A prick of joy seemed to lift his grief for a moment. Despite everything, there was new life in the camp.

Wind Runner nodded toward a tiny shape lying at the edge of the den.

Emberkit.

He crossed the soft earth and picked up the dead kit's body. He was shocked by how light it felt—hardly more than a bundle of feathers.

"I'll watch the others," Hawk Swoop told Wind Runner as Gray Wing carried Emberkit out into the clearing.

Wind Runner hurried past him and led him out of camp. She crossed the clearing and ducked along a rabbit trail through the heather.

The sprigs brushed Gray Wing's pelt as he followed. Emberkit swung beneath his chin. How could the grief of this day ever ease? As his thoughts darkened, the heather opened into a clearing, bounded by gorse. He padded out after Wind Runner.

The moor cats were already gathered around the grave Gorse Fur had dug. Shattered Ice stood beside Acorn Fur. Lightning Tail pressed against his sister, his eyes hollow. Thunder stood rigidly beside the earth piled next to the grave, while Cloud Spots and Dappled Pelt faced him, Tall Shadow and Jagged Peak at their side.

"He's too young to be dead," Sparrow Fur wailed. She huddled with Owl Eyes against Rainswept Flower. Pebble Heart hung back. They watched Gray Wing with glistening eyes as he padded forward and laid Emberkit in the hole. Shadows swallowed the tiny kit as his body dropped stiffly into the earth.

Gorse Fur stood like stone as Gray Wing joined the kits. Pebble Heart backed away. "It's okay, Pebble Heart." Gray Wing began to reassure him, but Pebble Heart was reaching for a pile of loose leaves.

The kit grabbed a wad between his jaws and carried them to the graveside. He dropped them into the grave. "They are burnet leaves," he mewed. "They will give him strength for his journey."

"Thank you, Pebble Heart." Gorse Fur nodded solemnly as Pebble Heart took his place beside his littermates. He looked at Wind Runner. "We wish we'd had Emberkit for longer," he meowed. "We had so much love to share with him. But we will remember him with pride. He would have grown into a fine tom."

Wind Runner didn't move or speak, only stared into the grave.

Tall Shadow watched, gaze fixed on the shadows that had swallowed Emberkit. For a moment it seemed as though every cat was frozen in grief. Gray Wing curled his tail till it arched protectively over Sparrow Fur, Owl Eyes, and Pebble Heart.

Then Thunder padded forward and began pawing earth into the grave. It showered silently over Emberkit's soft pelt, until it landed with muffled thuds.

"No!" Wind Runner's wail split the air. She lunged forward, eyes wide with panic. "Get him out! You can't bury him. He's my kit!"

Gorse Fur hauled her back with his forepaws and held her until she stopped wailing. "Let's go back to the other kits," he whispered to her gently. Helping her up, he guided her into the heather.

Gray Wing stared after the grieving pair, then turned back to Emberkit's grave. He padded to the edge and gazed down at the half-covered body. "Finish it," he told Thunder, fighting despair.

Thunder caught his eye. "I wish we could bury Turtle Tail too." He looked exhausted by grief.

"It's too late," Gray Wing told him hoarsely. Who knew what they'd find? He knew foxes roamed Twolegplace at night. "It's better we remember her covered in petals."

"I guess." Thunder's ear twitched.

As he began to push more earth into the grave, Shattered Ice and Lightning Tail hurried forward to help. Working together, they covered Emberkit, filling the hole until it was a mound rising from the grass.

Gray Wing lifted his gaze. Clouds scudded across the pale blue sky, like cats chasing each other. "Turtle Tail, I know you'll always be with me," he called. "You waited a long time for our love to grow and it won't die now. I'll fight for you, Turtle Tail, and I'll make sure that your kits have a future on the moor, safe among friends." The clouds touched, becoming one. "I will not fail you." Calm enfolded him. As birds began to sing in the new day, Gray Wing felt strength seep back into his limbs. He glanced around, suddenly aware he'd spoken aloud.

Lightning Tail dipped his head. Tall Shadow and Thunder did the same. Soft murmurs of approval rippled around the moor cats. Cloud Spots met his gaze, his eyes glistening.

Gray Wing nodded and, wordlessly, led the others back to camp.

Thunder caught up with him as he reached the clearing outside the hollow. Gray Wing halted and watched Rainswept Flower nudge the kits toward their nest. "Do you think they'll be okay?"

Thunder touched his muzzle to Gray Wing's shoulder. "My mother died," he murmured. "I'm sad she's not here, but I don't have to face the world alone." He glanced toward Acorn Fur and Lightning Tail as they sifted through what was left of yesterday's prey pile. "Nor will Turtle Tail's kits."

"You must rest today." Tall Shadow meowed as she

approached. "Both of you. The meeting with Clear Sky is tonight."

Gray Wing's pelt felt suddenly as heavy as mud. How could he face a dumb argument over territory after this? His weary eyes glazed. What would Turtle Tail tell him?

You must do this, Gray Wing. His ear fur rippled as he imagined her words. *Only you can stop Clear Sky from dragging us into war.*

CHAPTER 17

Thunder glanced over his shoulder. Gray Wing was in the clearing, pacing back and forth. His shadow slid over the worn grass, sharp under the bright full moon. Thunder tried to catch his eye, but the sleek gray tom was absorbed in his own thoughts. *Is he thinking about Turtle Tail? Or Clear Sky?* Thunder hoped he was focusing on the meeting ahead rather than his grief but, with each turn, Gray Wing's gaze flicked toward the nest in the tunnel where Rainswept Flower was nestling Turtle Tail's kits.

Owl Eyes stared blankly into the distance, while Sparrow Fur washed his ear distractedly. Pebble Heart watched Gray Wing, his amber gaze steady.

There was a solemnity in the kit's gaze that sent shivers rippling along Thunder's spine. *He looks like he's lived longer than Tall Shadow.* "Are you ready?" Though he had just been thinking of her, Tall Shadow's mew surprised him.

"Yes." Thunder faced her.

Gray Wing will do the talking," Tall Shadow reminded him.

"I know." Thunder curled his claws into the dewy grass. It

was obvious that Gray Wing had far more sympathy for Clear Sky than any other moor cat. Guilt jabbed Thunder's belly. *Should I feel sympathy for him? He is my father, after all.* He pushed the thought away with a growl. *Then he should have acted like one.* Thunder lashed his tail. "When do we leave?"

Tall Shadow lifted her muzzle and gazed around the clearing. Shattered Ice sat beside Hawk Swoop, a thrush lying half eaten between them. Cloud Spots was showing Frost the prey heap. It was the white tom's first trip out of the gorse den and Thunder was pleased to see he was hardly limping. Wind Runner lay in the long grass, cozy in the nest Gorse Fur had built her. She'd refused to stay in the gloomy bramble den, even though he'd tried hard to persuade her they'd been more sheltered there. "Kits need to feel sunshine, and wind in their fur," she had told him. Now, the kits clambered blindly over her, their fur fluffier than owlet feathers. One of them mewled hungrily. Thunder felt a twinge of sadness as he noticed that Sparrow Fur didn't even lift her head at the sound. She'd been so excited about helping Wind Runner with her kits. But, since Turtle Tail's death, she hadn't even crossed the clearing to sniff them.

Tall Shadow cleared her throat. "I want you all to stay in camp until we get back," she announced. Her voice carried clearly through the still night air.

Gorse Fur padded from the long grass. "Some of us should stand guard near the hollow," he growled. "Just in case."

Dappled Pelt gazed from outside the gorse den. "Clear Sky can't be trusted."

Thunder glanced at her, surprised at the darkness in the tortoiseshell's tone.

"This is a meeting, not a battle," Tall Shadow told her firmly. "Clear Sky knows that we just want to talk."

Gorse Fur met her gaze. "What does *he* want?"

Thunder wished he could reassure the tom, but he didn't trust Clear Sky any more than the rest of them.

He saw Tall Shadow take a step forward. "Gray Wing." The black she-cat's call seemed to jerk Gray Wing from his trance. His eyes flashed in the moonlight as he turned toward her. Then, nodding sharply, he padded toward the gap in the heather.

"Gray Wing!" Rainswept Flower called from his nest. "Aren't you going to say good-bye?"

Gray Wing glanced toward the kits huddling beside Rainswept Flower. "Of course." Shaking out his fur, he hurried across the clearing. "Rest, my dears," he told them, touching his muzzle to each of their heads. "I'll be back before long."

Owl Eyes stared at him anxiously. "You'll be okay, won't you?"

Gray Wing pressed his cheek to the young tom's. "Of course." His purr sounded forced. "I'm going to meet with my brother. And I've got Thunder and Tall Shadow with me."

Sparrow Fur glared at him. "You're going to meet *Clear Sky,*" she mewed. "The meanest cat ever."

"He's still my littermate," Gray Wing reminded her softly. He glanced fondly at Pebble Heart. "Will you be okay?"

Pebble Heart's eyes reflected starlight. "Be careful, Gray

Wing," he mewed. "Danger lies in the hollow."

"I will." Gray Wing dipped his head.

Thunder narrowed his eyes, curious. Why was Gray Wing taking advice from a *kit*? What did Pebble Heart know of conflict between cats? Unease moved in his belly as Gray Wing crossed the clearing and followed Tall Shadow out of the camp. He tasted the air warily, wondering at the foreboding creeping beneath his pelt. Was a storm coming? The faint scent of rain tinged the breeze. He checked the sky. For now, it was clear, the stars sparkling high above.

"Are you coming?" Gray Wing called to him over his shoulder.

Thunder bounded after him. As Tall Shadow ducked into the heather ahead of them, he whispered in Gray Wing's ear. "What did Pebble Heart mean by *danger lies in the hollow*?"

"I don't know." Gray Wing followed the black she-cat.

Thunder nosed his way among the springy branches. The trail was cracked and jabbed his pads as he wove one way then the other through the thick bushes. It was a few moments before he caught up to Gray Wing again. "What do you mean you don't know?" he hissed at Gray Wing's tail.

Gray Wing didn't answer. As he broke from the heather, Thunder saw Gray Wing and Tall Shadow already climbing the grass slope toward the hollow. They were veering away from the quickest route.

He broke into a run until he reached them, then fell in beside Gray Wing, matching his pace. "Why are we going this way?" Across the wide slope, he could see treetops shimmering in the hollow. Tall Shadow seemed to be leading them around it.

"We're heading for the sunhigh slope," Gray Wing told him. "It's clear of brambles and ferns. We decided that Clear Sky would feel more at ease if he saw our approach clearly."

"Who *cares* how he feels?" Thunder growled.

Gray Wing's pelt brushed his. "We need him to feel calm."

Thunder snorted. "It's like feeding prey to a buzzard. He'll take as much as he can get and *still* try to claw your pelt off."

Tall Shadow turned her head, her dark gaze glowing through the gloom. "We have to try." She flicked her night-black tail toward the top of the steepening slope. "I'll go on ahead to check it's safe. My pelt will be hidden better in the shadows."

"Don't go into the hollow until we get there." Gray Wing called as she bounded ahead.

"Shouldn't we stay with her?" Thunder watched her go uneasily. What if Clear Sky had planned a trap?

"She'll be careful." Gray Wing kept his gaze fixed ahead. "I don't want to arrive out of breath."

Thunder stiffened. "Is your chest still tight?"

"A little." Gray Wing's tail twitched. "But I'll be fine."

Thunder watched Tall Shadow disappear into the darkness at the top of the slope. "Perhaps *I* should go with her."

Gray Wing glanced pointedly at his wide white paws, pale against the grass. "Her pelt won't be seen. We don't want to alarm Clear Sky."

Thunder flexed his claws angrily. Were they going to spend

their whole lives tiptoeing around Clear Sky? *The meanest cat ever.* Sparrow Fur's words rang in his mind. *Danger lies in the hollow.* He looked to Gray Wing, remembering Pebble Heart's words. "If you don't know what Pebble Heart meant, why did you look so worried when you left?"

Gray Wing's paws brushed the grass.

"Well?" Thunder pressed.

"Pebble Heart has dreams," he murmured at last.

Thunder frowned. "We all have dreams."

"Not like Pebble Heart's."

A soft wind lifted Thunder's fur. "What do you mean?"

"You never knew Stoneteller. She was our leader in the mountains." Gray Wing kept walking. "She shared with the ancients in dreams. They warned her of darkness to come and showed her the way forward when we were unsure."

Thunder's heart quickened. "Do you think Pebble Heart shares with the ancients?"

"I don't know." Gray Wing scrambled up the last steep rise and stopped at the top. Starlight glittered behind him. He was breathless from the climb. "But I think he's special."

Thunder caught him up. "He's like *Stoneteller?*"

Gray Wing shrugged. "His dreams are important. That's all I know." He gazed toward the hollow. It opened like a wound at the edge of the moorland.

Thunder flattened his ears against the rustling of the forest beyond.

"He dreamed of death," Gray Wing murmured. "Before Turtle Tail was killed."

Thunder's fur spiked as surprise jolted through him. "You mean he saw it coming?"

"He didn't know it would be Turtle Tail." Gray Wing stared at him. "You're the only one I've told. Keep it to yourself while Pebble Heart's a kit. He's young and we don't want to put pressure on him."

"Why tell me *now?*"

"Just in case."

Fear dropped like a stone in Thunder's belly as Gray Wing held his gaze.

"Some cat needs to know, in case something happens to me."

Thunder's mouth grew dry. "Pebble Heart's had a dream about the meeting, hasn't he?"

Gray Wing bounded forward. "Let's catch up." He crossed the grass following Tall Shadow's trail.

Thunder charged after him, his pelt bristling with frustration. "Is there something you need to tell me?"

Gray Wing stopped at the top of the hollow where Tall Shadow was pacing the lush grass. He gave Thunder a warning look.

Thunder swallowed back the questions spinning in his head and scrambled to a halt. He stared down into the hollow. The four oaks swished, their leaves rippling like water in the moonlight. At the bottom he could see a great rock between them, thrusting from the ground like a massive paw. Silhouetted at the top, he recognized Clear Sky's broad shoulders, and saw his father's confident pose. For a moment, Thunder thought he was getting a glimpse at the cat Clear Sky once was—the young cat of the mountains.

He hoped that this would make him easier to negotiate with.

Tall Shadow shifted her paws. "He's not alone."

Thunder opened his mouth, letting the cool night breeze bathe his tongue. A jumble of cat scents made him stiffen, his fur prickling. "He's brought every cat in his territory."

"Every cat?" Gray Wing snapped his head around.

Falling Feather, Quick Water, Leaf, Petal. Thunder recognized all the scents of his old camp mates. And newer scents he didn't know. Had Clear Sky recruited more rogues?

Tall Shadow was peering down into the hollow. "I can't see any cat except Clear Sky."

Thunder fought to steady his breath. "They're hiding."

"Is it a trap?" Tall Shadow narrowed her eyes.

"Gray Wing!" Clear Sky's yowl sounded from below. "I know you're here. With Thunder and Tall Shadow. Why not show yourselves? You came to talk, didn't you? Then let's begin."

Thunder hesitated as Gray Wing stepped forward. He felt his breath catch. *I hope he's wrong about Pebble Heart's dreams.*

CHAPTER 18

"Keep your hackles down," Gray Wing murmured as he descended the slope.

"What are you doing?" Thunder stared after him, paws rooted to the grass. "We're outnumbered."

"He won't attack." Gray Wing glanced over his shoulder.

"Why bring his whole camp if he doesn't mean to attack?" *And what about Pebble Heart's warning?* Thunder couldn't believe that Gray Wing was being so reckless.

Tall Shadow padded after him. "What will he gain by harming us?"

Thunder watched her go. "Clear Sky hurts cats just because he can."

"I don't believe that." Gray Wing paused and met Thunder's gaze. "Are you coming or not?"

Thunder took a deep breath. *I'm no coward.* Forcing his fur to lie flat, he followed. The grass was slippery with dew beneath his paws. The musky scents of the forest cats filled the hollow. His gaze slid sideways as they reached the bottom. Shapes moved in the shadows on the slopes. He could see them slipping between the ferns like fish through reeds. But the moonlit clearing was deserted.

That's just like Clear Sky. I bet he told them to stay hidden because he knows a hidden enemy is more intimidating. "Just face us, you cowards," he muttered under his breath.

"Hush!" Tall Shadow's hiss was sharp.

Gray Wing padded to the foot of the great rock looming at the end of the clearing. He slid around the side and a moment later appeared at the top, facing Clear Sky.

Thunder flexed his claws. He felt uncomfortable, exposed.

"Join us!" Clear Sky called down.

Something about this felt wrong. A chill ran down Thunder's spine.

"Come on." Tall Shadow headed toward the rock.

Thunder followed. At least, he told himself, up there, they'd be safe from the reach of claws and teeth.

"What do we do if they attack?" he whispered to Tall Shadow as she crouched, ready to jump.

"Let's hope they don't." She leaped, landing on a narrow ledge halfway up before jumping to the top.

Thunder sighed. That wasn't much of a plan. "I hope you're right," he muttered, bounding after her.

The top of the rock was smooth, still warm from the day's heat. Gray Wing sat a tail-length from Clear Sky, who rested on his haunches, paws splayed as he washed his chest.

Tall Shadow circled Clear Sky slowly, her eyes never leaving him. She stopped and narrowed her eyes. "Why did you bring the others?"

Clear Sky lifted his head slowly and met her gaze, drawing

his paws neatly in front of him. "Why did Gray Wing bring *you?*"

Thunder bristled. "Because we don't trust you," he growled.

Gray Wing nudged Thunder backward as Tall Shadow settled beside him. "Thank you for coming, Clear Sky," he meowed evenly.

Clear Sky lifted his chin. "This meeting is long overdue." His voice rang across the hollow.

Thunder scanned the shadowy slopes, searching for movement. Clear Sky seemed to be addressing every cat, as though he was leader of them all. His hackles lifted. "Stop acting like it was your idea."

"Be quiet, Thunder," Gray Wing growled softly.

"Yes, Thunder. Be quiet." Clear Sky's eyes flashed scornfully in the moonlight.

"Don't tell me what to do!" Thunder flashed back at him.

"I forgot," Clear Sky meowed silkily. "You were always Gray Wing's cat."

"That's not true!" Claws seemed to rake Thunder's heart. "I tried to be the son you wanted me to be."

"Is that right?" Clear Sky stared at him coldly, the moonlight gleaming on his pelt.

"You wanted me to be cruel, like you!" Thunder thrust his muzzle toward his father. "But I'll never be cruel!"

"Thunder!" Gray Wing hissed at him fiercely.

Tall Shadow wove past Thunder, nudging him backward, as Gray Wing shifted his paws.

"I'm sorry about Thunder," said Gray Wing. "He's young and impulsive."

Thunder struggled to swallow his rage at the politeness in Gray Wing's mew. *How dare you apologize for me!*

Gray Wing went on. "The silence between us has festered like warm prey. Talk will clear the air and perhaps we can go back to how things were when we first arrived from the mountains."

Clear Sky's ear twitched but he didn't speak.

"Do you remember how it was?" Gray Wing prompted. "What it was like to be warm for the first time? To have full bellies? To feel soft grass beneath our paws instead of snow and rock? We were proud that we'd made such a dangerous journey. We were united in our determination never again to cower, hungry, in cold caves." He reached his muzzle closer to Clear Sky. "Surely, you remember?"

Clear Sky cocked his head to one side. "I remember the cats who died on the way. Have you forgotten Bright Stream?" His gaze glittered like ice. "And, when we arrived, the rogues didn't exactly welcome us to their land. We had to fight for it."

"That's not true!" Gray Wing objected. "What about Wind and Gorse?" He flicked his nose toward the shadows moving at the edges of the clearing. "What about Nettle and Fircone? All these rogues! They're your allies now."

"Like *Fox*?" There was a sneer in Clear Sky's mew.

As Gray Wing flinched, Thunder leaned closer. He'd heard about the tom Gray Wing had killed. "Fox died defending boundaries that *you* created!" he snarled.

"Hush!" Tall Shadow breathed in his ear. "Control your-self, Thunder. Now isn't the time to settle scores with your father."

He met her dark gaze, anger churning in his belly. She was right. They were here to bring peace to the forest and the moor.

She stepped forward and lifted her face so that moonlight drenched her muzzle. "The stars have looked down on this place for countless seasons. The stone beneath my paws has stood for endless moons."

Movement flickered at the corner of Thunder's vision. The cats below were slinking from the shadows. Falling Feather's white pelt glowed. He recognized the small frame of Quick Water at her side. Nettle and Fircone hurried closer, fur rip-pling. Petal, Leaf, and Snake jostled to get near. Thunder spotted a dull, black pelt moving like a shadow after the oth-ers. Was that Jackdaw's Cry?

As silent as hunters, they gathered beneath the rock. Their eyes shone with curiosity. Above them, bats flitted, swoop-ing this way and that like ghostly swallows. The cats ignored them and lifted their gazes to Tall Shadow.

She turned to them. "This great rock did not rise from the ground for me to sit on. These trees did not grow to give you shelter." She flicked her muzzle toward the moor. "The grass did not cover the moor to soften our paw steps. The rab-bits didn't hollow burrows for us to shelter in." She turned her gaze suddenly to Clear Sky. "The forest did not burn to destroy your home."

Thunder saw him shiver. She'd reminded Clear Sky of how vulnerable he'd been when flames threatened to engulf his camp. He'd needed their help then. He'd never have survived without it.

Tall Shadow pressed on. "This land isn't ours. We live here for a few short moons then disappear. But the land lives on. It isn't ours to claw into morsels and share like prey. We must honor it and protect it. It feeds us and shelters us." Her gaze swept back to the cats below. "Can we be united in that?"

Quick Water glanced at Falling Feather. Leaf rounded his eyes, intrigued. Fircone shifted his paws.

Were they considering Tall Shadow's plea?

Thunder looked at Clear Sky. His father's gaze had widened. Suddenly, he looked young, his ears pricked, his whiskers quivering. Had Tall Shadow convinced him that they could share the land in peace?

Hope surged beneath Thunder's pelt as Gray Wing stepped forward, reaching his muzzle out to his brother.

"Got you!" A triumphant yowl sounded below.

Thunder spun, heart lurching as he saw Jackdaw's Cry leap and swat a bat from the air. The black tom leaped on it and began gnawing, a warning growl rumbling in his throat.

"How dare you!" Petal turned on him, hissing. "That's forest prey."

"This is no cat's land." Jackdaw's Cry looked up at her, bat flesh hanging from his jaws. He flicked it into his mouth and swallowed hungrily.

Petal leaped and hooked the bat away. "That belongs to us!

Clear Sky forbid you from eating our prey!"

"No!" Gray Wing's eyes rounded in horror.

Thunder blinked. They were so close to an agreement. They mustn't fight now. Not over prey!

Clear Sky growled from the edge of the rock. "Stop!"

Petal and Jackdaw's Cry froze and backed away. The bat lay between them, pooled in blood.

Clear Sky's gaze swung toward Jackdaw's Cry. "What's he doing here?"

Petal looked up at her leader. "We couldn't leave him alone with Birch and Alder."

Jackdaw's Cry snarled. "You think I'd harm kits?"

Leaf showed his teeth. "Never trust a hungry cat."

"Whose fault is it I'm hungry?" Jackdaw's Cry threw an accusing glare at Clear Sky. "You haven't let me eat since I got to the forest."

What? Outrage pulsed through Thunder. He pictured the piles of prey in the forest camp, rotting because there was too much to eat. Hadn't they shared *any* with Jackdaw's Cry? "You *starved* him? But . . . you *swore* that you would never again see another cat go hungry."

Clear Sky turned on him. "Don't you dare speak! You've no right to be heard after everything you've done!" Hurt blazed in his eyes. "You're disloyal and ungrateful. First, you left Gray Wing. And then you left *me!*"

Thunder shrank beneath his pelt. *Disloyal?* Was that how Gray Wing saw it, too? "You told me it was destiny." His mew was barely a whisper.

Clear Sky's eyes narrowed. "Your destiny has nothing to do with me." He barged past Gray Wing and thrust his muzzle into Thunder's face. "You betrayed Gray Wing and you betrayed me!" He drew back, teeth glinting. "Isn't that right, *brother?*" He glared at Gray Wing.

"Leaving the moor wasn't a betrayal," Gray Wing protested. "He thought he was doing the right thing."

Clear Sky snorted. "He can't be trusted." His gaze swung back to Thunder.

Thunder backed away, his paws trembling. He knew he'd come to despise Clear Sky . . . but he didn't realize his father hated *him*.

"I know what you've been doing on the moor," Clear Sky accused, leaning close to Thunder again. "You've been training cats for battle—"

"I haven't!" Thunder defended himself. "I've been trying to persuade them *not* to fight!"

Clear Sky wasn't listening. "You've been seen. Telling them how to turn hunting crouches into fighting moves! But don't forget, you mean nothing to any cat, no matter how much you try to prove yourself. *No cat* trusts you anymore!"

Sudden darkness shrouded the hollow. Thunder jerked his gaze up. Past the towering oaks, he searched for the moon, but clouds had swallowed it and hidden the stars.

Clear Sky's mew dropped to a whisper. "You may as well not exist." His breath stirred Thunder's ear fur.

Thunder gasped, shock pulsing through him as he saw coldness harden his father's gaze.

Clear Sky turned his head toward the cats below. "Attack!" He reared and hooked his claws into Tall Shadow's pelt and hauled her over the edge of the rock.

Yowls of excitement erupted as she landed among the forest cats.

"Tall Shadow!" Thunder stared in horror as they turned on her, claws flashing in the moonlight.

Jackdaw's Cry plunged into the sea of writhing pelts, snaking his way to Tall Shadow's side. Back to back, they reared and hit out at their attackers.

Petal hurled herself at Tall Shadow, hissing. Snake lunged low, nipping at her paws. With a hefty blow, Nettle caught Tall Shadow's cheek. Tall Shadow staggered, unbalancing Jackdaw's Cry. He teetered forward and Fircone grabbed his scruff and dragged him onto the ground.

"We have to help them." Gray Wing's panicked mew sounded in his ear.

"Let's get them up here. It'll be easier to defend ourselves," Thunder hissed back.

"Then what?" Gray Wing's gaze flashed with fear.

I don't know! Thunder froze, staring down at the forest cats as Tall Shadow and Jackdaw's Cry disappeared beneath them.

Clear Sky pushed past him. "That's right," he hissed. "Stay up here and watch your friends die." He leaped down from the rock.

"Quick!" Thunder slithered after him. Gray Wing landed heavily beside him. They exchanged glances, then Thunder hurled himself into the battle. He grabbed Petal, digging his claws deep into her pelt, and dragged her backward. She yowled and turned, lips drawn back. Thunder ducked as she snapped at his muzzle, feeling a fierce tug at his whiskers as her jaws slammed shut dangerously close to his cheek. He dodged forward, thrusting himself beneath Nettle's belly. Pushing up, he heaved the tom off his paws and sent him sprawling.

"Thunder!" Jackdaw's Cry exclaimed. The tom's gaze lit with hope.

"Get to the rock!" Thunder ordered.

Tall Shadow jerked her head around, catching Thunder's eye.

"Watch out!" Thunder's heart lurched as he saw Fircone lunge for her.

Tall Shadow spun and met the tom's attack with an outstretched paw. She raked his muzzle, then threw her full weight against him, sending him staggering back against Quick Water and Leaf.

Pain seared Thunder's flank. He turned as Snake sunk his claws deep. Fury rose in his belly. He dragged himself free and snapped at the rogue's throat. Snake dodged away. Thunder leaped after him, grabbed his scruff between his teeth and shook him hard.

Claws hooked his shoulders and dragged him backward.

"Did you really think this battle could be avoided?" Clear Sky hissed in his ear.

"This isn't a battle!" Thunder grunted with pain as Clear Sky pinned him to the ground with outstretched claws. "It's slaughter." Thrashing desperately, he spotted Gray Wing dragging Jackdaw's Cry free of Fircone and pushing him toward the rock.

"Use the ledge to jump to the top!" Gray Wing ordered. He turned back for Tall Shadow.

Thunder writhed in Clear Sky's grip. "We're not going to make it easy!" As fast as a rabbit, he tucked his hind paws under his father's belly and thrust him backward. Clear Sky's eyes lit in surprise as he staggered backward and tripped over Snake.

Thunder leaped to his paws.

Tall Shadow streaked past him.

Gray Wing was on her tail. "Come on." He paused to nose Thunder toward the rock.

Thunder ran, following Tall Shadow as she leaped onto the ledge. He scrambled to the top of the great rock a moment after her. Jackdaw's Cry was trembling at the top. Gray Wing landed beside him.

"Now what?" Tall Shadow's eyes were wide.

A hiss sounded from the ledge. Thunder looked down and saw Snake, halfway up. The rogue jumped. But Thunder was quick. He lashed out and sent him sprawling to the ground. Scrambling to his paws, Snake threw a menacing look to the top of the rock. Around him, the forest cats circled, low growls rumbling in their throats.

"We're trapped!" Jackdaw's Cry blinked at Gray Wing.

"They can't keep us here forever," Gray Wing reasoned.

Clear Sky padded to the center of the clearing and called up. "What's your plan now, Gray Wing?" he snarled triumphantly.

"Are you going to let us watch you starve up there? Or are you going to come down and fight like real cats?"

Thunder glanced up at the oak branch swaying a tail-length above their heads. "We need help," he said.

Jackdaw's Cry followed his gaze. "Do you think the birds are going to come and teach us to fly away?"

"If I could just get back to camp, I could fetch more cats." Thunder murmured.

"You'll never get past them." Tall Shadow nodded toward the cats below.

Gray Wing narrowed his eyes. "Are you thinking about climbing out of here?"

Thunder met his gaze. "If I could get into the tree and climb along that branch." He nodded toward a bough stretching toward the slope. The moor rose beyond. "I might make it to the camp for help."

"It's dangerous." Tall Shadow's eyes darkened. "They'll try and stop you."

"We'll distract them," Gray Wing promised.

Thunder peered down at the circling cats. "Stay up here," he warned. "I want you safe when I return with the others."

"Will they come?" Jackdaw's Cry stared at him anxiously.

Thunder straightened. "Do you think Acorn Fur, Lightning Tail, and Hawk Swoop would leave you here?"

Jackdaw's Cry lifted his tail. "Never!"

"Be careful," Tall Shadow warned, her eyes glistening with fear.

Thunder dipped his head. "I'll do my best."

Gray Wing padded to the edge of the rock and called down to the forest cats. "Look at your leader," he growled. Clear Sky was in the middle of the clearing, his eyes gleaming. "Does he make you proud? Watching while you fight his battle for him."

"How dare you?" Clear Sky lashed his tail.

As every cat's gaze flicked toward Clear Sky, Thunder leaped for the branch. He hooked it with his forepaws, his hind paws churning the air desperately. Panic flashed though him. He had to make it before the cats noticed. Leaves showered around him as the branch shook under his weight. Swinging his haunches, he hooked a hind paw onto a jutting twig. Growling under his breath, he heaved himself upward, gasping as he dragged himself onto the branch.

He peered through the leaves.

Clear Sky was padding toward his cats. "Why are you even listening to a cat who only left the mountains because he was following his littermate? He was *born* to follow. I was born to lead!"

Thunder growled. *Arrogant fox-heart!*

He crept along the ancient branch, the bark rough beneath his pads. It thickened as he neared the trunk. He paused at the crook, relieved to see another branch jutting half a tail-length away. He leaped onto it, following the branches around the wide trunk like crossing stones in a river. Before he knew it, he was balancing on the branch that stretched toward the slope. He padded along it, his heart pounding, hoping that the leaves would conceal him. As he neared the end, his paws spilled over the sides of the branch—it was growing thinner.

He unsheathed his claws, curling them into the thick bark as it quivered beneath his weight. He dropped to his belly and slithered forward. Gazing down, he saw the slope several tail-lengths below. Could he risk jumping down yet? He pulled himself farther along the fast-thinning branch. Suddenly, it dipped. His chest tightened in terror. *I'm too heavy!* With a crack, it snapped, sending him hurtling him toward the ground. He twisted clumsily, sucking in a yowl of alarm, and landed with a thump on his side.

Am I hurt? Fear pulsed through him as he lay winded, checking for pain. *Nothing.* Just the dull shock of landing. He drew in a shuddering breath.

"Where's Thunder?" Clear Sky's alarmed mew sounded from the clearing.

"He's gone!"

"Where is he?"

He glanced down into the clearing. The forest cats were scanning the hollow, ears pricked.

Thunder leaped to his paws and raced uphill.

"He's heading for the moor!" Nettle's cry ripped through the night air.

Thunder ran harder, cresting the top of the slope, and hared onto the moor. Angry yowls rose from the hollow. He tore over the grass. Glancing back, he saw two shapes appear at the hollow's rim. The moonlight glinted off sleek pelts. *Snake and Petal.* Their eyes flashed as they saw him. More cats loomed behind them.

Panic raging, Thunder fled. He could hear the yowls of the

cats behind him as they gave chase. Gulping air, he looked back.

Snake was gaining on him. Small and wiry, the rogue moved fast over the grass. Thunder would never outrun him as far as the camp.

If they catch me, the others are lost! Scanning the moorside, he spotted a dip in the grass. A burrow?

I can use the tunnels!

Gray Wing had shown him the maze beneath the moor when he was younger and told him how to tell a good tunnel from a bad. Would a forest cat dare follow him into the darkness?

I hope not. Chest burning, pelt on end, Thunder skidded to a halt beside the dip and dived into the tunnel.

Earth scraped his flanks, soil crumbled beneath his paws. Scrambling inside, his nose wrinkled at the rank air. As moonlight faded behind him, the tunnel grew damp. *Where am I heading?* Slick mud walls slid past his pelt. *Just keep going!* He wasn't even sure where the tunnel led. *You have to save Gray Wing and the others!*

How could this have happened? They'd gone to reach an agreement. Instead they faced battle. How could his father have betrayed his own brother? *How could he have betrayed me?* Rage burned beneath Thunder's pelt. He growled as he pelted through the darkness. *You'll pay for this, Clear Sky. With blood.*

CHAPTER 19

❧

Never follow stale air.

The words carried back to him from his kithood, when
Gray Wing had begun to teach him the tunnels beneath the
moor.

Distant yowls echoed along the tunnel behind.

"You moor cats aren't cats! You're worms!"

"Come out and fight, you mouseheart!"

Snake and Petal were calling into the darkness. At least
they hadn't followed.

Thunder picked up his pace, ignoring the musty, cold air
of the tunnel, and the endless ache in his paws. He had to get
back to camp. There was no turning back.

His heart lurched, as the ground sloped down steeply
beneath his paws. *Only follow a downward slope if you can retrace
your steps.*

"Sorry, Gray Wing," Thunder muttered under his breath.
There was no way he could follow the older cat's advice now.

"We'll guard the entrance." Snake's growl echoed along
tunnel behind. "If he comes back out, we'll get him!"

Thunder swallowed, hoping he was heading in the right

direction. *The camp* must *be this way.* The tunnel hadn't curved since he entered it. His forepaws slipped as the slope suddenly sharpened. *What if it just keeps going deeper?* No. *It can't,* he told himself. *It must lead somewhere.* As he calmed himself, the slope flattened and began to widen. Hope sparked in his chest. He slowed to a trot. The tunnel was straighter than crow-flight. *It'll take me to the camp.* As he began to imagine bursting out beside the hollow, the air changed.

Thunder halted. Damp scents bathed his tongue. Blind in the darkness, Thunder reached forward with his muzzle. His nose touched earth. A dead end? It couldn't be. The damp smell must be coming from somewhere. And there was only stale air behind. He reached forward with one forepaw. It flapped in thin air. So did his other. He frowned, puzzled. His nose touched earth, yet each paw reached into empty space. The tunnel must split into two! *Which way do I choose?* Heart pounding, Thunder sniffed first this way, then that.

One tunnel smelled dry and musty, the other damp and fresh.

Could it be dew? If he could smell dew, there must be grass and sky and air. Thunder headed along the damp tunnel. His paws pattered over mud. Hope flashed fresh with every paw step. The trail must start to rise soon.

His whiskers brushed close to earth on one side. The tunnel was curving. Was it leading away from camp? He followed the bend, anxiety curling in his belly. *Have I gone the wrong way?* The curve tightened. Thunder slowed. *Should I go back?* Uncertainty weighted his paws. *Gray Wing's depending on me.* Suddenly the tunnel turned back on itself. *Now where?* Disoriented, Thunder pressed on.

He could picture Gray Wing, Jackdaw's Cry, and Tall Shadow on the rock. What if Clear Sky's cats attacked? If enough of them climbed the ledge together, they might be able to push the moor cats back and overrun their sanctuary. Breath quickening, Thunder broke into a run, pulling up again as he felt the tunnel narrow around him. Within paw steps, it was pressing on his spine, then his flanks, until he was hauling himself through a narrow gap, earth dragging against his belly.

I should have taken the other tunnel. Fear crawled beneath his pelt. But the damp fresh scent of dew still bathed his muzzle. This tunnel *must* lead out onto the moor. Once he was in the open, he would be able to find his way back to camp. He dragged himself forward, relief flooding his fur as the space opened out, feeling like a great weight being lifted off his back.

He scrambled to his paws and raced onward, mouth open, hoping to smell a familiar scent. Had he been in this tunnel before?

Gray Wing's mew sounded in his ears. *Jackdaw's Cry knows these tunnels as well as he knows the rabbit runs through the heather. You must learn them too. Who knows when you'll need their shelter?*

If only he hadn't spent so much time in the forest with Clear Sky. Bitterness caught in his throat. *I could have been learning these routes. I might have made it back to the camp by now.*

Whiskers twitching as he felt for open space ahead, he hurried through the blackness. His heart lifted as light showed ahead. *How?* The tunnel hadn't sloped upward. He couldn't be near the surface. He hurried toward the brightness, realizing as he neared that moonlight was seeping through a deep crack in the earth. The scent of grass, rich with predawn dew, washed over him. He scowled with disappointment and halted, straining to see ahead.

A scuffling sound made him stiffen. Fur was brushing the earth. Thunder's belly tightened as a familiar stench touched his nose.

Badger!

He backed away. Had he stumbled into a set? Heavy paws scuffed the ground in the shadows farther down the tunnel. Thunder's pelt lifted as eyes glinted in the muted moonlight streaming from the crack. He could make out the white stripes of a badger face.

A growl rumbled toward him.

"I'm sorry," he whispered. "I didn't mean to—"

Claws scraped the earth as the badger lunged. Fighting panic, Thunder turned and raced back along the tunnel. As it narrowed around him, he dived forward, reaching out with his forepaws to haul himself through. Behind, he felt hot breath on his tail and heard jaws snap, an angry snarl following him as he dragged himself forward.

Heart thrumming against the earth, he heard heavy paws scraping the earth behind. The badger was too big to fit through.

Unsheathing his claws, Thunder heaved himself through

the narrowest part of the tunnel, gasping for breath as he scrambled out the other side.

He stopped and pricked his ears. Trembling like prey, he listened as the badger snorted before lumbering away. Thunder's thoughts began to race. Petal and Snake were at the entrance. A badger blocked this way. There was only one way to go.

He raced back to the split and headed down the other tunnel. *Please let it lead to the camp!* Ignoring the stale air, he raced through the darkness, fur bristling as he braced every moment to hurtle headlong into a dead end. But the tunnel seemed to open before him like a fern leaf unfurling. It twisted this way and that, but a deep sense in his belly told Thunder that it *had to be* heading for the hollow. As the ground began to slope up beneath his paws, sharp night air touched his nose. There must be an opening ahead. He kept running until he saw moonlight. He raced for it, bursting out onto grass.

A cool breeze ruffled his fur and he breathed it deep into his chest. Relief washed his pelt. Above, the clouds had cleared and the moon shone, full and bright. He gazed around, searching for familiar markers. The hillside was dappled with heather, gorse, and grass so that it looked like a tortoiseshell's pelt in the moonlight. But Thunder could still recognize the dark shadow that betrayed the dip where the camp nestled. *The hollow!* He raced toward it, crossing a swath of grass and plunging through heather. He zigzagged along a rabbit trail and burst out the other side. With a rush of excitement he recognized the heather wall of the camp.

He raced for it and leaped through the gap, skidding to a halt in the clearing.

The eyes of his camp mates swiveled toward him, flashing in the moonlight.

"Thunder!" Lightning Tail jumped up in alarm. But Thunder was heading for Gray Wing's nest. He had to speak to Pebble Heart.

He stopped at the edge of the nest. Owl Eyes, Sparrow Fur, and Pebble Heart were nestled against Rainswept Flower. They stared at him with bright round eyes.

Thunder looked right at Pebble Heart. "What was your dream?" he demanded.

Rainswept Flower leaped to her paws behind the kits and hissed: "Thunder, what is this about? You're scaring them!"

Sparrow Fur scanned the shadows behind Thunder. "Where's Gray Wing?"

"He's still at the hollow," Thunder told her quickly, his gaze fixing on Pebble Heart. "What was your dream?" he repeated sharply.

Owl Eyes jumped up and shielded his brother. "Leave him alone!"

"It's okay." Pebble Heart nosed Owl Eyes softly aside and hopped out of the nest, meeting Thunder's eyes. "Did Gray Wing tell you about it?"

"Thunder!" Shattered Ice's mew sounded across the camp. Frost's white pelt glowed at the corner of Thunder's gaze. Paw steps scuffed the grass behind him. The cats were gathering in the clearing.

"Why did you come back alone?" Gorse Fur asked uneasily.

Thunder faced him. "Gray Wing, Tall Shadow, and Jackdaw's Cry are in trouble." He searched the anxious gazes of his campmates. Would they be prepared to fight to protect their friends? "I came back to get help."

"Help?" Gorse Fur murmured.

Cloud Spots slid from beneath the gorse. "What's the trouble?"

Shattered Ice growled. "I knew Clear Sky couldn't be trusted."

"He's a fox-heart," Frost hissed bitterly.

Thunder turned to Pebble Heart. "I must know what your dream was about." He lowered his voice as the moor cats murmured behind him.

Pebble Heart gazed at him solemnly. "I saw a fight beneath a great rock," he breathed.

"How did it end?" Thunder ignored the panic throbbing through his chest.

Pebble Heart blinked at him. "I don't know." Confusion clouded the young cat's gaze. "It didn't make sense."

Thunder flicked his tail in frustration.

"I'm sorry," Pebble Heart mewed.

"It's not your fault." Thunder turned away. There wasn't time to worry—he needed to act. He leaped onto the flat rock. The smooth stone felt strange beneath his paws. This was Tall

Shadow's place, not his. But Tall Shadow wasn't here.

He gazed down at the moor cats. "Clear Sky has betrayed us!"

Shattered Ice flattened his ears. "I told you—"

Thunder cut him off. "He brought his cats with him. Too many to count. Rogues and loners I've never seen before. Tall Shadow, Gray Wing, and Jackdaw's Cry are stranded on the great rock in the hollow. I don't know how long they can hold Clear Sky's cats off. I'm going back to help them. Who will come with me?"

Gorse Fur stepped forward, chin high. "I will!"

"Me too!" Shattered Ice stood beside his friend.

"I'm coming!" Lightning Tail lashed his tail.

"So am I!" Frost's blue eyes sparkled like ice. "If there's a fight with Clear Sky, I want to be part of it!"

Acorn Fur paced beside him. "We'll all go!" she yowled.

Thunder shook his head. "Someone must stay with Wind Runner and the kits." He could hear mewling from Wind Runner's nest in the long grass. He narrowed his eyes, waiting for someone to offer to remain in the camp.

Rainswept Flower met his gaze wordlessly. Jagged Peak stepped from the shadows, his face grim with determination. Dappled Pelt joined Cloud Spots and stared at Thunder, unflinching.

Pride surged beneath Thunder's pelt—every cat wanted to fight for their friends. "You are brave," he yowled. "And I'm honored to fight beside you, but *someone* must stay behind." What if the battle ended in death? He pictured Owl Eyes,

Pebble Heart, and Sparrow Fur trying to comfort Wind Runner and her kits as they waited in vain for someone to come home. Wind Runner couldn't hunt for them all. "Jagged Peak." He stared at the lame tom. "You'll be more use here."

Jagged Peak glared back at him stubbornly. "But I want to fight!"

Thunder ignored him, turning to Dappled Pelt. "Wind Runner and the kits need you more than Gray Wing and Tall Shadow do."

Dappled Pelt's hackles lifted. "But—"

Cloud Spots pushed past her. "If Dappled Pelt wants to go, then she must. She's nimbler than me. It'll make her a good fighter. I'll stay behind with Wind Runner and the kits."

Dappled Pelt glanced gratefully at her friend. "Are you sure?"

Cloud Spots nodded. "I'll be more use here."

"Jagged Peak?" Thunder turned back to the tom.

Jagged Peak's eyes were still blazing with indignation. "I'm coming with you! This is as much my battle as yours." He limped forward. Thunder could see his shoulders rippling with muscle. The weakness in his hind leg had given him strength in his forelegs. But he was slow. Clear Sky's cats would shred him the moment he set paw in the hollow.

"I know you are strong, Jagged Peak," Thunder told him. "And brave. But this is a fight to the death. Clear Sky will take advantage of any weakness." Guilt pricked through him as he saw hurt sharpen Jagged Peak's gaze. "Your strength is in guarding the kits. Wind Runner will need prey if she's to feed them. You can hunt better than you can fight. You are needed here."

Jagged Peak held his gaze for a moment, then dipped his head. "Okay."

Thunder felt a rush of gratitude. "Thank you."

"Tell Clear Sky I would fight by *your* side to the death," Jagged Peak growled. "But I wouldn't lift a claw to help *him*."

"I will," Thunder promised, his heart swelling.

Sparrow Fur circled Rainswept Flower anxiously. "Are you going with Thunder?"

Rainswept Flower met the young she-cat's gaze solemnly. "I have to help Gray Wing."

Sparrow Fur's ears flattened with terror. "What if you don't come back?"

Like Turtle Tail. Thunder leaped from the rock and padded toward her. "Gray Wing needs us," he told her softly.

Sparrow Fur stared at him. "Will you bring him home?"

Thunder nodded. "I promise." The words caught in his throat. He'd made the same promise about Turtle Tail. This time he would keep his word.

"I want to come." Owl Eyes flicked his fluffy tail.

"You're too young." Thunder touched his muzzle to the young tom's head.

Owl Eyes scowled. "But I know how to fight."

"Hurry!" Shattered Ice was pacing the gap in the heather. Acorn Fur kneaded the ground beside him.

Overhead, clouds were surging toward the moon, driven by a rising wind. Thunder felt it lift his fur as he left the kits and headed past Shattered Ice, breaking into a run as his paws touched the soft grass outside camp.

"I'm coming too!"

Wind Runner's yowl made him freeze. He turned, shocked to see the queen racing out of the camp.

Gorse Fur skidded to a halt beside Thunder and stared at his mate. "What about the kits?"

Shattered Ice, Hawk Swoop, Lightning Tail, and Acorn Fur streaked past, heading for the heather. Rainswept Flower and Dappled Pelt followed, Frost at their heels.

Wind Runner held her ground. "Our kits are tough," she growled, glancing back into the camp. "Besides, they'll have Jagged Peak and Cloud Spots."

Gorse Fur flattened his ears.

Wind Runner's growl was determined. "Don't try and stop me. I want my kits to grow up somewhere safe, and the moor will never be safe as long as Clear Sky thinks he can tell any cat what to do!"

Thunder eyed the queen. "We have enough orphans already," he told her grimly.

"They won't be orphans." Gorse Fur lifted his chin, his gaze flashing as it caught Wind Runner's. "She will not die today. I won't let her."

Wind Runner's eyes glistened as she stared at her mate. "Thank you," she murmured.

Thunder pricked his ears. Paw steps were thrumming away over the moor. Hawk Swoop and Lightning Tail were already leading the others toward the battle. "Come on." He dived into the heather. The bushes shook around him as Gorse Fur and Wind Runner followed.

As he burst out on the far side, he saw his camp mates already crossing the slope toward the hollow. Their pelts moved like shadows over the grass. He pushed harder to catch up. They had to meet Clear Sky and his rogues side by side and fight together if they were to stand a chance of winning this battle. At his side, Gorse Fur matched him paw step for paw step; just in front, Wind Runner's lithe body moved easily over the grass.

Ahead, Hawk Swoop reached the top of the slope first. Lightning Tail, Rainswept Flower, and Shattered Ice pulled up beside her and waited motionless in the starlight. Acorn Fur and Dappled Pelt scrambled to a halt and paced around their camp mates while Frost peered over the edge. As he neared, Thunder could see that the white tom's pelt was bristling.

His heart lurched as he strained to hear sounds from the hollow. It was silent. Had the battle already been fought? He swallowed back dread. What if he reached the top of the slope to find the bodies of Tall Shadow, Gray Wing, and Jackdaw's Cry—plucked from their perch and slaughtered in the clearing?

He scrambled the last few paw steps and slowed, weaving past Lightning Tail and Hawk Swoop. Holding his breath, he stared down. *Where are they?* Clouds swallowed the moon. Flanks heaving, Thunder strained to see over the ferns. He narrowed his eyes. Beneath the branches of the oaks, he could make out the great rock. Three figures sat like stone at the top. *They're alive!*

"Welcome back, Thunder." Clear Sky's yowl rang from below.

Thunder froze. His father stared at him from the middle of the clearing.

"I can smell your fear-scent," Clear Sky sneered. Ripples of amusement sounded from the cats collected behind him.

"I'm not scared of you!" Thunder's tail bushed with anger.

"*Really?*" Clear Sky padded to the bottom of the slope. "Then why did you bring so many cats?"

"We're here to rescue Gray Wing and the others."

Clear Sky lifted his tail. "Then come and get them."

CHAPTER 20

Thunder glanced at his camp mates. "Ready?"

Hawk Swoop met his gaze grimly. "How many cats does Clear Sky have?"

"More than us," Thunder told her.

Lightning Tail squared his shoulders. "We have to save Gray Wing, Tall Shadow, and Jackdaw's Cry."

Shattered Ice glared into the hollow. "We have to show Clear Sky he can't tell us what to do."

Growls rumbled in the throats of his camp mates.

Frost showed his teeth. "Just let me get my claws into him."

Thunder drew in a deep breath, fear darkening his thoughts. Clear Sky's cats were ready for them. *We're ready for you.*

"Attack!" He plunged down the slope, crashing through the ferns. Fear turned to energy fizzing in his paws as they hit the open clearing.

Pelts swarmed toward them. The air stank of the carrion scent of rogues. Didn't Clear Sky care who fought for him? Shrieks seemed to claw at the night air as the moor cats raced among the forest cats.

Matted brown fur flashed at the edge of Thunder's vision.

He ducked as Snake leaped at him, dodging beneath the tom's belly and slashing out with his forepaw as a tabby reared up. His claws pierced Snake's fur, digging into flesh as he raked the tabby's cheek.

"This is a battle you can't win!" Snake hissed. "You're out-numbered—and we've been *training* for this."

"At least we know what we're fighting *for!*" Thunder glanced at the great rock, relieved to see Gray Wing leap down into battle. He landed squarely on Dew's back. The rogue she-cat yowled, eyes lighting with rage. Jackdaw's Cry thumped onto the ground beside her. Tall Shadow slid into the sea of writhing pelts.

Pain sliced through Thunder's muzzle. Snake had caught him with a vicious jab, and now blood sprayed the earth. He dodged low and sank his teeth into Snake's forepaw, gasping as jaws clamped his neck. His heart lurched as he felt Snake bite down. Mind whirling, he tried to twist free before Snake could crush his spine like he would crush prey.

"Get off him!" Lightning Tail yowled. And then suddenly Snake was gone. Thunder leaped to his paws and saw Lightning Tail hauling Snake backward. The rogue's hind paws churned the air as Lightning Tail lifted them off the ground, his claws hooked into Snake's flanks. With a grunt, Lightning Tail heaved Snake away. Snake staggered backward and disappeared into the mass of writhing pelts.

"Are you okay?" Lightning Tail crouched beside Thunder.

Thunder straightened and shook out his fur. His scruff was wet with his own blood. "Yes," he growled.

"They're fighting to kill!" Lightning Tail's eyes were wide.

"So will we." Fury pulsing beneath his pelt, Thunder scanned the battle. Dappled Pelt reared to meet the slashing blows of a long-furred rogue. Shattered Ice struggled beneath a mottled brown-and-white she-cat. Wind Runner tore at Quick Water's spine-fur with punishing hind claws. Gray Wing backed into the shadow of the great rock. Dew slashed at him, eyes slitted. Gray Wing fought back with a flurry of blows that sent the she-cat staggering, blood welling at her muzzle.

As he drove Dew toward her camp mates, Petal darted forward. The small yellow she-cat's eyes flashed with hatred as she barged past Dew. "This one's mine!" Hissing, she threw a hefty blow that caught Gray Wing on his ear.

He flinched.

"That's for my brother, you murdering snake-heart!" Petal leaped onto Gray Wing's back, sinking her teeth into his tail as she pounded his head with her hind paws. "You had no right to kill Fox!"

Dew lunged and bit Gray Wing's forepaw. He stumbled and fell, Petal clinging to his back. Dew lunged again, claws outstretched, and raked Gray Wing's flank, opening long, scarlet wounds in his pelt.

Thunder dived forward, shouldering his way between thrashing bodies. "Gray Wing!" Panic pounded in his ears. He reached out and dug his claws into Dew's thick gray fur. Snagging flesh, he pulled her backward and tossed her to one side. She landed clumsily at Shattered Ice's paws, eyes wide with surprise. Shattered Ice glanced down at her, then rearing, he slammed his paws hard into her exposed flank.

Thunder backed away as Gray Wing stretched onto his hind legs. Petal clung like a burr to his back. He twisted, snapping at her hind leg and she shrieked as his jaws clamped down on the bone, releasing her grip and thumping onto the ground.

Thunder leaped in beside Gray Wing. Tails to the rock, they faced the battling cats.

"Thanks," Gray Wing panted. Blood streamed from his flank. His ear tip hung, torn and loose.

Thunder could feel his own pelt matted with blood. The air was rich with its stone tang as the screeching cats fought. "We're not finished yet."

"You're not finished until Gray Wing's dead!" Petal reared in front of them, claws glinting in the half-light. A tabby rogue slid in beside her and glared at them. As Petal dove for Gray Wing, he lifted his forepaws. Thunder reared as the tabby leaped at him. Together, he and Gray Wing met their attackers with a flurry of blows, batting them backward, step by step. Gray Wing knocked Petal away with a swinging blow that sent her reeling. She collapsed onto Gorse Fur, who turned and met her with another swipe.

Thunder's hind legs trembled beneath him as he hit out at the tabby. His muscles burned until, panting, he lost his balance and collapsed onto all fours. The tabby dropped heavily onto his shoulders, and agony scorched through Thunder's pelt as claws dug into the wounds Snake had left. Thunder struggled, stumbling as Gray Wing tugged the tabby sharply away.

Flanks heaving, he watched Gray Wing wrestle the tabby to the ground, hind paws scrabbling at the rogue's belly. Beyond them, Rainswept Flower fought two toms, snapping at one, then the other as they drove her backward, away from her camp mates to the edge of the clearing.

A yowl from the far side of the battle jerked his attention away. He recognized the agonized shriek.

Wind Runner!

Leaf was pinning her to the ground, drawing back his lips as he prepared to sink his teeth into her spine.

"No!" With a roar, Gorse Fur let go of Petal and pelted for Wind Runner. He charged into Leaf, knocking him away with such force that the thump of the tom's flank on the hard earth sounded over the yowls of rage and pain. Wind Runner leaped to her paws beside Gorse Fur. Together they drove Leaf backward until, eyes bright with panic, he ducked past them and streaked into the heart of battle, his gray-and-white pelt disappearing among his camp mates.

Thunder's mind whirled. How could this end? As he flattened his ears against the shrieking, paws slammed into his side. He staggered, gasping. *Fircone.* He recognized the tom's mottled brown-and-white pelt. Turning to defend himself, he caught Fircone's eye. "This must stop!"

"This is Clear Sky's territory!" Fircone arched his back. "We're just fighting to defend what's ours."

"The hollow belongs to no cat!" Thunder blinked. Fircone

had been one of the cats to beg him to *stop* Clear Sky expanding his borders. Now he was fighting to protect land Clear Sky hadn't even claimed! "You asked me to stop him!"

"Times change." Fircone thrust a paw out, catching Thunder's ear.

Thunder ducked away as he felt the tip tear. What had Clear Sky told these cats to persuade them to fight so bitterly?

Claws snagged his scruff and he fought to stay on his paws as Fircone hauled him sideways.

Black fur streaked past his vision. Tall Shadow crashed between them, shoving Fircone away. The tom's eyes widened in surprise as Tall Shadow leaped on him. Thunder froze, watching Tall Shadow's bristling pelt as she pressed Fircone onto his spine and sliced his belly with thrashing claws. The she-cat trembled with fury as she lashed out.

Fircone shrieked in pain, then fell still.

Tall Shadow leaped away and stared at the tom. Blood streamed from his lifeless body, coloring the earth.

Thunder's mouth felt as dry as the dirt. He'd told Lightning Tail they would fight to the death. The idea had sent courage surging beneath his pelt. Was *this* what courage did? He stared at Fircone's corpse. The rogue would never taste prey scent again or feel the sun on his back or the wind in his fur. "You killed him."

"So?" Tall Shadow's gaze raked the battling cats. "Clear Sky's cats are showing no mercy. We must fight or die."

Rainswept Flower was on her back, a tabby rogue pinning her shoulders to the ground while a tortoiseshell scraped at her flank. Thunder prepared to leap, but Acorn Fur was already racing toward her camp mate. She charged the tabby, bowling him over. Rainswept Flower leaped to her paws and, hissing with rage, began swiping at the tortoiseshell.

Lightning Tail rolled, shrieking, across the clearing. Thorn had him in a badger-grip, pulling his head backward and exposing his throat. His hind paws hacked lumps from Lightning Tail's pelt. Yowling, Lightning Tail twisted in Thorn's grip and, fast as a snake, sank his teeth into the rogue's shoulder with a snarl.

As Thorn screeched and let go, Frost's yowl rang across the clearing.

Thunder turned. The white tom was pressed against the trunk of an oak. Blood splashed the bark as Snake slashed at Frost's muzzle. Frost ducked, hissing, and dived for Snake's hind leg. His blue eyes flashed in the gloom as he tugged Snake's leg from under him. Snatching his pelt with a forepaw, he hooked him onto his spine. Snake tried to roll away, but Frost lunged for his throat.

Thunder blinked. *Let him go!* None of this made sense. Did they need to kill each other? For what? A shriek jerked him from his thoughts. Snake had knocked Frost onto his side. He sliced the white tom's throat with a flailing paw. Frost's scruff darkened in the moonlight as blood spread through his fur. Groaning, he twitched, then fell limp.

Thunder's heart dropped like stone, heavy in his chest. Tall Shadow was right. *We must fight or die.*

"Mouseheart!" Falling Feather chased Acorn Fur, lip

curled and eyes shining with hate. She streaked past Thunder and leaped for the young cat, hauling her onto her side.

Dread hollowed Thunder's belly. He wasn't going to watch another tribe mate die. "Get off her!" He leaped for Falling Feather and sank his claws into her pelt. As he dragged her off Acorn Fur, she twisted, thrusting her muzzle forward to nip at his throat. But Thunder was quicker, heaving her onto her belly and scraping his hind claws along her spine.

Clear Sky's pale gray pelt caught his eye as it flashed toward Rainswept Flower a tail-length away. Clear Sky hit her like a swooping eagle, sending her reeling.

Thunder stiffened, holding Falling Feather firmly. He ignored her snarls as she wriggled beneath him, his gaze fixed on Clear Sky.

"Is this worth it?" he heard Clear Sky hiss at Rainswept Flower.

Scrambling to her paws, she faced him. "What do you mean?"

Clear Sky flattened his ears menacingly. "Are you ready to die just to stop me from making borders?"

Rainswept Flower curled her lip. "You'll keep stealing land as long as we let you."

"*Stealing* land?" Clear Sky's mew trembled with rage. "I'm just making sure my cats never starve."

Rainswept Flower's gaze flitted around the lush slopes of the hollow. "How could any cat starve here? There's so much. Wanting more is just *greedy!*"

"How dare you!" With a snarl, Clear Sky leaped for her,

grabbing her throat between his jaws. Her paws flailed desperately, lashing out at thin air as he shook her like prey. Then she hung still.

Clear Sky dropped her, gazing coldly at her lifeless body. "You never understood. I'm not greedy. I'm just *strong.*"

The whole forest seemed to fall silent around Thunder. All he could hear was rage pounding in his ears. He let Falling Feather go. She scrambled from beneath him and backed away, hissing. He barely heard her over his chaotic, fighting thoughts.

Clear Sky was *glad* he'd killed another cat. *I'm not greedy. I'm just strong.* He'd rejected Jagged Peak and thrown Frost out of his territory because he thought they were weak. *You're wrong!* Frost had given his life defending his camp mates. Jagged Peak was guarding kits and Thunder knew he would fight to the death to protect them.

A growl rumbled in Thunder's throat. Clear Sky had only ever caused misery. He'd driven away any cat who had ever loved him. Thunder stalked toward his father, his belly burning.

"You killed her!" Dark fur barged past Thunder as Gray Wing leaped for Clear Sky. "You killed Rainswept Flower!" He swiped his brother viciously across the muzzle.

Clear Sky staggered back, shaking his head, before turning to face his littermate. His eyes were as cold as stars. "If I hadn't, some other cat would have."

With a roar, Gray Wing leaped for him.

Clear Sky ducked, rolling sideways, but Gray Wing was

ready, as though it was a move he knew well. He turned as he landed and slashed at his brother's cheek. Clear Sky hissed, taking the blow without flinching. The fur on his spine spiked into a ridge. Tail lashing, ears flat, he lunged forward.

Gray Wing tried to leap clear of the attack, but Clear Sky grabbed his hind paw as he skidded beneath his belly.

Thunder felt like he was watching a fight rehearsed for moons. *They play fought as kits.* He narrowed his eyes. They knew each other's moves better than any cat. But now they weren't playing. Now they were out for blood.

Clear Sky flicked Gray Wing's hind paws from beneath him. Gray Wing landed on his flank with a grunt.

Clear Sky was on him in a moment, pressing his cheek to the ground with a wide-stretched paw. "Why do you always have to challenge me?" he demanded. "You should have just let me make my boundaries as I wanted! Instead, you bring me war." He pressed harder, drool hanging from his lips.

"You've betrayed the cats who were once your kin," Gray Wing grunted, his mew muffled. He spat earth from his mouth. "The cats who traveled here with you from the mountains. Is that what you wanted?" His words turned into a groan as Clear Sky pressed harder, but Gray Wing went on. "Is *this* why we left the mountains? To kill each other?" Gasping with effort, he pushed his shoulders up. Clear Sky stumbled, unbalanced, and Gray Wing scrambled to his paws.

"I'm glad Storm is dead," Gray Wing hissed. "She would never have wanted to see this!"

Clear Sky's gaze darkened. "Don't mention her name!" He

hurled himself, hissing, at Gray Wing.

Thunder rushed forward, but claws grasped his tail. He spun around. Falling Feather was staring at him, her eyes gleaming with malice. "We've not finished," she snarled, hurling herself at him.

Thunder staggered back, shocked by the force of her attack. His mind was whirling as he fell. "But Gray Wing!" He landed with a thump on his back and felt claws curling into his chest. "You traveled from the mountains with him—you can't let him be killed by Clear Sky!"

Falling Feather's muzzle was a whisker from his. He saw her eyes narrow and felt her hot breath as claws raked deep across his belly.

Pain spiraled into panic as he felt blood well where she'd struck. *She's ripped out my belly!* As terror rose in his throat, green eyes glinted beside him. Black fur brushed across his face. The strong scent of Jackdaw's Cry filled his nose.

Falling Feather yowled as the black tom knocked her sprawling onto the ground.

Gasping, Thunder scrambled to his paws and found himself facing Leaf.

The rogue growled at him as Jackdaw's Cry and Falling Feather rolled away, snarling. "I'll finish you," he hissed.

Fury roared louder in Thunder's ears. Falling Feather and Jackdaw's Cry were littermates, just like Gray Wing and Clear Sky! This had to stop. He lashed out at Leaf. "Get out of my way!"

Leaf blocked him, slamming his paws down onto Thunder's

shoulders. Growling, Thunder shrugged off Leaf and headed toward Gray Wing.

Claws dug into his flanks.

"Get off, Leaf," he snarled as the tom attacked again.

"Never!"

Thunder turned and lashed out. Leaf gasped as claws raked his throat, his fur and flesh ripping, blood spurting from the wound like water, turning to a glistening pool on the ground.

Leaf stared at him, eyes glazing with shock, then dropped to his belly.

Thunder froze. *What have I done?* He was trying to *stop* the killing. "Dappled Pelt! Help him!" he cried desperately to his camp mate. She knew how to heal.

The tortoiseshell looked up. Blood stained her muzzle. At her paws, a panting rogue clawed weakly at her. She struggled free and raced around the battling cats. Crouching beside Leaf, she sniffed his wound. "It's okay. This is bleeding that will stop." She pushed Leaf onto his side and pressed her paws against his neck.

Shaking with relief, Thunder started to turn back to Gray Wing.

"No!" Falling Feather's horrified yowl caught his ear. He glanced sideways to see Jackdaw's Cry bite hard into his sister's spine. She jerked, flinging out her paws, then slumped onto her belly. Thunder recognized the prey-look of death. He stared at Jackdaw's Cry. The tom's black pelt was slick with blood. He staggered, eyes glazing, then collapsed lifeless onto his sister's body.

Thunder staggered as grief sliced though him. *They killed each other!*

"Clear Sky! Don't!" Acorn Fur's panicked yowl jerked him back from despair.

Clear Sky stood over Gray Wing. "Just give in!"

Gray Wing lay on the ground, gasping for breath. His flanks heaved desperately as he stared up at his littermate. "Never." He aimed a weak blow at his brother's muzzle, but it missed clumsily.

"*Give in!*" Clear Sky growled threateningly. He lifted a paw. Thunder froze.

Gray Wing pushed himself onto his paws, his legs trembling. "Kill me," he rasped at Clear Sky. "Kill me and live with the memory. Then tell the stars that you *won*."

Clear Sky held his gaze. "Don't make me do this, brother." His mew quivered. "All I want is for every cat to be safe. To have borders to protect us and make sure we have prey."

Gray Wing staggered closer. "You want to tell every cat what to do," he wheezed. "You always have and you always will. You're so greedy for power, you'll kill your own littermate to get it."

Clear Sky let his paw drop and turned away. "I can't . . ." His gaze flitted over the bodies littering the clearing. Cats fought on weakly, staggering more unsteadily with every blow.

"Stop!" Clear Sky yowled. "This battle is over."

CHAPTER 21

❧

A voice buzzed in Clear Sky's mind, blocking everything else out. *You're weak. You don't deserve to lead other cats. You can't even kill.*

"Clear Sky?" Petal was staring at him.

Clear Sky returned her gaze numbly. "Just go," he growled.

Snake cocked his head, eyes clouding with confusion. "It's over?"

"Who won?" Nettle padded toward his leader.

Clear Sky hissed at him. "*No cat won!*"

Nettle glanced at Petal uncertainly. "Now what?"

She shrugged. "I guess we go back to camp." She turned and headed for the slope.

Clear Sky hardly heard her. He was watching Thunder pick his way between the bodies.

"What would Stoneteller say?" The young tom stared hollow-eyed at the fallen cats, stiffening as his gaze fell on an orange pelt, sticky with blood. "Hawk Swoop?" He stopped, nudging her with his muzzle. "You can't be dead. . . . How can you be dead?"

Lightning Tail raced to Thunder's side, while Acorn Fur hung back, her eyes brimming with grief.

"Hawk Swoop?" Lightning Tail crouched beside his mother, his flanks trembling.

Clear Sky looked away. "They're acting like kits," he muttered.

"They *are* kits." Gray Wing's mew sounded beside him. His brother had staggered to his side and was staring at Thunder and Lightning Tail. "They're *her* kits."

"Thunder is *Storm's* kit," Clear Sky snapped.

"But Hawk Swoop was the cat who raised him," Gray Wing murmured.

Clear Sky's heart twisted. *I did this to my son.* He pushed the thought away and glared at Snake. The rogue was lingering beside Fircone's body. "Why are you still standing there? I said *leave*," he growled sharply. "All of you—get back to camp!"

Snake heaved Fircone over with a paw. "What about the dead?"

"They're not going anywhere," Clear Sky muttered.

Snake padded across the clearing and nosed Dappled Pelt away from Leaf. "We can look after our own."

As Dappled Pelt backed off, Snake helped Leaf to his paws. Taking Leaf's weight against his shoulder, he helped him limp toward the slope.

Dappled Pelt called after them. "Put some spider's web on the wound to stop the bleeding."

Quick Water eyed her warily and followed Snake. Nettle, Dew, and Thorn padded after her, the other rogues at their heels. Their tails dragged over the dry earth, leaving blood in their wake.

"Gray Wing? Are you okay?"

Clear Sky stiffened, his heart quickening, as Shattered Ice padded toward them. He suddenly realized he was alone with the moor cats.

Gray Wing lifted his head, his chest trembling as he struggled for breath, which rattled like dry grass. "I'll be okay," he growled. "I just need to rest."

"I'll get you some coltsfoot." Dappled Pelt hurried across the clearing and began to climb the slope.

"Go with her," Gray Wing told Shattered Ice. His gaze flicked to Lightning Tail. Clear Sky saw that tufts of fur hung from the young tom's pelt, which was matted with blood. "Go back to the hollow and get Cloud Spots to treat your wounds."

Lightning Tail nodded and pulled himself away from Hawk Swoop. Acorn Fur watched him, quivering. He padded slowly past the bodies and touched his nose to her cheek. "Come on." Gently, he began to guide her up the slope.

Tall Shadow crossed the clearing and stopped in front of Gray Wing. "I'm not leaving you with *him*." She shot a look at Clear Sky.

He flinched at the hate in her gaze.

Thunder looked up from Hawk Swoop's body, his eyes glistening in the darkness. "I'm not leaving until she's buried," he growled.

Gray Wing dipped his head.

Wind Runner stepped forward. "Nor me." She glanced around the bodies.

Gorse Fur stood beside her. "Then I'm staying too."

Clear Sky stared at him bleakly. "What for?"

Wind Runner answered. "We will sit with our camp mates while there is warmth in their bodies," she growled. "We owe them that much."

Clear Sky swallowed. This battle was supposed to prove that he could decide his own borders, and take as much territory as his cats needed to survive. But it hadn't proven a thing, except that the moor cats were as willing to fight to the death as the forest cats. He watched Thunder rest his chin on Hawk Swoop's flank. Then he spotted Falling Feather's body; Jackdaw's Cry was slumped across it. He'd known these cats since kithood. He'd traveled from the mountains with them. Had they really come here only to die?

A leaf drifted down and landed on Rainswept Flower's body. *Did I kill you?* Clear Sky's thoughts blurred as he tried to remember the battle. Rage had pulsed through him so fiercely, it felt like another cat had been fighting, not him. Then he had come face to face with Gray Wing. *He was at my mercy. And I couldn't kill him.*

Clear Sky swayed on his paws, dizzy with confusion.

Ferns swished near the top of the hollow. He jerked up his gaze. Was Dappled Pelt back already? The fronds rippled as a pelt moved through them. Clear Sky narrowed his eyes, glancing at Gray Wing. "Who's coming?"

Gray Wing lifted his head numbly. His nosed twitched. "River Ripple."

Clouds still covered the moon and shadow gripped the

hollow but, as the long-furred tom stepped into the clearing, Clear Sky recognized his silver pelt. "What are you doing here?" he asked gruffly. This was none of the rogue's business.

River Ripple glanced around the bodies. "I watched the battle."

Thunder stared at the rogue. "And you didn't try to help?"

"Who would I have helped?" Sadness glistened in River Ripple's eyes as he leaned down to sniff Fircone's body. "This battle was not mine." He turned to Clear Sky, his gaze sharpening. "Why did you leave the mountains? Did you need something to fight over so badly? Before you came, we hunted and slept and lay in the sun. We fought over prey, but no cat ever killed another." He blinked. "You brought death here."

Clear Sky met his gaze stubbornly, trying to ignore the shame that burned beneath his pelt. "This wasn't my fault," he insisted. "I just wanted to make sure there was enough prey for every cat."

River Ripple glanced down at Fircone's body. "There'll be plenty now," he muttered dryly.

Fur brushed the ground beside Clear Sky. Gray Wing had dropped into a crouch. His breath was hoarse, thickening his mew as he spoke. "We let it go too far."

Tall Shadow growled. "There never would have been a battle if Clear Sky hadn't started setting borders."

River Ripple dipped his head. "It's done now."

"What next?" Wind Runner lifted her chin. "I'll fight

again if that's what it takes to make the moor safe for my kits."

Gorse Fur looked at her, his ear twitching. "You fought well, but the moor isn't worth it. We can take the kits somewhere else."

"Never." Wind Runner glared at her mate. "The moor is our home now."

Clear Sky narrowed his eyes. "And the forest is *mine*," he snapped. "I was just fighting to defend it."

Wind Runner jerked around to stare at him. "You were fighting to take *our* land too. You're greedy."

"No." Gray Wing blinked. "Clear Sky was never greedy. In the mountains he gave his food up for Fluttering Bird. No cat changes *that* much."

Clear Sky stared at Gray Wing, surprised.

Gray Wing returned his gaze. "Why can't we live side by side, in peace?"

As he spoke the wind lifted. The clouds cleared from the moon and starlight drenched the clearing, sparkling on the pelts of the fallen cats, turning them silver.

Clear Sky stiffened as he saw something else move on the slope. *Who is it now?* He strained to see over the ferns and caught sight of a pair of eyes.

His breath caught in his throat.

A cat was heading into the hollow. She stared at him, her gentle gaze so familiar that it broke his heart to return it.

It can't be!

She padded into the clearing, her silver pelt sleek in the moonlight.

She's dead.

Clear Sky's fur prickled along his spine. "Storm? Is that you?"

CHAPTER 22

Gray Wing stared at his brother. How could it be Storm? *I saw her die.* Heart racing, he followed Clear Sky's gaze.

It *was* Storm.

She stood beyond the littered bodies, her silver pelt seeming to sparkle as though the stars were woven through her fur.

He struggled to his paws, his chest tightening until it hurt to breathe.

"What's happening?"

Gray Wing jerked back as Thunder leaped up with a wail of terror. The young tom was staring at Hawk Swoop's limp body as a glittering, silvery shape rose from it and drifted around him.

"Hawk Swoop?" Thunder gasped, eyes wide. "Are you . . . *alive?*"

She purred. "No, my dear Thunder. But don't grieve. I will never truly leave you."

As she spoke, more spirits rose, glittering, from the other broken bodies.

Gray Wing swallowed, fear spiraling through his belly as he gasped for breath. *What's happening?* He glanced down at his paws, half expecting to see his own fur sparkle with starlight. *Am I dying?*

Gray Wing reasoned with himself. Thunder wasn't dying. Nor were Clear Sky and Wind Runner—he could tell by their bristling fur. Around them, Gorse Fur backed away, while River Ripple was shaking his head as if to clear his thoughts.

Tall Shadow padded forward, muzzle stretched, her nose twitching. "Rainswept Flower?"

"Hello, Tall Shadow." The brown tabby she-cat faced her camp mate, eyes bright, as she stepped away from her body. There was no wound at her throat, and no blood matting her pelt.

The spirit-cats did not carry the wounds that had killed them. Their pelts were sleek and thick. Frost's white pelt shone brighter than in life. Fircone, Falling Feather, and Jackdaw's Cry gazed about themselves, as if trying to figure out where they were and what had happened to them.

"Falling Feather." Jackdaw's Cry stared at his sister, his round eyes glistening with grief. "I'm sorry."

She padded forward and touched her muzzle to his. "I forgive you. I hope you forgive me, too. . . ."

Thunder picked his way past the bodies, his gaze flitting around the spirit-cats. He stopped beside Gray Wing and pressed against him, trembling. "What's happening?"

"I don't know," Gray Wing whispered, unable to drag his gaze from the spirit-cats.

"Stoneteller would know," Clear Sky whispered.

"But Stoneteller isn't here." Gray Wing fought panic. This

didn't make sense. He stiffened as he saw more cats appear on the slope.

Bright Stream!

Shaded Moss, Fox, and Moon Shadow padded into the clearing after her. Every cat who had died since they'd left the mountains. His mind whirled until a single thought made him gasp. "Pebble Heart's dream!"

Thunder moved beside him. "Did he know this would happen?"

"He knew *something* would happen," Gray Wing murmured. "He just couldn't put it into words. This must be it." As he spoke, a familiar pelt appeared from beneath the great rock. A tortoiseshell crossed the clearing toward him. His heart rose like a bird. "Turtle Tail!"

A kit scampered ahead of her.

"Emberkit?" He reached down his head to meet the tiny tom as it skidded to a halt in front of him.

"Hi, Gray Wing." The kit glanced around the hollow. "Where's Wind Runner?"

"I'm here!" The lithe she-cat was already bounding across the clearing. Scrambling to a stop, she stared at her kit. "You're safe!"

The kit purred. "I have Turtle Tail."

Wind Runner purred back, sniffing Emberkit's starry pelt.

Turtle Tail lifted her chin. Her eyes sparkled with amusement as she gazed at Gray Wing. "Aren't you going to say hello?"

Gray Wing fumbled for words. He could hardly believe

how well she looked—plump and sleek, her tortoiseshell markings more beautiful than ever. Was she *really* here, or was he dreaming? The tightness in his chest began to loosen. He drew in a deep gulp of air. "I never thought I'd see you again."

Thunder pushed past him. "I'm sorry we left you in Twolegplace, Turtle Tail. We should have given you a proper burial."

Turtle Tail dipped her head. "You left me among the petals where my kits wouldn't see me. I could ask for no more than that." She turned to River Ripple. "Thank you for helping them. Without you they might never have found Sparrow Fur, Owl Eyes, and Pebble Heart." Her mew lingered on their names, her eyes glistening with loss.

Gray Wing's heart ached—he could not imagine just how much she missed them.

River Ripple dipped his head. "Thunder would have found them," he murmured. "It might have taken a little longer, that's all."

Turtle Tail swung her gaze around the living cats. "You think of River Ripple as just a rogue. But he is more than that. He has an old soul. He walked this land before the mountain cats arrived. He has seen more of life than you think—and what he hasn't seen, he has the power to imagine." She turned back to River Ripple. "Did you imagine our coming?"

River Ripple shook his head. "What cat could?"

Clear Sky stepped forward. "You're a dream! You have to be." He blinked at Gray Wing. "They *can't* be real."

Turtle Tail narrowed her eyes. "You fool, Clear Sky," she hissed. "When did you forget where you came from?" She glanced over her shoulder at Rainswept Flower. "When did you decide it was okay to kill the cats you were raised beside?"

Clear Sky backed away, his tail low. "I only wanted to protect my own."

Turtle Tail showed her teeth. "Killing only ever leads to more killing. Let your mistakes teach you." She whisked her tail. "Leave us now. I must speak with Gray Wing."

Clear Sky backed away. Thunder followed. Wind Runner guided Emberkit toward the edge of the clearing, where Gorse Fur hurried to greet him.

Gray Wing shifted his paws as Turtle Tail stepped closer. He reached out his muzzle, feeling for her warm breath and the musky smell of prey. But the air shimmering around her was cold and scentless. Anxiety stirred in his belly. "Can you stay?" he asked. "The kits will want to see you."

"You're not foolish enough to believe that, Gray Wing," she told him softly.

"But how can I go on without you?" His eyes blurred but he dared not blink in case she disappeared.

Turtle Tail's ear twitched disapprovingly. "Don't be a mouseheart! Of course you can go on. The kits need you. Your camp mates need you."

"But you're here *now*! Can't you stay?" He reached closer, desperate to feel the soft fur of her cheek, but his nose passed through her as though she wasn't there. He drew back, shock sparking through his pelt. *It's too cruel! She's here but she's not!* "It'd be better if you'd never come at all," he growled bitterly.

Turtle Tail's eyes narrowed. "I never thought you were a

selfish cat, Gray Wing. Don't prove me wrong. Don't you realize I'm not here just for you? We came to tell all cats what they must know if they are to survive here."

"What?" Gray Wing pricked his ears.

But Turtle Tail was backing away. Behind her, the spirit-cats gathered, reflecting starlight.

Storm padded forward, her gaze fixed on Clear Sky.

Clear Sky moved toward her.

"You can't touch her," Gray Wing warned. He didn't want his brother to suffer as he had. He must know these cats weren't real.

"I don't want to," Clear Sky called back. "I just want to hear what she has to tell us." He faced Storm, chin high. "What message do you bring?"

Gray Wing looked back to Turtle Tail, his belly fur trembling. He wasn't sure if he really wanted to hear what the ghost cat had to say. . . .

CHAPTER 23

✤

Clear Sky forced his paws to stop trembling. Love ached deep in his heart as he gazed into Storm's eyes. How had he ever let her go? She stared at him now, her face shimmering in the moonlight. Her gaze was stern.

"Is this what you planned?" She flicked her tail toward the bodies, keeping her eyes fixed on Clear Sky.

Clear Sky glanced past her. The bodies lay unmoving. Their blood glistened in the moonlight. His mouth dried as he searched for words. Did she think he'd meant for this to happen? "I—I was trying to do the right thing," he mumbled.

"And you didn't guess that this is how it would end?" Storm demanded.

"I followed my instincts." The ground seemed to sway beneath his paws.

Storm narrowed her eyes. "Your *instincts*?" The scorn in her growl pierced his heart like claws.

"I had to protect my cats."

"*Your* cats?"

"I'm their leader. I'm responsible for them."

Storm tipped her head to one side. "And have you protected them?"

Clear Sky tried not to look again at the bodies of his camp mates, but their lifeless pelts seemed to draw his gaze like prey scent. He shuddered, guilt twisting in his belly. "I have not."

"You've been greedy, Clear Sky," Storm murmured. "You wanted power over every cat."

"That's not true!" Clear Sky protested. "I had to make difficult decisions. That took *courage*."

Storm said nothing. She just stared at him.

"You must understand," Clear Sky wailed.

Slowly, Storm turned and gazed at Rainswept Flower's battered body. Blood pooled around her muzzle. "Was killing her *courageous*?"

Clear Sky stared desperately at Thunder and Gray Wing. They gazed back in silence, while Rainswept Flower's spirit watched him with accusing eyes. Would no cat defend him? "I didn't want to see any cat starve. I was scared my heart would break if I ever had to see another cat die like Fluttering Bird."

"*Fear* is what drove you." There was relief in Storm's mew. She turned back to him, her gaze softening suddenly. "Fear is a powerful instinct that only the strongest cat can resist. But now you see there's no need to be afraid. We have shown that death is nothing for you to fear. It's not the end."

Clear Sky stared at her, hope lifting in his chest. Could it be true? As he opened his mouth to beg her to tell him, paw steps thrummed toward the clearing.

Cloud Spots scrambled to a halt at the edge. He held a wad of green leaves in his mouth. He dropped them and stared across the bodies, his gaze fixing on Gray Wing. "Dappled Pelt told me you needed coltsfoot." He spoke blankly, his eyes widening as his gaze flicked back to the bloodstained bodies, and then the starry pelts of the spirit-cats. "What's happening?"

Storm glanced at him. "We have brought a message."

Cloud Spots stared at her, disbelief clouding his gaze. "Message?" he echoed hoarsely.

Storm turned to Thunder. "My dear son. I could not be more proud of the cat you've become. Do *you* know why we've come here?"

Thunder narrowed his eyes, puzzled. "To show us that death is not the end."

"No." Storm rolled her eyes. "You must know that already. You've heard tales of Stoneteller, the cat who learned to speak to the ancients. Did you think she *imagined* the cats who had gone before her?"

"Then why *are* you here?" Thunder asked.

"Do you remember what I told you?" Storm asked gently.

Thunder frowned as though trying to remember. "That I would know when to make things right."

Storm purred approvingly. "*Now* is the time."

"Now?" Thunder lifted his muzzle. "What do I have to do?"

"Can't you guess?" Storm glanced again at the bodies. "After all this death, don't you know?"

"Tall Shadow!"

Clear Sky stiffened as another spirit-cat stepped forward. Tall Shadow stretched her muzzle toward it, sniffing. "Shaded Moss!" There was joy in her mew as she greeted the older cat.

Shaded Moss returned her gaze. "Did I die in vain?"

"What do you mean?" Tall Shadow frowned.

"I thought you could lead the cats when I'd gone." The spirit tom's star-specked gaze darkened. "But where did you lead them? To *this*?"

Tall Shadow backed away, hackles lifting. "I had no choice!"

Shaded Moss nodded toward Fircone's body. "You *had* to kill him?"

"He was going to kill Thunder!"

"How do you know?" Shaded Moss challenged. "And who are you to decide whose life is more important?"

Tall Shadow glared at him. "I had no choice," she repeated fiercely.

"All cats have a choice," Shaded Moss countered. "A cat who follows only one path, never stopping to question where it leads, is as dumb as the prey she hunts."

Fircone's spirit shimmered closer, stopping in front of Gorse Fur. "We hunted as rogues," he purred. "Do you remember?"

"Of course." Gorse Fur lifted his chin.

Fircone nodded to Wind Runner. "You were always faster than us both."

Emberkit was still at her paws. "Were you fast?" He stared up at her with round eyes.

"As the breeze," Wind Runner told him proudly.

"But you're happy now," Fircone meowed. "Being part of a group."

"Yes." Wind Runner met his gaze. "We are stronger with allies. Our kits are safer."

Storm purred suddenly. "Have you guessed our message yet?" As Wind Runner gazed blankly back, she turned to River Ripple. "What about you? Do you know?"

River Ripple sat down, curling his tail across his paws. "I think so," he mewed softly.

Clear Sky watched him closely, frustration pricking in his pelt. How did he know what they didn't? He was just a rogue!

"The fighting must end," River Ripple mewed. "It has torn us apart and—"

Clear Sky thrust his muzzle toward him. "How dare you come here, acting like one of us? This has nothing to do with you. You don't belong!"

Storm jerked around and glared at him.

Clear Sky stiffened, shocked at the fury burning in her gaze.

"Stop arguing!" she spat. "For once in your life, stop telling every cat who *belongs* and who doesn't. *You* don't get to decide!" Her pelt bristled. "Why do you think I left the forest?" Her gaze flashed toward Gray Wing. "You came here from the mountains and brought nothing but death. This is your chance to make amends. *All* of you!"

Clear Sky shifted his paws. Shame washed over him. She was right. If they'd stayed in the mountains they'd have starved. But the rogues that had died here today would still be alive. *Storm* would still be alive. As his thoughts began to whirl, shadows swept the clearing. Clear Sky looked up. Between the rustling branches of the oak, he saw a cloud cross the moon. Beside it, bright light flared.

A falling star!

It streaked across the crow-black night.

Hope flashed through Clear Sky's pelt. He glanced at Gray Wing. His brother's eyes were glowing, fixed on the falling star. Thunder was watching it too.

"It's a sign." Cloud Spots lifted his tail as he watched its glittering trail.

"You all live under the same stars," Storm mewed.

Fircone tipped his head. "And a single moon shines onto all your nests."

Shaded Moss gazed fondly at Tall Shadow. "We came to tell you only one thing," he purred. "Unite or die."

"Don't let these deaths be wasted," Storm added. "This must never happen again."

Clear Sky gazed deep into her eyes. His heart ached with understanding. "We'll unite," he promised. "From now on, we live as one."

Thunder whipped around, staring at his father. "How? Gray Wing could never live beneath trees. And you hate the moor. It's impossible."

"You'll find a way." Storm headed toward the slope, her shimmering fur fading as she neared it.

Fircone's spirit returned to his body and curled down into it as though returning to his nest.

Rainswept Flower dipped her head to Tall Shadow. "Unite or die," she breathed.

One by one, the spirit-cats began to pad away.

Wind Runner's eyes glistened with sadness as Emberkit trotted after Turtle Tail.

"Good-bye, Gray Wing," Turtle Tail called fondly over her shoulder as she disappeared into the ferns, Emberkit at her heels.

Grief ripped through Clear Sky. He could see the ferns through Storm's vanishing pelt. "Don't go. . . ."

She glanced back at him, her gaze growing pale. "Return to the four trees next full moon," she told him. "Be ready."

Clear Sky swallowed. *For what?*

A breeze swept through the hollow and, like mist, the spirit-cats disappeared.

Clear Sky drew in a deep breath, the tang of blood bathing his tongue once more. He blinked at the dead bodies, lying as still as stones, in the clearing. The wind ruffled his fur as it strengthened, and he wrinkled his nose as he smelled rain. The cloud that had covered the moon was thickening, rolling in from the moor.

As the first drop of rain touched his pelt, he watched Gray Wing weave his way between the bodies. Tall Shadow followed him, her tail drooping as her gaze slid mournfully over her fallen camp mates.

Uncertainty suddenly pricked in Clear Sky's paws. "What did we just see?" he called.

Gray Wing turned to look at him. "I'm . . . not sure."

Rain began to thrum the hard earth.

River Ripple padded to the great rock and settled in its shadow, flattening his ears against the squall. "Did the dead walk among you in the mountains?"

Tall Shadow shook her head. "Stoneteller shared with our ancestors. We never saw them."

"Perhaps you never needed to," River Ripple murmured.

"Because you never died like this before." Thunder padded heavily to Hawk Swoop's body and, nudging it with his nose, moved her so that she looked as though she were curled asleep. Gently, he lifted her tail and draped it over her muzzle. Then he settled beside her and, as the rain drenched his pelt, pressed his flank to hers.

"What do we do now?" Clear Sky called through the downpour.

"I don't know." Wind Runner nodded toward the bodies as the rain washed the blood from their pelts. "Whatever we decide, we have been given hope. We know that we can make a better future than this."

"We can." Tall Shadow shook out her sodden fur. "But first, we must bury the dead."

DAWN OF THE CLANS

WARRIORS

THE FIRST BATTLE

BONUS SCENE!

Read on to see how Wind met Gorse. . . .

PROLOGUE

Wind glanced across the river toward the reed marshes and licked her lips. "Are you sure we couldn't share some of those cats' fresh-kill?"

Her companion, Branch, bristled. "You want to eat *fish*?"

"I'm so hungry I'd eat anything." The sharp breeze whipping across the moor sliced through Wind's fur. Snow clouds were piling at the moortop. Flakes whisked around her. Soon they would thicken and swallow the whole hillside, then wrap the forest in white.

"Don't you trust me to find us food?" Branch huffed.

"We've been hunting all day." Wind's belly ached with hunger. The sudden chill had driven the moor prey underground. The group of cats who lived near the river had said that they had hunted fish before the river froze. But Branch had refused their kind offer to share their prey.

Even the sour taste of fish would be better than an empty belly, Wind thought.

"Come on." Branch stalked across the grass, his mottled tabby pelt rippling as snowflakes caught in his fur. Wind knew that it wasn't only the snow that was ruffling his pelt; she'd upset him. Branch had looked after her since her mother and sister had died of sickness in the last cold season. She knew that he felt responsible for her. He wanted to be the only one who hunted for her; why else would he have refused the fish?

Guiltily, she hurried after him. She and Branch would hunt together and make camp together. Perhaps, one day, they would even have kits together. *He will always take care of me.* Her heart felt warmed by the thought.

As she fell into step beside him, an ugly scent touched her nose. "Wait!" She stopped. "I smell dog."

Branch swished his tail. "It's a long way off," he grunted. "The breeze is carrying the scent, that's all."

Wind opened her mouth. Snowflakes speckled her tongue and froze the roof of her mouth until she wasn't sure *what* she could taste. Shaking out her fur, she hurried after him.

Branch had halted, his head turning as he scanned the moorside. As Wind stopped beside him, he nodded toward a brown shape bobbing across the grass.

Wind squinted through the snow, her mouth watering as she recognized the scent. *Rabbit!* She dropped into a crouch. Branch signaled with a sharp flick of his tail that he wanted her to stay where she was. They'd used this hunting technique before. She watched Branch trace a wide arc up and around the rabbit, stalking it from the far side.

The rabbit paused and sniffed the air, blinking through the snow, then bent to nibble at the grass.

Wind forced her paws to stay still. Her empty belly growled again as Branch crept closer. The rabbit would see him at any moment and then rush toward *her*. She huddled lower in the grass so that her brown pelt looked like no more than a shadow against the hillside.

The rabbit's head jerked up, its eyes widening as it spotted Branch. Turning, it dashed away from him.

Wind stiffened with excitement, fixing her gaze on the rabbit as it fled toward her. Another few tail-lengths and she would pounce.

Suddenly the rabbit froze. Wind blinked with surprise. What was it doing? Branch was closing in on it. *Come on!* As Wind willed it closer, she saw Branch slither to a halt. *What's wrong with you both?* Wind watched their gazes dart fearfully upslope. *What are you staring at?*

She spun around just in time to see snarling jaws lunge at her.

Dog!

Terror pulsed through her body, then pain as teeth clamped around her hind leg. Digging her claws into the grass, she tore out clumps of earth as the dog hauled her backward.

Her mind reeled, fear draining from her as she felt herself being shaken like fresh-kill. Numbness infused every hair on her pelt until she felt like she was watching from very far away. This must be what it was like for captured prey. *Am I dead?* Through her haze of shock, she heard Branch yowl. Then the dog let her go. She slumped onto the grass, vaguely aware of shrieking and barking beside her. Turning her head stiffly, she saw Branch clinging to the dog's shoulders, his forepaws slashing at its face. Yelping in agony, the dog shook Branch off and fled up the hillside.

"Wind?" Branch was standing over her, panting. "Are you okay?"

She gazed at him helplessly, feeling the distant throb of pain. "My hind leg," she croaked.

Branch turned to sniff it. "It's a bad bite. We have to get you somewhere sheltered. Can you walk?"

"I'll try." Dazed, Wind struggled onto her three good legs. She felt Branch's shoulder press into hers and leaned against it, grateful for his support. Dragging her hind leg, she began to limp beside him. Her pain was spiraling, growing sharper and hotter until she could hardly see the moor. Snow whipped her muzzle, but it did nothing to cool the agony burning through her body.

"We're nearly there," Branch puffed, guiding her out of the snow between stiff bushes of heather. Wind groaned with pain as the bristly branches scraped her wounded leg.

"Here." Branch stopped and let her slide gently onto cold, peaty earth.

Wind collapsed, panting. "How bad is the wound?" She didn't have the strength to look.

Branch's gaze fixed on hers, glittering with fear.

Her heart quickened. "Am I going to die?"

"I'll find some moss to make you more comfortable." He turned away and disappeared through the heather.

Wind let her head drop onto her paws, her flank trembling as she felt the air strangely warm around her—as though the heat of her own body were filling the hollow. And yet she was still shivering, cold reaching her bones. She closed her eyes; perhaps if she slept, she'd heal more quickly. Her thoughts whirled. She heard Branch's yowl as she saw the big dog chasing the rabbit. The images swirled and jumbled as she slid into unconsciousness.

She woke to the feeling of soft moss pressed around her. Someone had laid sprigs of heather over her so that she was warmly cocooned in a nest. "Branch?" She lifted her head weakly, relieved as she saw his eyes shining through the gloom. The sun must have set; pale moonlight filtered into the gloomy den.

"How do you feel?" Branch blinked at her slowly.

Wind leaned toward him, puzzled as he seemed to flinch away. "My leg hurts." The pain was throbbing now, as though invisible jaws gnawed at her wound.

"Are you hungry?" Branch blinked again.

Wind shook her head.

"You'll need food anyway," Branch told her. "You should keep your strength up."

Wind stared at him. There was hardness in his mew. Was he angry with her? She pushed the thought away. *He's just frightened.* "I'll be okay," she reassured him. "I can hunt with you after I've rested."

Branch straightened. "I'll fetch you food now."

Before Wind could reply, he had pushed his way through the heather, the tip of his tail snaking out of sight.

She laid her head on her paws and closed her eyes, relieved to be warm. She was lucky to have Branch. He'd bring her food until she was well enough to hunt for herself. He'd always looked after her. Giving in, she let pain swallow her and slid into darkness.

When she woke, there was no sign of the mottled tom.

Pale sunlight showed through the heather roof of the den. How long had he been gone? Her wounded leg stuck out stiffly, the fur dark and spiked where blood had dried. Then she spotted the carcass of a young rabbit lying beside her. Branch must have brought it. But where was he?

Pushing herself awkwardly up onto her forepaws, she stretched her muzzle forward and dragged the rabbit closer. She had no appetite, but Branch's words rang in her ears. *You should keep your strength up.* She forced herself to tear off a piece of flesh and swallow it, her belly heaving as she did. She swallowed two more mouthfuls before collapsing.

She stared at the gap in the heather where Branch had disappeared. Had the dog attacked him too? A chill reached through her fur and she began to shiver. She could feel her breath hot on her paws. She must have a fever. *Come back, Branch. I need you.*

Wind lost track of the days. The rabbit carcass rotted beside her, but gradually she felt the pain in her leg loosen its grip and her fever subside. Branch had still not returned, and when Wind woke one morning, feeling brighter than she had since the dog attack, she forced herself to her paws. *I must find him.*

She shook the twigs and moss from her pelt, her paws trembling as she nosed her way through the heather, relieved to get away from the stench of sickness and death.

Her belly twisted with hunger. She was thirsty too and lapped greedily at the snow that lay on the ground. When she'd had enough, she scanned the hillside for paw tracks. The snow lay smooth and undisturbed; the sky was bright and blue above. Stiffly she struggled through the deep snow, her injured leg dragging behind. It was still too painful to put weight on. Limping around the wide swath of heather, she made her way back to the part of the slope where the dog had attacked. She sniffed cautiously.

There was no scent of dog on the crisp, icy air. Nor of Branch.

Neither of them had been here for days.

She halted, her heart aching. *Did Branch leave me to die?*
He wouldn't.

But she remembered the hardness in his mew and the distant way he'd stared at her.

Had he left her the rabbit as a parting gift?

The thought stung. She tried to push it away. But doubt dragged like a stone in her belly. Every harsh glance and sharp word Branch had ever flashed at her burned suddenly like a fresh wound. She knew how he relished the freedom of the moor. Why would he want to be tied down with a lame companion?

Wind swayed on her paws. The glare of the snow seemed too bright to bear.

I'm alone! Fear broke over her like a wave of icy water.

No! She lifted her chin. Her leg would heal, and she could fend for herself. *I can hunt, I can fight—I can survive!*

She ignored the grief tearing at her heart. That would heal too. No cat would ever abandon her again, because she wouldn't be dumb enough to trust again. Squaring her shoulders, she limped across the moor, crouching low against the freezing wind. Her thoughts narrowed to a single goal—*find something to eat.*

CHAPTER 1

❧

Wind raced across the grass, a rabbit's white tail bobbing ahead of her. Beyond it, the forest stood green against the bright, blue sky. Around her, the heather bloomed, filling the hot air with its sweet scent. It hadn't rained in a moon, and the moor was as dry as old bone. But clouds were rolling in from the mountains, and Wind could feel the air thicken. She looked forward to the coming storm; its cooling rain would soften the grass and nourish the heather.

The rabbit raced as quickly as a bird over the moorside, but it would never outrun her. *I'm as fast as the wind!* She pushed harder against the coarse, dry grass, her injured hind leg healed now and as strong as ever. The rabbit's scent, tainted with fear, bathed her tongue. As she drew near, the rabbit scooted down a burrow. Wind dived after it. Dirt sprayed her muzzle as the rabbit scrabbled to escape into the darkness. Wind hooked her claws into its haunches and dragged it out onto the moor, its squeals still echoing in the tunnel as, with one bite, she killed it.

The rich tang of its blood felt sweet on her tongue, and her belly rumbled with satisfaction. She'd grown strong since the sickness and near-starvation of leaf-bare. Feasting on the rich prey of the moor, she was hardly ever hungry. She wanted to eat as much as she could. There would be another leaf-bare soon enough, and she would face it alone. Hunger couldn't frighten her so long as she ate well during the prey-rich moons.

Wind picked the rabbit up in her jaws and padded toward the holly tree that stood alone on the hillside. Thick gorse bushes crowded at one side, their spikes and narrow leaves sharper than ever, dried by the relentless heat. She dropped the rabbit on the shady earth on the other side, where a hollow among the roots would make a good place to eat. Thunder rumbled in the distance. She glanced up, pleased to see the storm clouds swallowing the blue. Cooling rain would arrive soon.

Licking her lips, she crouched to take a bite.

"Tansy! I'm hungry!" A small mew sounded from beneath the gorse.

"I smell rabbit!" Another mew rang out.

Wind pricked her ears. *Kits?*

"I know, my dears." The soothing purr of a queen touched Wind's ear fur. "I'll hunt soon, when I've got my strength back."

"Hunt *now*!" a mew demanded.

"I can't run fast enough to catch anything yet." The queen sounded apologetic.

"I'll do it then!" The gorse rustled as a tiny gray tom ducked from under its shelter and stomped across the grass.

Wind narrowed her eyes. Rabbit scent was filling her nose.

But she didn't eat. She watched the kit stride across the moor. On the far horizon, lightning flashed against the darkening clouds.

A second kit popped out from beneath the gorse. She was a pale tabby with bright blue eyes. "Frog! Come back! Tansy said you were to stay near her!"

The tom glanced crossly over his shoulder. "If I stay with her, we'll *all* starve. I'll be back once I've caught something."

Wind scrambled to her paws. The moor wasn't safe for such a young kit. She glanced at the sky, checking for hawks. The tiny tom would make an easy meal for a hungry marsh harrier. She called out: "Wait!"

He turned and gaped at her, his pelt bushing. "Who are you?"

Wind dipped her head. "I'm Wind. I live on the moor."

"Frog! Run! Tansy warned us about moor cats!" His sister's mew was sharp with fear.

"I won't hurt him." Wind nodded toward her rabbit. "I have food if you're hungry." Instantly she felt a pang of doubt. Should she give her prey away so easily? Wind was used to looking after herself; she wasn't sure if she wanted to look after other cats.

"See, Willow? I told you I smelled rabbit!" Frog was already padding toward her.

The she-kit stared at Wind with round eyes. "We are very hungry. Tansy's milk has dried up and she's too sick to hunt."

Wind watched Frog sniff the rabbit. "What's wrong with Tansy?" she asked distractedly.

"She got a thorn in her paw," Willow mewed. "I managed to pull it out this morning, but her pad is all red and fat."

"It's probably infected. Now the thorn's out, it should heal—as long as she washes it regularly." Wind nudged Frog away from the rabbit. Perhaps she should just tear off a few strips for them, enough to keep their bellies from rumbling. After all, they weren't *her* kits.

Frog stared at her defiantly. "You *said* we could have it."

Wind prickled crossly. "Not *all* of it."

Willow hurried to her brother's side. "I'm sorry about Frog," she mewed quickly. "He's always been greedy. And it's hard being hungry."

Wind remembered with a jab of grief her first moon after Branch had abandoned her, lying through long, cold nights, too frightened to sleep in case she didn't wake up. She had nearly starved. "You can have it." Leaning down, she grabbed the rabbit between her jaws, then marched toward the gorse bush.

Tansy was squeezing out from under the branches as she approached. Spikes stuck out of the queen's thick gray pelt, and she was holding a forepaw gingerly off the ground.

Wind dropped the rabbit in front of her. "I'm not surprised you get thorns in your paws if you make your nest under a gorse bush." She frowned, irritated that any moor cat could be so mouse-brained.

"I didn't know where else to shelter." Tansy's gaze was on the rabbit, her nose twitching eagerly. "We used to be strays in Twolegplace. I thought the moor would be a safer place to raise my kits."

Wind snorted. "No place is safe for a cat who doesn't know how to look after herself."

Tansy bristled. "I'll learn!"

"I hope so," Wind answered darkly.

Frog and Willow crowded around the rabbit, their tails twitching excitedly.

Wind jerked her nose toward the wide swath of heather coating the moorside. "You should make your den in there. There are more dips and hollows than there are rabbits on the moor. And the heather sprigs make good nests."

"Is that where your nest is?" Tansy asked her.

"I have no nest." Wind flicked her tail. "I have no mate. Or kits. Why would I need a den?" She nudged the rabbit toward Tansy. "Here. Eat this."

"All of it?" Tansy blinked at her, surprised.

Wind shrugged. "I can catch another."

"Please share it with us," Tansy begged. "You caught it, after all."

Wind backed away. It had been so long since she'd shared prey with any cat, she felt more comfortable eating alone. "No, thanks."

Willow looked up from the rabbit. "Why not?"

Frog was already tugging at its fur with his small, sharp teeth.

"I'm a loner," Wind told the kit. "I don't share."

Tansy blinked at her. "But you shared this prey with us."

"I gave it to you." Wind turned away. She didn't want to get involved with these cats. If they wanted to live on the moor, they'd have to learn how to survive just as she had.

"Thank you!"

She heard Tansy's call but didn't look back, heading back across the slope, her eyes scanning the grass for rabbit tracks.

"That was kind of you."

A deep mew took her by surprise. She spun, pelt bristling, and saw a gray-striped tom stalking from the heather. His face was lean and handsome.

Wind narrowed her eyes. "I wasn't being kind. Starving cats attract disease."

The tom glanced at her, but he didn't comment until thunder rumbled over the moortop. "I hope the rain arrives first."

Wind was surprised. *"First?"*

"Before the lightning," the tom explained. "I've seen the moor burn when the heather's as dry as this." He glanced back at the bushes, and Wind noticed for the first time that the tips of their branches had begun turning brown, as though already scorched. "Lightning will start a fire as easily as a careless Twoleg."

Wind carried on walking. She didn't want to waste her time chatting to a stranger—she had prey to find.

Paw steps followed her. "Let me help you catch another rabbit."

Wind didn't turn her head as the tom fell in beside her. "I *prefer* to hunt alone."

"So I've noticed."

She tried to stop her hackles lifting. Had he been *watching* her? "Who are you?"

"I'm Gorse." The tom's mew was friendly. "My mother must have known I'd end up living on the moor when she named me." A purr rumbled in his throat.

"Weren't you born on the moor?" Wind felt a flash of annoyance as she realized Gorse had drawn her into conversation.

"I was raised among the reed beds, beside the river. But I left them a few moons ago. I prefer it up here." He swished his tail. "Plenty of fresh air and no fish."

Wind's whiskers twitched. "Do you hate fish too?"

"I like my prey dry," Gorse rumbled.

Wind's belly tightened. What was she *doing*? Talking to a strange tom! *I'm a loner!* She curled her claws. "I have to hunt now."

"You'll catch something quicker if I help you," Gorse meowed cheerfully.

"I don't *need* help," she snapped, glaring at him.

Gorse dipped his head. "Okay." Flicking the tip of his tail, he headed toward the heather. "See you around."

Wind watched him go, her irritation growing. *Not if I see you first!*

Movement caught her eye. A lapwing was swooping low over the heather, then across the grass. Clouds of midges swarmed ahead of it. The lapwing cut through them and landed on a tussock. Wind's tail twitched eagerly as the bird began to root through the coarse grass. A moment later it plucked out an earthworm.

Wind dropped into a hunting crouch and drew herself forward. She kept her tail still, lifting it above the ground so that
she moved soundlessly over the grass. The lapwing dipped its
beak again, searching for more worms. Wind was only a tail-
length away. Another paw step and she could pounce. Her
heart pounded harder. Why did Gorse think she needed *help*?
What a mouse-brain! She bunched her hind legs beneath her,
preparing to jump.

Lightning flickered at the edge of her vision. A moment
later thunder crashed overhead. The lapwing cried in surprise
and, unfolding its wings, struggled into the air.

Frustration scorched through Wind. She leaped desperately, catching the lapwing's claws with an outstretched paw,
but it flicked itself free and fluttered up, its wings beating the
air as it flew away.

"Mouse dung!" Wind landed with an angry hiss. Why had
she given the rabbit to those cats? They didn't even *belong* on
the moor. Another flash of lightning streaked through the air.
She'd better take cover. The rain would come soon, and no
creature would be dumb enough to stay out in a storm like
this—not even prey.

As she hurried toward the heather, thunder rumbled overhead. Lightning split the air with a deafening crack. A roar
exploded behind her. Wind spun, her pelt bushing. The gorse
beside the holly tree was on fire! As the dry leaves crackled
swiftly into flame, a shriek of terror sounded from beneath
the branches. Wind froze.

The kits!

CHAPTER 2

❧

Wind hared toward the burning gorse. Tansy had already limped
from beneath the bush and was nosing Willow away from the
flames.

The she-kit's eyes were wide with terror. "Frog!"

Wind skidded to a halt beside them, flinching from the
heat. The sound of the fire roared in her ears. "Get away!"
She tried to nudge Tansy and Willow back, but they dug their
claws in deep and stared in horror at the holly tree.

She followed their gaze. Frog was scrambling up the trunk.
With a squeal of panic he reached the lowest branch and disappeared among the prickly leaves.

The flames from the gorse burned harder, sending sparks
flashing up into the holly branches. If the sparks caught, the
holly would blaze like dry heather.

Frog will be burned alive.

"Come down!" Tansy wailed.

Frog stuck his head through the spiky leaves, his eyes wild.
"The fire will burn me!"

Wind forced herself closer to the heat. "If you don't come
down *now*, it'll be too late!"

Frog disappeared, and Wind saw the branches shiver as he climbed higher.

Willow shrieked. "He's climbing *up*, not down!"

"Get back!" Wind ordered Tansy. "Get Willow to safety." She dodged around the flaming gorse and leaped at the holly trunk. Her claws sank deep into the gnarled bark, and she pulled herself upward.

"Stop!" Gorse's cry rang behind her.

She glanced over her shoulder and saw the gray-striped tom staring up at her from beside Tansy.

"You'll be killed!" he yowled.

"I have to save Frog!" She dragged herself higher up the trunk. When she reached the lowest branch, she flung her forepaws over it, hauling herself up.

The heat from the fire grew fiercer. She coughed as smoke engulfed her. "Frog!" she cried desperately. "Where are you?" Her heart pounded in her ears. Her throat was raw with fear. Blindly she reached up and squirmed around the thick branches, climbing higher and higher, the prickly leaves scraping her fur.

As she cleared the worst of the smoke, she scanned the holly, trying to glimpse Frog's gray pelt. Her eyes streamed, stinging like fury, but she blinked away her tears and pulled herself onto the next branch.

A panicked mewl sounded ahead, and she saw a scrap of gray fur near the very end of the branch. "Frog!" She began to pad toward him, the bough creaking beneath her paws.

Suddenly the tree jerked and trembled. Unbalanced, Wind

dug her claws in, her heart lurching. She glanced over her shoulder, panic sparking in her chest.

Gorse!

The gray-striped tom was hauling himself up into the holly, his weight shaking the tree. "Stay where you are!" His gaze fixed on her, glittering with fear. "That branch is too thin. It might break!"

"I have to get to Frog!"

The kit was clinging to the very tip, which dipped under his weight.

"Wait!" Gorse nosed his way through the leaves, wincing, and began to pick his way along a sturdy branch below. "Keep him calm until I get below him," he called up to her. "Make him trust you."

Wind fixed her gaze on the frightened eyes of the kit, forcing her mew to remain calm. "We're going to save you."

Lightning flashed around them. Thunder cracked. Frog squealed with terror.

"You'll be fine!" Wind called through the rising gusts. She dropped onto her belly and pulled herself along the branch, her breath stopping as it began to dip. Halting, she reached a forepaw toward Frog. The kit was trembling. "Gorse is right underneath you."

Frog looked down as Gorse picked his way along the branch below. It seemed thicker, easily holding his weight as he neared the stretch below Frog.

The tree lit up as another crack of lightning split the air. The roar of the burning gorse swelled beneath them. Wind dared not look down to see if it had reached the trunk yet. *Let the wind change,* she pleaded silently. *Make it blow the fire away from the tree!*

"Frog!" Gorse was balancing on his haunches on the branch below, his belly showing as he lifted his forepaws toward the kit. "I'll catch you!"

Wind nodded. "Let yourself drop, Frog," she urged.

"I'll fall right down to the ground!" Frog wailed.

"Gorse will catch you," Wind promised.

"How do *you* know?"

"I just do!" Frustration wormed beneath Wind's pelt. The flames were getting closer. "You can trust him."

"I don't *know* him!" Frog cried.

"You didn't know me until today, but I gave you my rabbit!" Wind argued.

Frog looked at her, his eyes glistening with doubt.

"He'll catch you," Wind promised again. "Just let go."

Her breath stopped in her throat as she saw Frog shift his paws. He was uncurling his claws from the bark. With a squeak, he let go and slithered down from the branch. She jerked her muzzle over the edge in time to see Gorse snatch Frog's falling scruff in his teeth.

The gray-striped tom wobbled as the weight of the kit swung from his jaws. But his claws were dug firmly into the bark, and with a grunt he regained his balance.

Wind slithered down onto the branch below and stared at him. "Now what?" She glanced over her shoulder. The flames were licking the holly trunk. They couldn't get down that way.

Gorse stared back at her. Fear glittered in his gaze as Frog squirmed beneath his chin.

He doesn't know what to do! Wind squared her shoulders. "We'll have to jump down." She glanced toward the earth. It seemed so far away! But if they scrambled down through the branches to the lowest one, the leap to the ground wouldn't be too hard. They just needed to make sure they landed on smooth earth. If they caught a paw on one of the gnarled roots snaking from the ground, they could really hurt themselves.

"Follow me." As Wind hopped down onto the branch below, a gust of wind blew smoke into her face. She screwed up her eyes, digging her claws into the bark to keep her balance. A raindrop splashed onto her back.

Rain! She blinked her eyes open. Water was dripping down through the holly leaves. She peered out and saw the moor darkened by driving rain. Behind her she heard the fire crackle and hiss as the downpour smothered it.

Gorse landed on the branch beside her, hope sparking in his gaze. Did he think the rain would put out the fire right away?

Wind shook her head. "The rain won't save us if the holly catches."

"Put me down!" Frog squealed as he hung from the tom's jaws.

"Not until we're safe," Wind told the kit firmly. She jumped down to the next branch, then the next, until there was nothing between the tree and the ground but air.

Gorse landed nimbly beside her and caught her eye.

"I'll jump down first," she told him. "Wait until I've found my paws. I'll try and steady you as you land with Frog."

Gorse blinked his agreement, and Wind peered over the edge. It was a long way down. Tansy and Willow stood trembling in the rain, their pelts slicked against their thin frames.

Wind took a deep breath, picked out a spot between the roots, and jumped.

Air rushed around her as she fell, but she was ready. As her paws hit the ground, she dropped into a crouch, her belly brushing the earth as she absorbed the landing. Pain spiked through her old injury, but her hind leg held firm.

Beyond the tree, the fire was crackling, trying to outlast the rain. Flames licked the trunk of the holly, climbing the bark like deadly ivy.

Wind looked up at Gorse through the downpour. "Hurry!"

Gorse jumped. Wind stepped back, reaching up as the tom and the kit fell toward her. She caught Frog between her paws, shielding him from the hard earth as Gorse thumped against the ground.

Paw steps pounded toward them.

"Is he hurt?" Tansy nosed past her, sniffing at her kit.

Frog tugged himself free of Gorse's grasp and stood up. "I could have jumped by myself," he mewed crossly.

Wind glanced at Gorse.

The gray tabby tom was panting, his pelt dripping with rain.

Worry sparked in Wind's belly. "Are *you* hurt?"

Gorse's eyes lit up with sudden mischief. "Do you care?"

Wind snorted and lifted her tail. "I'm not heartless!"

"I know. You just *prefer* to hunt alone," Gorse teased gently.

Tansy nosed between them and brushed her muzzle along Wind's cheek. "You saved my kit! I owe you so much."

"Just get them to shelter," Wind told her briskly. "Somewhere that's not going to catch fire this time." Before the queen could say any more, she headed across the grass.

"Wait!" Wind heard Gorse hurrying after her.

"What do you want?" Wind narrowed her eyes against the driving rain.

"To find some shelter from this rain," Gorse told her.

Wind glanced at him out of the corner of her eye and kept walking. "Why are you following me, then?"

"I assume even loners need shelter." He didn't turn his head.

She huffed. "I'm independent, not dumb."

"You're brave and smart," Gorse murmured softly.

Wind tried to ignore the admiration in his mew, but the warmth of it seemed to pierce her heart.

Gorse pulled ahead. "There's a gap between the rocks in that stretch of heather." He jerked his muzzle toward the great stones that stood like guards on the hillside.

Thunder rumbled from the dark clouds above them.

"Come on." Gorse broke into a run and ducked into the heather.

Wind followed and found herself chasing him along a zigzagging path between the bushes until she reached the stones.

As he slid into the gap between the two largest, she skidded to a halt outside and peered into the shadowy cleft.

"It's okay." Gorse's mew echoed from the darkness. "There's no one here except me."

Flattening her ears against the rain, Wind padded warily inside.

The earth was dry. The rocks met above their heads and closed at the far end, forming a shelter against the driving rain. Crushed heather stems lined the floor, springy beneath her paws. Now that she was free of the driving rain, exhaustion swept over her. She crouched on her belly, limp.

Gorse sat beside her, curling his tail across his paws. "Why don't you sleep while the storm passes?"

Wind yawned. "Aren't you tired?"

"No." Gorse half closed his eyes. "I'm just happy to be out of the rain."

Weariness dragged at Wind's bones, and she let her head droop, feeling suddenly safer than she had in moons. Gorse was beside her, and she felt deep in her belly that she could trust him. She rested her nose on her forepaws and let herself slide into sleep.

When she woke, Gorse was gone.

Disappointment jabbed her belly. She sat up and shook out her pelt, which had dried while she'd slept. *Of course he's gone,* she told herself briskly. *It's not like we're friends. We were just sheltering from the storm while it passed.* Her disappointment lingered. *Stop being so soft! I walk alone!* She flicked her tail and stretched. Her belly rumbled. She still hadn't eaten today. She glanced at the dark rocks, suddenly aware that the thrumming of the rain had stopped. Prey would be returning to the moor. She could hunt.

As Wind headed for the entrance, heather rustled outside. She stiffened, tasting the air. "Gorse?" She smelled his scent a moment before he slid into the cave. He held a fresh rabbit in his teeth.

He dropped it at her paws. "I thought you'd be hungry."

She blinked at him, suddenly realizing that she could smell his scent infusing the cave. Not just *fresh* scent, but stale, too, as though he'd slept here for moons. "Is this your *den?*" Hadn't he taken a risk leading her—a stranger—to his home?

"Do you like it?" Gorse tipped his head to one side. "It's warm and dry and easy to guard." He nodded toward the opening they'd come through. It was too narrow for a dog, and unwelcome cats could be easily driven off with a few well-aimed jabs through the gap.

Wind dipped her head. "You must feel safe here."

"I do." Gorse nudged the rabbit closer. "Eat. You look hungry."

Wind felt a purr rumble in her throat, surprised to feel how happy she felt.

Gorse came back.

KEEP WATCH FOR

DAWN OF THE CLANS

WARRIORS

BOOK FOUR:
THE BLAZING STAR

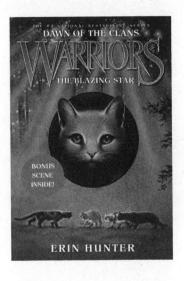

Read on for a sneak peek!

CHAPTER 1
❧

"It's time to bury our dead," Tall Shadow declared.

The black she-cat's words dragged Thunder's attention back to the death and devastation all around him.

Everywhere beneath the branches of the four oak trees the moonlight showed him pools of drying blood and tufts of torn-out fur. Cats lay on their sides in the trampled grass, their eyes open and their faces frozen in expressions of pain or shock. The anger that had made them fight had vanished like mist under the morning sun. Now every cat looked vulnerable, the living as well as the dead.

Thunder caught the flapping of a black wing from the corner of his line of vision, and turned to spot a crow as it alighted on a low branch. Its tiny, bright eyes flicked greedily from cat to cat. A shudder ran through Thunder from ears to tail-tip, and his fur bristled.

Tall Shadow is right. No cat should be left here as food for scavengers, not when they've given their lives in such a bloody battle.

He felt as if he were carrying a heavy, wet rock in his chest in place of his heart—somehow, he knew that everything had been leading up to this terrible battle: no matter what any cat could do, *nothing* could have stopped it. Cat against cat, claw against teeth—all because of arguments over territory. A vision of blood splashing against bark flashed behind his eyes and he shuddered. Spirit-cats had come to visit them in a vision, to tell them that fighting must stop. *I want it to,* Thunder thought now. *But how do we claw our way back to peace?*

Thunder struggled to find meaning in this devastation, but it was like groping blindly through thick fog. *Now we've all seen that fighting tooth and claw over territory brings nothing but death and destruction, pain and grief.* Thunder wondered whether the cats they had lost today had died so that could be understood.

"There are so many," Thunder meowed as he moved forward to stand beside Tall Shadow, picking his way carefully among the bodies. "How can we protect them?"

Tall Shadow stretched out one foreleg, and thoughtfully slid out her claws. "This is what spilled blood," she responded. "And this is what will make things right."

Make things right? Thunder thought, bewildered. He knew what the she-cat meant, but almost unbearable pain pierced him at her words. *What could possibly make things right?*

"However long it takes," Tall Shadow went on, "we will make a hole in the ground, big enough for all our fallen friends to lie in together. In life, they were torn apart; in death, they will be united."

Thunder felt every hair on his pelt prickle at the words Tall Shadow had chosen. *Unite. That was what the spirit-cats told us at the end of the battle. Unite or die.* "Yes, this is what we should do," he mewed hoarsely.

Gray Wing, Wind Runner, and River Ripple gathered around, murmuring their agreement.

"It will take a lot of effort from every cat," Gray Wing warned them.

"Then we must make that effort," Tall Shadow insisted. "Only the earth will be able to protect our fallen denmates from crows and foxes."

As she and the other cats began to scrape at the ground, Thunder noticed that his father, Clear Sky, was standing silently a couple of fox-lengths away. He looked reluctant to step forward and join in.

Thunder padded over to him, reflecting that it was not so long ago he and his father had been fighting to the death. At his approach, Clear Sky dipped his head, deep shame in his blue eyes. "I caused this," he rasped, as if he was fighting the urge to wail aloud. "It was my anger that created the chaos, my anger that brought these cats into the battle that killed them. *So many of them . . .*" he added in a whisper.

Memories crowded into Thunder's mind: Clear Sky's first rejection of him when he was a kit; their long estrangement, followed by Thunder's shock at his father's harsh methods when he tried to live with him in the forest; their arguments and their latest parting when Thunder's paws couldn't walk his father's path any longer.

But in spite of all that, Thunder was unable to repress a surge of sympathy. "Come on," he mewed encouragingly. "Let's do right by those cats who sacrificed themselves."

When Clear Sky did not protest, Thunder led him across

to the others, who had already begun to dig in the shadow of the four trees. No cat spoke as they scraped and clawed at the ground, the hole growing bigger and bigger.

Already tired from the battle, Thunder felt his legs begin to ache as his paws grew black with dirt, and his vision blurred from exhaustion. Yet he forced himself to go on. The harsh caw of a crow sounded somewhere overhead, and he found himself digging even faster.

At last Tall Shadow stood back, shaking off the earth that clung to her paws. "That should be big enough," she panted. "Now let's bring our friends over here."

Most of the cats divided into pairs, gripping the dead cats with their jaws and dragging their limp, lifeless bodies over to the grave. But Thunder found himself alone, standing over the body of Hawk Swoop. Her orange tabby fur was clotted with blood, and a cruel gash gaped in her throat.

Thunder felt sharp claws clenching around his heart as he remembered how Hawk Swoop had cared for him when Gray Wing first brought him to the hollow after he had been driven out of the forest by his father. His shoulder fur bristled as his gaze scoured the clearing and alighted on Clear Sky; he was padding up to the body of Rainswept Flower, whose life Clear Sky had taken just before the battle began.

They knew each other since they were both kits, Thunder thought, revulsion welling up inside him.

Then he heard his father's voice, a low, grief-stricken murmur. "I'm so sorry."

Clear Sky was truly mourning his dead friend.

The guilt will hurt him more than any cat's claw ever could.

His heart still weighing heavy in his chest, Thunder dipped his head to take Hawk Swoop's scruff in his jaws. Her fur was soaked with the taste of death, and he had to fight hard not to recoil. Her body was limp and heavy now that the life had run out of her. *I can see why the other cats worked in pairs,* Thunder thought as he tugged her toward the hole.

Before he had gone many paw steps, he caught a flash of black fur. He turned his head to see Lightning Tail, with his sister, Acorn Fur, hovering behind him.

"Please let us help," Lightning Tail meowed.

Thunder nodded, knowing how right it was that the two younger cats should help to bury their mother.

The black tom gripped Hawk Swoop's tail, his green eyes filled with sorrow as his teeth met in her orange tabby fur. Acorn Fur worked her shoulder underneath her mother's belly. With their help, Hawk Swoop's body suddenly seemed lighter, and in only a few heartbeats Thunder, Lightning Tail, and Acorn Fur carried her to the edge of the grave.

Panting as he recovered from the effort, Thunder took a step back. Lightning Tail and Acorn Fur stood over their mother's body, their heads drooping and their shoulders sagging. Exchanging a grief-stricken glance, they put their noses to the ground and pushed Hawk Swoop into the hole. At the last moment their eyes closed as if they couldn't bear to see her tumble and flop onto the pile of bodies.

"No day could ever be worse than this one."

The raspy, wheezing voice startled Thunder, who whipped

around to see Gray Wing. Beyond him, through the trees that still bore their last few ragged leaves, Thunder could see the line of the moor, bare and bleak under the frosty sky.

"The days ahead can only be better," the gray tom mewed.

Thunder straightened up, raising his head with an instinctive pride. *Gray Wing is right,* he thought determinedly. *We'll make sure we never feel grief like this again.*

"Hawk Swoop, I'll never forget you." Lightning Tail spoke from the edge of the grave, his voice throbbing with sorrow.

"Neither will I," Acorn Fur added. "We'll both miss you so much."

At their words, other cats gathered around the hole to gaze down at their fallen friends.

Shattered Ice crouched at the side of the grave, his gaze fixed on his friend Jackdaw's Cry. "We'll never dig out tunnels together again," he mewed in a voice rough with grief. "The hollow won't be the same without you."

"But you have not died in vain," Cloud Spots added, standing so close to Shattered Ice that their pelts brushed. "None of you have. We shall learn from this terrible day, we promise you."

More cats took up his words, raising their voices in wails of anguish. "We promise! We promise!"

As the yowling died away, Thunder drew back from the graveside, and found himself beside Tall Shadow. As if something invisible was tugging at their paws, River Ripple and Wind Runner padded up to join them.

A couple of heartbeats later, Clear Sky drew closer with

reluctant paw steps. His eyes seemed fixed, as if he was staring at something very far away, looking through the other cats at a vision they could not grasp. He halted a little way from the other four, who stood in a line facing the rest of the survivors.

We look like we're guarding the grave, Thunder thought.

Gray Wing limped to his littermate and sat beside him, though Clear Sky kept his distance from Thunder and the others.

"Listen to me, all of you!" Tall Shadow yowled, her gaze raking across the huddle of grief-stricken cats. "This must *never* happen again. We should listen to the cats in the stars, to the warning they gave us. From now on we have to work together peacefully, and at the next full moon we must return to this clearing to hear more messages from the spirit-cats."

"Yes!" Clear Sky's voice was a shaken purr. "At last there are cats who will tell us what we have to do."

Sudden understanding flashed into Thunder's mind like the dazzle of sunlight on water.

"So *that's* why you've been so protective and so hostile!" Gray Wing turned to his brother, his gaze full of compassion. "All this time your responsibilities have been too much for you. You tried to do the right thing, but you asked too much of yourself."

Clear Sky turned his head away in shame. "I'm so sorry. . . ."

For the first time in many days, Thunder felt hope stirring inside him. *Clear Sky will get guidance from the spirit-cats now, so maybe . . .* Then he shook his head. *Nothing will make me believe that these cats needed to die.*

THE TIME HAS COME
FOR DOGS TO RULE THE WILD

SURVIVORS

BOOK ONE:
THE EMPTY CITY

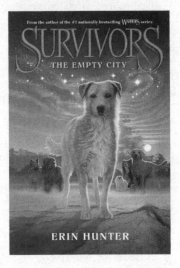

Lucky is a golden-haired mutt with a nose for survival. Other dogs have Packs, but Lucky stands on his own . . . until the Big Growl strikes. Suddenly the ground splits wide open. The longpaws disappear. And enemies threaten Lucky at every turn. For the first time in his life, Lucky needs to rely on other dogs to survive. But can he ever be a true Pack dog?

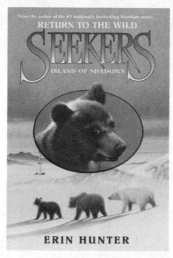
Toklo, Kallik, and Lusa survived the perilous mission that brought them together, and now it's time for them to find their way home. When the group reaches a shadowy island covered in mountains and ice, Kallik is sure they're almost back to the Frozen Sea. But a terrifying accident leads them into a maze of abandoned tunnels, unlike anything they've ever seen before—making them question their path once again.

ENTER THE WORLD OF
WARRIORS

Warriors: Dawn of the Clans

Discover how the warrior Clans came to be.

Warriors

Sinister perils threaten the four warrior Clans. Into the midst of this turmoil comes Rusty, an ordinary housecat, who may just be the bravest of them all.

Download the
free Warriors app at
www.warriorcats.com

HARPER
An Imprint of HarperCollinsPublishers

Warriors: The New Prophecy
Follow the next generation of heroic cats as they set off
on a quest to save the Clans from destruction.

Warriors: Power of Three
Firestar's grandchildren begin their training as warrior cats.
Prophecy foretells that they will hold more power than any cats before them.

Warriors: Omen of the Stars
Which ThunderClan apprentice will complete the prophecy that
foretells that three Clanmates hold the future of the Clans in their paws?

HARPER
An Imprint of HarperCollinsPublishers

All Warriors, Seekers, and Survivors books are available
as ebooks from HarperCollins.

Visit www.warriorcats.com for the free Warriors app, games, Clan lore, and much more!

   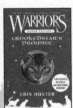  

Warrior Cats Come to Life in Manga!

HARPER

An Imprint of HarperCollinsPublishers

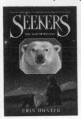     

  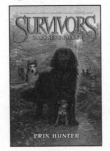